The Laughing Ladies

Karen Kanter

AuthorHouse™
1663 Liberty Drive
Bloomington, IN 47403
www.authorhouse.com
Phone: 1-800-839-8640

First published by AuthorHouse 5/12/2011

ISBN: 978-1-4567-4405-2 (e)
ISBN: 978-1-4567-4406-9 (sc)

Library of Congress Control Number: 2011903607

Printed in the United States of America

To Stan Tobin: my love and my rock, who unfailingly
told me how proud he was of my effort.

Special thanks to...

When a book takes shape, so many contribute. My thanks to all those who provided endless suggestions and encouragement, but there are some to whom I owe special thanks...

First to Pat Porter, good friend, watercolor artist and teacher, the inspiration for finding my passion. To my daughters, Tracey Woolrich and Amy Tannenbaum, their enthusiasm and pride gave me the confidence to keep writing. To Robbin Thompson, whose clear eyed vision and support made me think that I could actually be a writer. To Gay Walley, my writing coach, who turned my imaginings into a tightly woven story. To Bethene LeMahieu and Randye Farmer, who read the first chapters and asked for more, so I had to keep on producing. To Linda Small, who bravely edited the first version of the manuscript. Many changes, but she was always right. To Bob Tannenbaum, for his male point of view and careful scrutiny. Yes, Bob. The conductor would have flirted more with these lovely young women. To Paul Price, who listened to my thoughts and then designed the wonderful cover.

And finally, to the folks at Author House, who made it possible for you to read *The Laughing Ladies.*

Chapter One: Motivation

*Motivation - the reason for doing something
or behaving in a specific way*

"You might want to put your things on the overhead rack," Felicia heard a female voice behind her say. Felicia would never dream of talking to a stranger and was struck by the young woman's assured manner. She appeared quite comfortable initiating a conversation.

"Here, let me help you," the woman offered and stood up to move the bags onto the metal rack. Felicia took in her smart suit and the saucy straw hat perched on the reddest hair she had ever seen.

"Thank you," Felicia said, righting herself as the train lurched out of the station. She settled into the window seat and adjusted her skirts over her long legs. Tall and slender, she downplayed her shapely figure by selecting conservative outfits. She fiddled with her wool jacket, then took off her hat and patted her carefully arranged hair.

Anyone looking at her would never guess the apprehension roiling her insides. Her refined features were composed. That ladies never showed their emotions had been instilled in her since childhood and was second nature to her now.

What have I done? Maybe I should have planned this more carefully. Was running off really the smartest thing to do?

Her thoughts were interrupted by an offer of food from the same friendly woman who helped with her bag. Felicia hadn't even considered food.

What am I going to do? How expensive are meals on a train? How can I afford to eat my way across the country?

As if reading Felicia's mind, the young woman said, "You don't have any food with you, do you?"

She began to unpack her basket, assessing her traveling companion as she removed napkins and a sandwich. *She certainly looks like she could afford whatever she wants. Definitely rich, smart clothing, fancy jewelry, and she's got that same high-born manner as the women I used to sew for.*

Felicia extended her hand and said, "I'm Felicia Welles and obviously, I didn't think very far ahead. My only plan was to leave as fast as I could. I don't even have a ticket. I don't have a clue where I'm going."

She listened to herself with growing dismay. It had seemed so easy to just get on the train and go. But, here she was without food, without a destination, without a plan. Before she could berate herself further, she was being spoken to again.

"My name is Corinne Sullivan, and I'm going to Crystal Creek. It's in Colorado and a long way from Boston where I used to live. It sounded like a good place to me because it's a mining town, which means lots of men with lots of money to spend. And that's all I need to know about it."

"Then, that's all *I* need to know. I'm going there, too," Felicia declared, making her second instant decision of the day. "I want to get far, far, away and Colorado sounds far away enough to me."

"Then, two for Colorado, it is," Corinne exclaimed as she carefully divided a beef sandwich.

Each of them held their half aloft in a toast to their new friendship. With a laugh, Felicia bit into the sandwich. *Spur of the moment decisions might not be so bad after all.*

Inside Abigail's shoe was her ticket to freedom, purchased yesterday for today's train trip. When Mrs. Hale left the house at 1:00pm for her visiting rounds, Abigail planned to go to the railroad station and catch the outbound train. Her preparations were made. She had already packed her belongings in a battered suitcase, pressed her only good suit and polished her shoes. She hoped she would look like a traveler and not a runaway housemaid.

At precisely 1:05pm, Abigail started up the stairs to her room. Doubt stabbed at her, but she continued climbing. She had saved and saved, but little was left after she paid for her ticket. Cook packed her a wonderful basket so she wouldn't have to spend any money on food. Abigail didn't know what she would have done without the kindness and support of Cook. When she cautiously asked if there was any extra food, Cook immediately became suspicious. Abigail and all the other servants had plenty to eat. Without too much effort, Cook coaxed Abigail's plans out of her and decided to help.

She felt sorry for the girl, an indentured servant because her parents were poor and desperate. Cook remembered how long it took to work herself up from kitchen maid to cook. Circumstances were changing now. It would be good to see someone get away from this life of serving others. Abigail confided where she was going, and Cook hoped she would be able to take advantage of opportunities not available here.

Overcoming her fears, Abigail dressed, gathered

together her sparse belongings, picked up her food basket and hurried down the stairs. She would never once miss the maid's uniform neatly folded on the bed.

She headed towards the train station and made it to the platform without seeing anyone. Enormously relieved, she boarded the departing train.

Once she found a seat, Abigail's hands stopped shaking and her heart settled back into a normal beat. She wondered what would happen when Mrs. Hale discovered she was missing. Would Mr. Hale be angry enough to send the Pinkerton detectives out searching for her and demand she be brought back in handcuffs. Maybe Mrs. Hale wouldn't notice she was gone until the morning when she didn't appear for her instructions. By then, she would be a long distance away.

She checked the final destination on her ticket. Crystal Creek, Colorado. She liked the sound of the name and repeated it slowly to herself. She started to chant in time to the rhythm of the locomotive's wheels.

"Crystal Creek. Crystal Creek. Crystal Creek."

She didn't realize she was saying it out loud until she saw two women staring at her. They sat together sharing a basket of food. One was immaculately dressed in a navy traveling suit. A small straw hat was perched atop her flaming red hair. An amused expression played across her face when she heard Abigail.

The other woman was poised with her sandwich suspended in the air. She wore a tan velvet jacket with an old-fashioned cameo pinned to its lapel. A frilled white blouse peeked through the front. A large linen napkin was placed over her black wool skirt. A stylish hat covered with peacock feathers was beside her on the seat, and Abigail could see brown hair arranged in the latest style. She looked like what Abigail thought a lady should look like.

With an embarrassed shrug, she smiled timidly at the two of them.

Corinne got up and crossed the aisle. Her professional eye took in the outdated shiny dark green suit. Fashionable at one time, it was obviously some rich woman's discard.

Leaning across the empty seat, she said, "Please come and sit with us. We couldn't help but hear what you said and this may just be the Crystal Creek Express. We're both headed there as well."

Abigail looked over at the second woman who gave a little wave and beckoned to her. Suddenly, she didn't feel so totally alone. Her trepidation turned to anticipation as she rose to meet her fellow travelers.

For each of them, boarding the train was an act of defiance, a rebellion against the restrictions of a society which kept them in their place, a place they no longer chose to be. As the train rushed westward, they were leaving these old lives further and further behind. There would be no turning back.

Felicia, seated at the window, watched as mile after mile of forest passed by. The tall maple and oak trees formed a canopy with smaller ferns and bushes lining the ground beneath. An occasional sumac grew close to the railroad tracks. Since it was early spring, the larger trees didn't block out the light, and the young green leaves were transparent in the sunshine.

Felicia always wanted to explore the woods, but Stewart, her husband, thought it was a waste of time. And, if he didn't initiate an activity, it wasn't worth doing. She decided when she got to Colorado, she would take long, long walks and enjoy the scenery. She smiled at the thought, felt her body relax, and let the rhythmic drone of the wheels lull her to sleep.

Corinne, seated across from her, watched Felicia's eyes slowly close and her breathing became even. *What would make someone like her decide to pack up and leave? She apparently is well-off. Those are expensive clothes and her earrings must have cost a fortune.*

Corinne looked at Felicia's hands. *No wedding ring*, she noted. Closer scrutiny, however, revealed a thin, pale band around the finger on her left hand. *She's running away from her marriage*, Corinne decided and started to sort through the possible reasons. *I wonder if her husband hit her or cheated on her or maybe he gambled away her dowry or maybe he drank or...*

The rustle as Abigail re-arranged her few items broke into Corinne's musings. She turned to look at Abigail and thought, *She's so sweet-looking. Pretty shabby, but it's obvious she's tried her best to spruce herself up.* Although they were well worn, her shoes gleamed with new polish. Her suit was neatly pressed, but Corinne could see it once belonged to a larger woman.

Abigail was slight, but well shaped. Lighter colored streaks shone in her chestnut brown hair, worn piled atop her head and kept in place with a number of tortoise shell combs. The combs were a Christmas gift from Mrs. Hale, and Abigail always wore them, treasuring the feel of elegance they gave her. Her eyes were hazel, shaded towards green, and Corinne had noticed her perfect white teeth when she smiled.

Abigail propped her legs up on the seat opposite, exposing the darns in her stockings. She couldn't find a comfortable position and started to re-arrange her belongings again.

"Why don't you put one of your bags on the rack? No one will be getting on the train until the next stop and we're hours away."

Corinne stood to help. "Just hand me what you want me to put up here."

Abigail hesitated a moment, reluctant to part with her belongings. But, Corinne's manner exuded confidence and Abigail was used to taking orders.

With extra space, Abigail again tried to find a comfortable position. She couldn't lean her head back because the top of the seat only reached her shoulders. Felicia and Corinne, who were seated at the window, could prop their heads against it but Abigail was in an aisle seat. She slouched down as far as she could, again placing her feet on the seat across from hers.

Tired of watching Abigail's adjustments, Corinne offered to change seats. "I'm not at all tired, so I'll be reading for a while."

As soon as Abigail was in her new seat, able to lean her head against the window, she drifted off.

After re-reading the same paragraph three times, Corinne gave up and marked the place with a velvet ribbon. *Was leaving so precipitously the right choice?* She often regretted actions she took because of her quick temper, but, she had never been this reckless before.

In a fit of anger, she had walked out of Mrs. Corey's shop after not getting credit for the beautiful creation she had labored over for so long. The shop owner had just nodded modestly when showered with praise for the dress' originality and gorgeous tiny stitches and elaborate beadwork.

No more lowly seamstress for me. From now on, I want credit for what I do. I'm only going to work for myself and get so rich everyone will have to pay attention to me. And a town full of men is just what I need to help me.

Satisfied with the plan, Corinne returned to her reading.

A few chapters later, she stood up to stretch and decided

to take a walk to the end of the car. There were two seats on either side of the aisle with some of them turned to form a group of four, the configuration in which she and her new friends were seated. It was a cozy arrangement and made for good conversation. Right now, however, the other two conversationalists were dreaming.

The floor was carpeted and the seats were well stuffed and covered in what she thought was velveteen. She counted the rows as she navigated her way to the far end. There were sixty seats in all and about three quarters of them were full. She noticed a few women wore long coats made of linen over their ordinary clothing to protect them from the cinders that invariably came aboard.

When she returned to her seat, she saw the Buffalo, New York station coming into view. A number of women collected their suitcases and bags in the usual ritual of departing passengers. The train had left Albany early in the morning after changing to the New York Central & Hudson River line to carry them across the state. This was the second day of her journey and she still felt a frisson of excitement as she marked her progress west. *Only three more days to go.*

When the whistle blew, the prolonged, shrill sound awoke both Felicia and Abigail.

"Where are we?" asked Felicia as they slowed to approach the station.

"Buffalo, New York," answered Corinne.

"Are we getting off the train again?" Abigail asked, ready to gather up her belongings.

"Yes, we are. We have another train change to make."

Corinne had done her research and knew exactly how many different train lines and how many different stops there would be.

"It's 12:15 now and miraculously we are right on time,"

she said consulting one of her many schedules. Felicia and Abigail were content to let her lead the way.

The vendors at the station pressed in on them as they tried to cross the platform. The "news butchers" hawked sandwiches, coffee, fresh fruit, books, newspapers and candy, with precious little time to make their sales.

"Over here," Corinne called loudly to attract the attention of one of the vendors. "Soap and a towel, how much?" she asked when he approached her eagerly offering the two items she wanted.

"Fifty cents," he said and the transaction was made. Corinne happily clutched her purchases. She had used the sink in the lavatory, but not the public brush and comb tethered to a cord. The shawl wrapped around her shoulders became her towel because she refused to wipe her face on the public one provided.

Afraid to spend too much time on the platform and miss their connection, the three boarded their next train, the Lake Shore & Michigan Southern to Chicago.

When the train began to pull out of the station, Abigail looked at the clock which read 12:00. She turned to Corinne and asked, "Didn't you say it was 12:15 when we arrived?"

Corinne nodded.

"But the clock we just passed said 12 noon. How can we be leaving before we got here?"

Felicia checked the large clock on the receding station and confirmed both hands indeed pointed straight up. "I'm sure the conductor will know," she said and when he came through the car, she asked him the question.

"Each of the railroads has its own system of time," he explained. "The time on the New York Central, which you arrived on, is 20 minutes ahead of the local Buffalo time and the Lake Shore train, which you are on now, is 15 minutes behind. So you left before you arrived," he concluded, pleased with himself for holding the attention of three lovely young women and delighted to show off his knowledge.

He continued through the car, punching tickets, and when he reached the far end, turned, tipped his hat to the three of them and disappeared into the next car.

Chapter Two: Journey

Journey - a trip or expedition from one place to another

That night they slept fitfully, awoken by the noisy clangs when the conductor opened the compartment door on his nightly patrol. In the morning, they waited patiently for the lavatory. Corinne insisted they use her soap and towel and leave the community brush and comb for others.

In a few hours, they reached Chicago where they were to change trains again, continuing their trip on the Chicago and Northwestern to Council Bluffs, Iowa. They stepped down to the platform swirling with people intent on making their connections. Fashionably dressed women bustled along, guided by a husband's hand on their elbows. Young children were tightly gripped, not to be lost in the swiftly moving crowds. No porters were available, but they carried their bags to the next train without any problems. A four hour layover gave them plenty of time to make the transition.

The women, subdued by three days of travel and two nights of poor sleep, talked little as they took their seats. The conductor gave out his call of "All Aboard!" and a few minutes later the train, sounding its long, low whistle, departed for the trip across the prairie.

They tried passing the day gazing out the window. But mile after mile, they saw only flat, empty land. The horizon stretched out, unbroken by a tree or a building. Even the sun seemed to hover listlessly overhead.

"I wonder what it's like in Crystal Creek," said Felicia turning from the window. "I know it's a mining town, but do you think there will be any kind of cultural activities?"

"Well," guessed Abigail, "since it's in the mountains, it can't look as empty as this. Why would people want to live here? Can you imagine how much washing and ironing and dusting these women do?"

She wriggled in her seat thinking about all the chores she left behind.

"And what do they wear?" asked Corinne, picking a speck of ash off her skirt. "There's no place to dress up for, except maybe church."

"I hope we have a church where we're going. I would miss Sunday services," said Felicia. "Sunday was always a truce time for Stewart and me. I never put much stock in what the minister preached, but I loved the organ music. I would go home and play all the hymns again on my piano. I could listen to music all day. The minute I sit down on a piano stool, my mood gets better."

"We used to all go to church on Sunday," said Abigail. "I loved to get dressed up in my suit. Mrs. Hale always offered us her clothing at the end of each season. But, she didn't do it to be nice. She did it to make herself more important. Every time she looked at one of us wearing her cast offs, it reminded her she was better than us."

Corinne and Felicia exchanged glances. Perhaps Abigail wasn't as naïve as they originally thought. They didn't yet know all the hardships she had experienced in her short life. They only saw a sweet, round face with rosy cheeks.

"My mother was a good Catholic wife," Corinne said quietly. "She said her rosary every day. She took us to church on Sunday and even made my father go. But, she went alone to say prayers for all the dead people."

"All the dead people?" they echoed in unison.

"Yes, all the dead people," Corinne repeated. "My parents owned a funeral home, which they bought with my mother's inheritance. When she married my father, he naturally assumed control of her money, and he chose to buy a house which they turned into a funeral parlor."

"What's a funeral parlor?" asked Abigail. She turned to Felicia.

"Have you ever heard of a funeral parlor?"

"I think we had one in Saratoga Springs, but I never went inside," she answered.

"Well, my parents started one. At the time, it was quite new. Instead of the dead body lying in the family's parlor, it would be brought to our house and the family could receive their guests there and even have a formal service if they wanted. We lived upstairs and my mother ran the business with my father. She dressed the bodies and arranged them in their coffins. People would always tell her how natural their loved one looked. She planned the wakes, kept the lists of guests, and even took the pictures for the funeral cards."

"Funeral cards?" asked Abigail. "What are they?"

"They're photographs of the deceased in their casket. My mother would mount the picture on a stiff black card with an inscription written on it. And after the service, she would give them to people as a remembrance. Of course, she really made them because they advertised our funeral business on the back."

Abigail shuddered and said, "That's so creepy. I wouldn't want anyone to take a picture of me when I'm dead."

"What did your father do?" asked Felicia.

"My father embalmed the bodies and drove the hearse to the cemetery, but mostly he talked to people, trying to convince them he offered a service they needed. He had a terrific gift of gab and everyone loved him. But, basically, Mother did all the work and he took all the credit."

"Sounds pretty much like what you told us happened to you at Mrs. Corey's," said Abigail, again surprising Corinne with her insight.

The miles mounted as the train hurtled westward. The repeated mournful sound of the whistle reminded Felicia of music played in a minor key. She listened more intently as the train raced across the prairie. The rhythmic clatter of the wheels, the periodic blowing of steam and the low whistle became a symphony of sounds.

The time passed slowly, and the women kept themselves occupied discussing their plans.

Felicia hoped to find a job as a governess.

"I was tutored at home so I understand what's expected. And I play the piano. Maybe I can give piano lessons."

She'd inherited her musical ability from her mother, and one of her earliest memories was sitting beside her father while her mother gave them a private concert. He adored music, and Felicia's mother provided musical pleasure by playing classical selections and renditions of modern tunes.

She jumped up to reach for her bag on the overhead rack.

"I brought some sheet music with me. Let me show you the beautiful illustrations on them."

Felicia pulled on the bag, but misjudged its weight. It

toppled down onto the empty seat next to her. The catch sprang open and the contents spilled out, most landing in Corinne and Abigail's laps.

"I'm just grateful you didn't have shoes packed in there," laughed Corinne as she reached for a silk camisole on the seat.

"This is beautifully made," she said turning the top inside out.

"Oh, I am so sorry," an embarrassed Felicia apologized and tried to stuff the scattered camisoles, petticoats, and under things back into her suitcase.

"Don't cram them in like that," cried Abigail, appalled at how Felicia was treating her beautiful possessions. She scooped up whatever she could reach and said, "Let me help you fold them."

She fingered the edge of a lace-trimmed slip, comparing it to her plain cotton underwear. *Someday,* she vowed. *Someday I'll wear beautiful undergarments just like these.*

While she folded, Abigail related how she intended to find work as a bookkeeper.

"I'm really good with figures. When Mrs. Hale's housekeeper saw how fast I could add and subtract, she let me help with the household accounts. Mining companies should need someone to do their payrolls, don't you think? It can't be that different from what I was doing."

"I don't care what kind of job I get, it just has to pay me well," said Corinne. "The minute I save enough, I'm going to open up my own parlor house. That's where all the money is and I'm going to get my share. I refuse to wind up an underpaid, underappreciated dressmaker again."

Indignation swelling, she shoved her newspaper down into her seat.

"I'm so glad to get away from the kind of women who patronized Mrs. Corey's shop. I always read the newspaper to keep up with the local news because I thought I should be able to chat intelligently with the clientele. But those women led such vacuous lives, full of teas and parties and balls, only concerned with news if it appeared on the Society Page. They might have lots of money, but I wonder if their husbands ever let them decide anything important. It seemed the only decision they could make was what color their dress should be. What a horrible life to lead."

"At least they got to decide something," argued Felicia. "Any time I tried to express an opinion, I got cut off immediately. I don't know why I didn't see that before I got married. But, I guess we don't pick who we fall in love with, and once we do, we don't see any of a man's faults…or his real motives," she added bitterly.

She snapped her repacked bag closed, the lovely sheet music forgotten.

"Didn't your husband love you?" asked Abigail.

"He loved my "supposed" money more. When my grandmother died and he found out I didn't get a large inheritance, I discovered the real reason he married me. He thought Gran was rich and it would all be mine and then it would all be his. But, Gran mortgaged her house to get the money she spent on my tutors and music lessons and clothes. She wanted me to attract the right sort of man. She never liked Stewart, but I wouldn't listen. He courted me with flowers and gifts and I fell madly in love. I wouldn't listen to her."

She rose to replace her bag on the rack. Corinne leaned her head back and watched Felicia.

"Men are good for only one thing, paying for the life you want. No falling in love stuff for me. I did it once and learned my lesson. This time I'll pay my own way."

"What happened?" asked Felicia, sitting down and smoothing her skirts.

Corinne told the story of her romance with Thomas Sperling, a well established businessman. They met at the bank when both were making deposits. He struck up a conversation with her which led to a dinner invitation and another and another. She finally went to his bed when he made promises to her about marriage once he got his business problems settled. She had no idea how much money he needed until he met Clara.

Clara, with her plain face and dumpy figure, who at twenty-five never thought a man would be interested in her. Thomas convinced Clara of his infatuation, but Corinne knew her dowry was the main attraction.

"I don't care about love, either," declared Abigail. "I'm going to find myself the richest man I can and let him buy me all those beautiful things I dusted and polished in the Hales' house."

They congratulated each other on their courage, confident that they were headed towards a place where a woman could make independent choices and decisions about the direction of her life.

"Maybe, it's desperation not courage," suggested Felicia.

"More likely, anger fueled my decision," said Corinne. "I was furious I didn't get the least bit of credit for what I did. I'm not going to repeat my mother's mistakes."

Abigail just listened, afraid she would reveal too much if she spoke. A runaway maid was acceptable, but an indentured servant breaking a legal contract was a different matter. She wanted nothing to interfere with her plans to escape.

After one more long day and even longer night, they arrived in Council Bluffs, where they changed to yet another train. The Union Pacific would take them to Denver and finally, to Crystal Creek. This time, they didn't travel in a car exclusively reserved for women and the male passengers appeared unlike those who traveled on the eastern trains. Men, who looked like adventurers out to make their fortunes, filled the car. They had an intensity about them, much different from the easy manner of the vacationers and travelers on their previous trains. They were the only women in the car and were the recipients of longing glances, but no one approached them.

Felicia, completely exhausted, decided to take a sleeping berth for the last night of the trip. She flagged down the porter to inquire about the price and availability. When he told her the $8.00 additional fee for the Pullman car, she decided to spend one more night in her seat. She'd paid $17.50 for the entire trip and didn't plan to add half as much for only one night.

The fourth day passed even more slowly than the previous three. By now, they were all travel-weary, dusty, and growing apprehensive about what they had done. As the sun began to set, the train suddenly lurched and with a high-pitched squeal of brakes, it came to a complete stop. Windows were raised and a few of the men leaned out to see what happened.

Questions flew about the compartment. Minutes passed with no information and then the conductor entered the car.

"We've hit a cow and the poor thing is completely mangled," he told them. "Does anyone have a gun so we can put it out of its misery?"

Immediately, every man reached into his jacket pocket and extended his hand, offering all kinds of weapons to the conductor. They carried long barreled guns, short barreled guns, plain guns, guns with fancy engraved grips. He beckoned to one of the men to follow him and the others pocketed their firearms. The women noted they were the only three people in the compartment without weapons.

"Well, I for one feel well protected," commented Corinne.

"Glad to see that we are riding with armed guards," agreed Felicia.

Abigail looked from one to the other, unsure if they were serious or not.

The rest of the day went by without incident and, at last, the final night of the trip ended. When the train pulled into the Denver station early the next morning, Abigail asked, "What time is it?"

"I think we are now on Denver time which is one hour earlier than Chicago time and an hour earlier than Omaha time and two hours earlier than Boston time and probably time to stop figuring out what time it is," babbled Corinne, delirious from lack of proper sleep.

They boarded the last train of their long journey. Even though exhaustion dulled their senses, they were struck by the scenery, radically changed from the desolate landscape of the prairies to the magnificent mountains of Colorado. Even high up at 5,200 feet, they were surrounded by towering snow capped peaks.

The train chugged through the rugged countryside and slowly made its way up to Crystal Creek at 9,000 feet. They passed jagged rock formations shot through with veins of shining minerals, deep gorges cut into the sides of the mountains and tumbling waterfalls engulfed in mist.

"Crystal Creek is at almost twice the elevation of Denver," Abigail read from a leaflet she picked up at the Denver station. "Crystal Creek started in 1859 when prospectors came to search for silver. But, the discovery of gold in the mid 1880's led to its explosive growth."

She glanced at her two companions, who paid no

attention to her because they were busy watching the scenery.

"These gorges are beautiful," said Corinne, pointing to a particularly large one. Sheer rock walls extended down the sides of the chasm and seemed to plunge into a bottomless abyss.

"Yes, they're absolutely gorgeous," said Abigail, quite pleased with her pun as she looked out at the passing landscape.

"I believe gorgeous does literally mean full of gorges," Felicia said, sounding like the governess she hoped to become.

The tracks ran alongside a rapidly flowing river with water that crashed over any obstacles in its path. High walls of red rock rose on either side. The narrow pass eventually opened into an immense valley bursting with brightly colored wildflowers. The intense orange of the Indian paintbrush contrasted with the blues and yellows scattered amongst the tall grasses. The air current caused by the passing train rippled across the field turning it into a sea of flowers.

After stops at little towns with Spanish names, like Salida and Buena Vista, they climbed again into another mountain dotted with clusters of aspens, their white trunks parallel against the blue sky. As the train took them higher and higher into the mountains, the adrenaline of anticipation overwhelmed their fatigue. The three women became more and more animated.

And then, five days and five nights after they began their journey, they heard the conductor call out the name of their destination.

"Crystal Creek. Next stop is Crystal Creek."

Chapter Three: Arrival

Arrival – the reaching of a place after a long journey

Felicia was stunned when she stepped onto the Crystal Creek platform. As she crossed the country, she often imagined what the town would look like. Not once did she dream it would be such a hodgepodge of mismatched buildings facing a wide dirt street.

Abigail, right behind her, was speechless. She clutched her bag to her chest and looked around wide-eyed.

Only Corinne appeared unruffled as she shook herself out.

"What did you expect?" she asked. "It's a mining town, and probably better than others we could've picked."

"But, this is no more than a long dusty stretch of road. Look at it!" said Felicia.

Corinne pointed to the same street. What she saw was an abundance of men. It was exactly what she hoped for.

"You know what I see, ladies?" she asked. "Men, men and more men. Look at all of them."

"Are we the only women?" asked Felicia

Corinne and Abigail put down their bags and squinted into the sun.

"No one else appears to be wearing a skirt," commented Corinne in the droll tone she reserved for the obvious.

Abigail put her hand up to her nose. "What is that smell?"

Felicia pointed to the middle of the road. "Looks like a horse passed by recently."

Corinne shrugged her shoulders and said, "I only smell pine trees and money."

Despite their dismay, Felicia and Abigail both laughed at Corinne's determined optimism.

Store after store bordered both sides of the long main thoroughfare. Most of the buildings were made of wood with high false fronts on which various names were painted. "Saddle Shop and Leathery," "Wilson's General Store," "Finest Wines and Spirits," "Cohen's Dry Goods and Hardware," all identified the specific businesses. Elaborate artwork accompanied a few signs and others simply announced the type of enterprise.

A large white building, with many windows, dominated one corner. A second large structure anchored the far end of the street. A small brass plaque was fastened to the right of its front door, but was unreadable from where the women stood.

As they took in their surroundings, a stylishly dressed woman with a bright red mouth, walked out of the far building. She stopped and stared at the three of them. Then, she opened her parasol and started down the street towards them. Apparently changing her mind, she switched direction and went into the general store.

"There's a woman," pointed Corinne unnecessarily since they had all watched her progress with interest.

"We can guess how she makes her money," Felicia commented and rolled her eyes.

Even this early in the day, loud voices of men who were well into the bottle emanated from the saloon. Their raucous shouts could be heard all the way down the street. The women watched a well built, broad-shouldered man, with a white apron tied around his waist, escort a wildly gesturing drunk out of the premises.

Next to the saloon was The Crystal Creek Courier, a newspaper office. Behind the large window, they glimpsed a man wearing a hat with a green bill and a shirt with large white cuff protectors.

Wilson's General Store, with barrels stacked on either side of its entrance and two horses hitched in front, abutted the newspaper office. The wide open door revealed walls of well stocked shelves. In front of the store, two men, deep in conversation, sat on rough hewn chairs. A heavyset man, his paunch balanced squarely on his thick thighs, smoked a corncob pipe which he waved in the air to make his point. His companion listened intently and occasionally tugged on his wide suspenders.

An older, gray haired cowboy, a large red and white print bandana tied loosely around his neck, walked hurriedly into the telegraph office. His long, thin legs were slightly bowed as if he had sat on his horse for too many years. Large silver spurs flashed on his worn leather boots which clattered noisily across the boards.

Another man, young and fair-skinned, obviously a prospector, nervously paced on the planked walkway in front of the assayer's office. He looked like he had just raced down from the surrounding hills. His hat, with a line of sweat around the crown, was tilted back from his sunburned face. The top of his forehead was white where it had been protected from the sun. His dirt caked hands clutched a bag of ore as he anxiously awaited his turn to enter and register his claim.

The three of them, preoccupied with their inspection, didn't notice two rugged looking men approach them. They appeared slightly disreputable with too eager grins on their faces. The women were instantly on guard. But, much to their surprise, the larger of the two politely greeted them.

"Welcome to Crystal Creek, ladies. May we be of assistance to you?"

He reached down toward one of their bags. The second man, with a high-pitched voice that didn't match his beefy build, suggested, "Perhaps carry your bags to the hotel?"

Corinne turned on the charm with a friendly smile and answered, "Why thank you. How generous of you."

"Hotel? Sounds better already," mumbled Felicia wearily to herself, visualizing a large tub filled with steaming hot water. She was ready to wash away the grime of the trip and slip into a bed with a nice feather down quilt and clean white sheets. She gave her bags to one of the men and turned to see if Corinne and Abigail were coming.

Abigail nervously handed her satchel to the second man who hoisted it easily onto his shoulder, and then maneuvered Corinne's bags onto his other arm.

They quickly covered the short distance to the hotel. Another street ran perpendicular to the main one and the building was so large, it wrapped around the corner. The men led them to the main entrance, and they climbed the two steps of the wooden walkway in front of the hotel.

A large window with the name Crystal Creek Hotel painted on it in fancy gold letters faced the main street. The lobby was furnished with a small sofa and two chairs arranged in front of a large stone fireplace. The warmth from a crackling fire filled the interior. Straight ahead was a wide mahogany desk with a short and prim looking woman standing behind it. Her dark hair was pulled back severely and wire-rimmed glasses perched halfway down her nose. Her gray shirtwaist dress was neatly pressed and everything about her said fussy.

She was anxious to properly receive the new arrivals. Greeting men, not women, was commonplace for her. Men continued to pour in at a rapid rate from all over the country, but women were still a mere trickle. Not too many young women wanted to endure the rigors of the trip west.

"Welcome to Crystal Creek, ladies," she began in her official hotel voice. "You must be tired after your long trip, and I'm sure you're ready for a nice rest."

The two men reached the desk before the women and set the luggage down beside it. With a bow and a sweep of his hat, one of the men said, "If there's anything else we can do for you, just let us know. Vivian here can always find us."

Corinne again turned on her magnificent smile.

"Sure will," she said and reached for the pen to enter her name in the hotel registry. Felicia and Abigail quickly followed, all three relieved their long trip was finally over.

"Don't pay any mind to those two," the clerk said indicating the backs of the departing men. "They're harmless."

She turned the register around, read their names and kept on chatting.

"My name is Vivian Wallace and I run the hotel for Mr. Clovis. He built this hotel himself and he owns almost all the property on Main Street. Made his money at the Beulah Mine before the vein petered out, but he was smart and sold his shares in time."

Vivian rambled on, wondering why these women had come to Crystal Creek, but knew she would find out soon enough. Crystal Creek was an open town in more ways than one. But altogether too curious to wait, she tested her most likely theory by saying, "We run a clean business here so don't be thinking about bringing men upstairs to your room. It's not allowed here. If that's why you've come, take yourself down the street to Mrs. Woodley's. She's always looking for new girls."

Felicia, startled by Vivian's suggestion, looked up sharply. Abigail who was reaching for her suitcase froze, her hand outstretched in front of her. Corinne, although she remained silent, made a mental note of Mrs. Woodley's name for future reference.

Since no one responded to her implication, Vivian moved on to the necessary hotel information.

"The rate is $12.00 a week, and you have plenty of time to freshen up before dinner is served at 6:00pm sharp."

Taking a breath, she started across the lobby to the stairs.

"Please follow me. I'll show you to your rooms."

Felicia was bone tired, and all thoughts of a bath disappeared as she collapsed on the bed and fell instantly asleep.

Abigail, too over stimulated to relax, paced around the hotel room touching each object she passed. *This is the best hotel room I've ever been in*, she thought. She'd never been in a hotel room before, but it didn't make any difference in her excitement.

Corinne unpacked and coolly assessed what Vivian said about Mrs. Woodley. *She'll be a good place to start. I need to find out whatever I can about the parlor houses in this town. They're all going to be my competition.*

The women gathered for dinner at the hotel's restaurant where they attracted a lot of attention from the male diners. Two men, obviously Eastern businessmen by their well-tailored suits and unscarred soft white hands, were seated immediately to their left. They rose when the ladies entered the room and walked to their table.

Across the room was a round table at which five men were seated. They spoke with the easy camaraderie of old friends. Laughter burst out periodically and a lot of backslapping went on. All activity stopped when they saw the women.

At the far wall, three ranchers were studying roughly drawn maps. Their actions came to a halt when one of them pointed out the women entering.

Empty tables quickly filled with mine owners, local politicians, merchants, and a few solitary men who came for dinner. This room was clearly a social gathering place as well as a restaurant.

The hotel was proving to be a first class operation. The rooms were immaculately clean, well stocked and Felicia declared her bed heavenly. So far, the dinner was delicious. After almost a week of cold sandwiches and ill-prepared food purchased at the railroad stops, anything hot was greatly appreciated. The hotel cook apparently knew what he was doing in the kitchen. The soup was a delectable concoction of fresh vegetables. And now, the main dish of roasted chicken, browned potatoes and carrots seemed like a sumptuous banquet.

Corinne watched Abigail try to contain her excitement when she drank from a crystal wine glass, an experience she suspected was a first for her. Felicia, she noticed, didn't even glance at the table, obviously accustomed to sitting at one so well set.

It became impossible to enjoy a quiet meal. They were repeatedly interrupted by men who stopped at their table to introduce themselves. During a brief pause in the steady stream of welcomers, Corinne looked at her friends and said, "I think it might be easier than I thought to make good money here. All we have to do is lie down on our backs and let those eager men sprinkle us with gold dust."

Abigail, who was setting her glass down, quickly caught it before it spilled. In a shocked voice she said, "Corinne, you don't actually mean that do you?"

"Of course, I do. I've always said it's the fastest way to get what you want."

She nodded graciously at the next man who approached the table. He wore a flannel shirt and denim pants over his worn leather boots. Although he was dressed more casually than the other diners, his bolo tie cords ended in silver aglets and were secured with a silver dollar.

"May I buy you ladies dinner as my way of welcoming you to Crystal Creek?" he asked when he was close enough to be heard.

Before either Abigail or Felicia could answer, Corinne beamed at him and said, "We'd be honored."

He handed her his card and bowed with a flourish.

"Corinne! What were you thinking?" Felicia asked, horrified at her action.

"I'm thinking I didn't pay for my dinner." Corinne answered. "Now don't either of you start with me! I'm tired. I want to finish eating and go to bed."

After dinner, Felicia and Abigail sat silently and watched Corinne's progress across the dining room. She made her way through the tables, aware of the admiring looks which followed her. She tried to acknowledge as many of them as she could. When she reached the stairs, Felicia said, "I know she said her plan was to establish her own business, but she never said she planned to get the money with her body."

They looked at one another. Even though they were together night and day throughout their journey, neither one of them had guessed what Corinne was really thinking.

Abigail reached over and took Felicia's hand.

"I'm scared," she said. "What happens if that *is* the only way we can make money out here?"

Felicia patted Abigail's hand and replied in a voice she hoped sounded reassuring, "Let's call it a night. We're exhausted. Things will look different in the morning."

She pushed back her chair and left Abigail alone at the table. She finished the last of her coffee and thought about her first evening in Crystal Creek. She had enjoyed sitting at a table covered by a starched white linen tablecloth and set with fine dinnerware. She had felt like a lady when she was served her meal. No one would suspect only six days ago, she was the one doing the serving. It was especially gratifying not to pay for anything.

For the first time, she wondered what she would be willing to do to live like this all the time.

Chapter Four: Search

*Search - a careful and thorough examination
in order to find something*

The three women sat together at breakfast, but there was little conversation. Corinne, oblivious to any tension, ate her way through two eggs, bacon, a slice of toast and two cups of excellent coffee. Abigail absently pushed food around her plate, while Felicia buttered her toast with intense concentration.

"Sleep well?" Corinne asked, and signaled the waiter to bring more coffee.

Before either could answer, she continued, "What's our plan for today?"

"To find myself a job and not think about what you said last night," replied Felicia, still troubled by what Corinne intimated at dinner.

Abigail, made nervous by confrontation, quickly cut in.

"I'm going to talk to Vivian. She's sure to know what jobs are available. I bet she knows everything that goes on in this town."

"And I plan to walk over to the newspaper office to see if anyone is advertising for a governess," said Felicia.

"I think I'll come with you," Corinne said as she finished her breakfast. "Shall we?"

Much to Corinne's satisfaction, they again saw a large number of men on the street. Men on horseback, men walking and talking, men sweeping the wooden walkways, men carrying maps, portfolios, or sheaths of paper, lots of men, and only men. Most were eager to welcome the women and exchange a few words. The pair found themselves making slow progress towards the newspaper office.

"Do you see any other women?" asked Felicia, looking around as they crossed the street. She lifted her skirts to avoid them brushing the dusty road and kept a careful watch to make sure she didn't step into something unpleasant.

Corinne peered up and down the street, then replied, "Not a one."

They headed towards the newspaper office and passed a number of shops. Curious, they paused in front of each window to examine its contents.

"Look! There must be women here. This window is full of ladies' hats," said Felicia, stopping in front of an elaborately dressed window display.

They peered into the milliner's shop and Corinne saw the owner's sewing machine. She shuddered, "I don't choose to ever sit behind one of those again."

"Give it some time. You only quit a week ago. You might feel better about it, if your customers got to thank you, not Mrs. Cory."

"I think I would rather do anything but sew for other women again," said Corinne.

"I can't believe it! An opera house," exclaimed Felicia, pointing to a poster plastered on the side of the building. "And it's announcing a string quartet."

Her mood instantly elevated, she linked her arm through Corinne's and added, "I like this town better already."

They continued their stroll, trying to ignore the miners as they walked past the saloon. Whistles followed them down the street. They found it difficult to ignore the suggestive propositions called out.

"I never realized men could make the same request so many different ways," commented Corinne.

"I'm beginning to feel like one of those hurdy-gurdy girls I read about," said Felicia, glad to reach the newspaper office and escape the ogling.

The man behind the counter turned his attention from typesetting when they entered. He walked over to the counter to greet them. Of medium height and build, he wore a bright green visor pulled down over his forehead. Even though it was warm inside the shop, he wore a long sleeved shirt and a vest.

He looked at the two well dressed women and thought, *What a fine way to start the day. An interesting story for my readers is standing right in front of me.*

He acknowledged them with a big smile.

"Good morning ladies. I'm T.J. Hansen and I run this place. How can I help you?"

"We're here to ask about job advertisements," answered Corinne. "Being new in town, we thought the newspaper would be a good place to start."

She removed her black kid gloves and started to leaf through the paper lying on the counter.

"What kind of job are you thinking about?" asked T.J. "Not a whole lot in the way of employment for ladies like you."

"I'm hoping to find a position as a governess. Do you know any families who might be in need of such a person?" asked Felicia.

T.J. almost laughed when he heard her request, but hastily repressed his snicker when he saw the expression on Felicia's face.

"Didn't mean to startle you, Miss...."

"Felicia Wells," she said offering her hand.

T.J. looked at her extended hand, but did not take it. "Sorry. I'm not being rude, just don't want to get this ink all over your fingers," he said, pointing to the dark block in front of the letters. "I was just setting up for the next edition."

"Why did you start to laugh a minute ago?" asked Corinne. "What did she say that was so amusing to you?"

"Sorry, ma'am. It's just the thought of a governess. There aren't many families living in Crystal Creek. Oh, a couple of the mine owners brought their wives and children with them, but mostly it's just the men."

He snapped his fingers as he suddenly remembered, "Though, the schoolmarm is getting married and they'll be looking for a replacement for her."

"No, thanks. I don't think I could face a room full of children. I'd prefer tutoring one or two, at most."

"Can't help you there, ma'am," said T.J., regretfully shaking his head.

Felicia turned to Corinne and asked if she found anything of interest in the newspaper.

"Simpson's Boarding House is looking for a cook. Pony Express needs two riders to carry the mail between here and Denver. The stagecoach company is offering a job at their rest stop. And, if you want to mine ore, you'd probably be the first one hired," Corinne recited as she went through the ads.

"Ladies, I don't want to discourage you, but I can't think of many jobs for women like you," said T.J.

"How about women *not* like us?" asked Corinne.

"Neither of you looks the type to work at the saloon or at Mrs. Woodley's," he answered.

"Mrs. Woodley's? That's the second time we've heard her name," said Felicia.

T.J. pointed to a woman walking down the street.

"There she goes," he said as Mrs. Woodley entered the bank. "First thing in the morning. She doesn't like to keep money around her place."

"Can you give us any suggestions?" asked Felicia, not wishing to discuss Mrs. Woodley's comings and goings.

Seeing how disappointed the two women looked, T.J. wished he could be of more help.

"Ladies," he said, "I'm sorry I can't do more for you. I bet you came out here thinking there'd be plenty of jobs. And there are lots of opportunities if you brought enough money to start your own business, but not many jobs."

He stopped to think for a minute. "Let's see. There's Mrs. Callahan, she owns a cattle ranch and Mrs. Grayson runs her late husband's mine. Two new shops recently opened and they're both owned by women. And, of course, there's her."

He looked out the window, and indicated the retreating figure shaded by a parasol.

As he spoke, he thought, *There's one job these fine looking ladies can find for sure. When word gets out about new women in town, they'll be a stampede of proposals.*

"I don't suppose you're looking for a husband," he said.

His comment was met with stony silence.

"Well, thank you, Mr. Hart," said Corinne, putting on her gloves and taking Felicia by the arm. "You've been very helpful."

The pair walked back to the hotel, their enthusiasm drained.

"That wasn't too encouraging. Maybe Abigail's gotten better news," said Corinne.

"There must be something to do here," insisted Felicia. "I can't believe we won't be able to find some kind of work."

"Let's not get discouraged yet. We only just got here," said Corinne, although she didn't feel too optimistic either.

They entered the hotel and found Abigail huddled in the corner of the couch staring into the fire. She looked up when she saw them and asked, "What did you find out at the newspaper office?"

"No jobs," said Corinne. "And you?"

"Vivian offered me a job as a maid," said Abigail. "Can you believe it? How far did I travel to wind up hearing that?"

"Well, what's next?" asked Felicia. "I don't know how long my money is going to hold out if I don't find a job."

For the next two nights, they shared their inventory of refusals over dinner.

Abigail, nurturing the hope of using her mathematical skills, went to the Crystal Creek Mercantile Bank. She was shown into the manager's office and treated courteously. He even offered to buy her lunch.

"He said the bank didn't have any positions available. But, he wanted to be helpful and told me to contact the mining offices because they always had payrolls to be done. No luck. All three of them turned me down."

Felicia told how she tried the Opera House, hoping to capitalize on her piano playing ability and her knowledge of classical music.

"It was exactly what I thought. The performers bring their own accompanist," she said. With a big sigh, she continued. "Then I asked about ushering. I even asked about selling tickets. Nothing, nothing."

In desperation, Corinne convinced herself she could sit behind a sewing machine until she found a better job.

"Unfortunately, Hattie, isn't that a great name for a milliner, hired a new assistant a few days ago. When I told her I designed and made the suit I was wearing, she walked me over to the new dressmaker's shop. And, although Olga was impressed, her business is too new to consider hiring anyone."

"What are we going to do?" asked Abigail. "I'm going to run out of money soon."

"Me, too." said Felicia. "I can probably last about two more weeks at the hotel and then I'm broke."

"Maybe, you should both go home," suggested Corinne.

"I can't go back," said Abigail.

"I won't go back," said Felicia.

"Then what are we going to do?"

No one had an answer.

Chapter Five: Discussion

Discussion - a detailed consideration about a subject or idea

Corinne looked up from her breakfast and with a slight tilt of her head indicated the source of her interest. The woman with the bright red lips was headed right to where they were seated. They watched as she made her way across the room. Everything about her was exaggerated. Large mutton sleeves on a too bright blue jacket. A waist cinched in more than was humanly possible. Her curls piled ridiculously high on her head. She was not tall, but managed to look imposing.

"Good morning, ladies. May I join you for a moment?"

Indicating an empty chair, the three sat silently, watching her prop her parasol against the table. She settled into the chair and adjusted her skirts beneath her. Then, she leaned forward and in an unexpectedly refined voice, said, "My name is Claire Woodley and I operate The Crystal Creek Parlor House. It's a brothel, and I offer my customers the best women in town."

She looked first at Corinne. *Won't take much to win her over.* She instantly recognized the type of woman who came west eager to make lots of money. She knew the other two would need more convincing, but was confident they would come around. *Wait until they learn what the available jobs for women are. They'll either be on the next train out of here or knocking on my door.*

"And why do you think this would be of interest to us?" inquired Felicia, wondering if a new woman in town meant only one thing.

Mrs. Woodley straightened up in her seat and unbuttoned her jacket to ease the pull across her chest.

"Women don't travel across the country and put up with the difficulties of the trip without having a good reason. Usually, they think they can make lots of money fast or they're running away from something. Am I right?"

Felicia thought about getting up from the table, but good manners prevailed. Abigail sat immobilized, worried she would be found out. Only Corinne nodded her head.

"Tell me, Mrs. Woodley, what arrangements do you make with your...um... 'employees'?"

Mrs. Woodley stirred a spoon of sugar into the coffee the waiter placed in front of her. Before she could answer, Corinne went on.

"Vivian mentioned your name before the ink was even dry in the registry. She warned us about the high moral standards of the hotel. She said there were no such standards at your establishment."

With a hearty laugh, Mrs. Woodley exclaimed, "At $5.00 a visit, I would hardly think so."

"Five dollars?" gasped Abigail. "Some man pays $5.00 for a night?"

"For an hour, dear," Mrs. Woodley corrected.

"And how many men a night do your women see?" asked Corinne.

"As many as she can handle. I don't dictate a number to my girls."

"Your girls can make more than $5.00 a night?" Abigail asked. She was amazed at the amount. She remembered how long it took her to accumulate the money for her train fare. The ticket used up almost all her funds and now, with the hotel costs, she was left with little money. She paid closer attention to the conversation.

"Yes, they usually do," Mrs. Woodley confirmed. "Believe me, the number of men, ready and willing to pay never runs out. A lot of my business comes from well-paid overnight visits, which can run as high as $50.00."

Corinne calculated the amount of money she could make. She, too, was surprised by the figure, much more than she anticipated. She had other questions, but decided now was not the time to ask them. She remembered how her new friends responded to her previous comments and didn't want to antagonize them further.

Mrs. Woodley placed her cup back into the saucer and stood. Being a shrewd businesswoman, she knew she had given the three enough information to start them thinking. A few of her girls were moving on after two years, and she needed replacements quickly. She didn't suppose it would take these ladies too long to discover how few their options were.

Silently, they watched her cross the lobby and walk out the door. As soon as it closed behind her, Abigail almost exploded.

"What is going on in this town? First, Vivian thinks we're a bunch of prostitutes and now, Mrs. Woodley is here first thing in the morning trying to tempt us with her numbers."

"I sure did like those numbers," observed Corinne.

"Corinne, you aren't seriously thinking of becoming a

lady of the evening?" asked Felicia, reluctant to even take part in this conversation.

"Lady of the evening," snorted Corinne. "Felicia, a prostitute is no lady of any kind."

"You can't really be considering it, are you?" asked Abigail anxiously searching Corinne's face. Her expression had subtly changed. She looked like Mrs. Hale when she wasn't pleased. Abigail felt herself bracing for a reprimand and waited nervously for Corinne's reply until she remembered she was no longer subject to someone else's mood.

"And if I was? Can you think of a faster way to make money? It wouldn't be forever. If what Mrs. Woodley said is true, four or five months should get me enough money to open my own place. A whole lot quicker than I thought it would take."

Abigail, distressed by what she heard Corinne saying, just sat and stared at her. But, not Felicia.

"Corinne, you're talking about becoming a prostitute. Taking off your clothes and letting a man touch you wherever he wants and then, then..."

"Fucking you," burst out Abigail.

They both stared at her.

"I know enough to know I wouldn't want to do that!" Abigail exclaimed.

She'd heard her mother's moans and her father's grunts, but when she asked questions, her mother just warned her never to let a man come near her until she was married.

Corinne was annoyed with her two new friends. They were thinking like those awful women she left behind. She hated those righteous wives who came into the shop, lauding their wealth and looking down at her. And it had especially galled her to wait on Clara Smith, who with one wave of her money stole Thomas away.

No, I'm not going to think about Thomas Sperling. He made his choice and I wasn't it.

Corinne tried again. "We're women, and women are a valuable commodity out here. Let's use it to our advantage. What's so wrong with being a prostitute? How different is it from what a wife does? Especially a wife who marries her husband for his money. With a husband, it's a lifetime of getting paid for your services. Isn't it simpler to just get paid by the night?"

A gentleman's stifled chuckle alerted them that their conversation could be overheard. And once Mrs. Woodley left, Vivian managed to find one excuse after another to edge close enough to their table to eavesdrop. If her interruptions weren't enough, the curious glances of the men, and their obvious interest, made the three self-conscious. They decided to move their discussion to Corinne's room.

She dropped her key on the dresser and made herself comfortable on the bed with her legs crossed beneath her. She watched Felicia pull over one of the armchairs. Abigail tried to pace, but found it difficult in the limited space.

"Will you please sit down, Abigail!" exclaimed Corinne. "You are making me crazy."

Abigail bounced down on the bed, leaned against the headboard and picked up a pillow which she held in front of her chest.

"Well, I may do it," Corinne announced. "The men are lonely and the women are scarce. What are these men supposed to do? This town is all about striking it rich, no one cares about right or wrong. I don't care if the Church says it's sinful. My mother's mind-numbing life was the real sin and I don't intend to repeat it. I want my own money and lots of it."

"Do you really want to work for Mrs. Woodley?" asked

Felicia. "We've only been in town a few days, we're not desperate yet."

She rubbed her hands along her thighs and then primly folded them in her lap.

"I didn't come west to be a prostitute," protested Abigail. "I came west to marry a rich man."

"Working at Mrs. Woodley's might be the fastest way to find one," replied Corinne.

She got up and walked to the window.

"Look down there," she said, pointing to the street. "How many women do you see? If a man wants a wife, where can he find one?"

"I think I would rather try something else before I let a bunch of men use my body," said Felicia.

Corinne turned to face her.

"Well, let's see. You've already found out families don't hire governesses for their children. Maybe you could take in laundry. I bet you could make a tidy $3.00 a day."

"Three dollars a day?" gasped Abigail. "Mrs. Woodley said it could be as much as $25 a night."

"My point exactly," Corinne agreed. "How about being someone's maid, Abigail? You've got good experience and Vivian's already offered you a job."

"What an awful thing to say. I want to get married. That's why I came here."

"We know, Abigail. For god's sake, you've said it enough. So, let's think about this…"

Felicia broke in before Corinne could finish the sentence. Her neck was mottled with red blotches, and her hands shook as she asked, "Was this your plan all along? When you said you wanted to run a business, but not be one of the girls, did you lie to us?"

Corinne crossed the room and stood defiantly in front

of Felicia. Her redhead's complexion betrayed her anger at the insinuation, but she looked steadily at her as she spoke.

"When Mrs. Woodley threw those numbers around at breakfast, I realized it was the quickest way to make enough money to buy my own place. I am no naive young girl who doesn't know what I'll be getting into. You forget I've already been in some man's bed. And I didn't wind up $25.00 richer."

Felicia leaned back in her chair and closed her eyes. She was tired of the discussion. She had no intention of becoming a prostitute and she hoped a healthy dose of reality would end the conversation.

"You are not $25.00 richer. Mrs. Woodley takes her share, and I bet it doesn't end there."

"I don't understand. What else would we pay for?" asked Abigail.

"Besides paying for your room, she probably charges you to have your clothes laundered, and your sheets washed and ironed. She might even charge for meals," replied Felicia, listing some of the possible expenses.

She thought for a moment and added, "And what about clothes? You'll have to wear fancy gowns and expensive shoes, which means buying all new clothing. That won't be cheap."

"But, we would look glamorous, wouldn't we?" asked Abigail as she twisted and turned in front of the mirror, imagining herself in a fancy ball gown and feathers in her upswept hair.

"I would look so beautiful in my evening dress, all the men would be in awe of me. When I walked by, they would sigh with pleasure just to see me pass."

"And how beautiful do you think you would look if you caught some awful sickness from one of those men?" asked

Felicia. "Stop dreaming, Abigail, and think about what you would really be doing."

The conversation continued. Each argument Felicia made was a practical one. But, Corinne, brought up by a religious, no-nonsense mother, had rebelled and chose to let practicality be the last determinant of what she did.

"Think of it as a kind of adventure," she proposed. "When I left Boston, I swore I would only work for myself and get all the credit for what I did. And, most importantly, keep the money *I* earned, not turn it over to the likes of a Mrs. Corey. Money was the only reason Clara got Thomas away from me. This time, I'm going to be the one with money."

"I do agree about the money part," Felicia said. "Enough money makes you independent, and I don't ever want to rely on a man again."

She felt tears welling up and made an effort to force them back.

"And, I also agree about those so-called rules which dictate what we women can or can't do. But still, I'm not sure I can be what you're suggesting."

"Only one way to find out."

Corinne reached for her jacket and hat.

"Are you really going to Mrs. Woodley's?" asked Felicia, but knew the answer before Corinne nodded.

"I'm on my way. Anyone care to join me?"

Felicia went to the door. "I'll walk over with you, but just to listen. Don't think it means I'll work for her."

Abigail, still dreaming about gowns she had only seen on other women, said she would meet them in the lobby. When they were gone, Abigail gazed into the long mirror. She whirled around and held her drab skirt out to one side.

With a sigh, she slowly left the room.

Chapter Six: Information

*Information - the collected facts and
knowledge about something*

The three women created a stir when they walked down the street.

A cattle buyer, making a transaction at the bank, put down his papers and peered through the window. The two men seated in front of the general store stopped their ongoing argument long enough to watch their progress. Four miners, smoking outside the saloon, shouted a few ribald comments. One started towards them, but was pulled back by his cohorts.

"Just keep walking," said Corinne, keeping her eyes straight ahead.

"The wolves are ready to attack," Felicia laughed, and put her arm through Abigail's to hurry her along.

Speculations took a more interesting turn when they stopped in front of Mrs. Woodley's Parlor House. Two miners even checked their ready cash.

"Ready, ladies?" asked Corinne.

She raised the large brass knocker and brought it against the door.

Mrs. Woodley ushered them into the main parlor and invited them to be seated. She rang a bell and told the maid to bring refreshments. Then, she waited for someone to speak. An awkward silence filled the room.

A little obvious, thought Felicia as she ran her hand across the plush red velvet sofa. She smiled to herself, imagining what Grandmother Baxter would think of her sitting in this room. *Gran, who thought if you crossed your right ankle over your left, instead of the other way around, you were committing a breach of etiquette.* She wondered how many rules of etiquette she would breach this morning.

She noticed a piano draped with a tasseled Spanish shawl in front of a wall of mirrors. Its dark wood shone with newly applied polish. A well-worn depression in the leather piano bench was testimony to many nights of making music.

Facing her was a fireplace framed by a mahogany mantel. A large oil painting of a provocatively posed woman hung above it. Mrs. Woodley sat across from her, in an armchair upholstered with a deep red fabric. Several more chairs, strewn with fancy, embroidered cushions, clustered nearby. A thick rug covered the floor and heavy dark curtains barred the outside view. The table tops were filled with fancy glass containers and carved wooden boxes. All the clutter made Felicia uncomfortable.

Abigail, seated beside Felicia on the settee, did her own appraisal. She wasn't sure if she liked the flocked red wallpaper, but found the velvet drapes very impressive. The room was decorated in much brighter colors than the Hales' parlor. *And the wall of mirrors! Is this what a rich person's house looks like out here?*

As she studied the space, she imagined what it would be like to live there. From what she'd heard, her dinner would be served to her, her clothes would be laundered and her room dusted and cleaned. *And all I would have to do is entertain a few men a night, whatever that means.*

Corinne didn't waste any time looking around. "We've come to hear a little more about the arrangements you offer your employees, or whatever it is you call them."

"I call them boarders since this place is called a boarding house. But, of course, everyone knows what it really is."

She certainly got right down to business, Mrs. Woodley thought, confirming her sense that Corinne was the leader, and the one who would convince the others to follow.

"Tell me again. What are the different prices you charge your customers?" asked Corinne. The faster she could make money, the faster she could open her own parlor house.

"As I told you earlier, I charge $5.00 and up for a visit, and if someone wants to stay overnight, it's $50. There's an added charge of $25.00 for any special request. I suggest what extras the girls can offer, but I don't force them to do anything," she continued. "But don't worry about money. I take care of that part of the transaction."

"How long is a visit?" asked Abigail, but her real question was what she had to do when a man paid for her services.

"Once a customer is satisfied, he is expected to leave. Some girls entertain many customers in a night, others see only one or two. It depends on how much time the client wants to pay for."

She poured herself another cup of coffee and added two spoons of sugar. The conversation was going well and she wanted to keep them talking.

"More coffee?" she offered.

"You said you take care of the money transactions," said Corinne. "How exactly does that work?"

"None of my girls handle money since we are trying to foster an illusion of intimacy. When a customer comes in,

I'm the one who collects the payment. After he gives me the money, I give him what's called a brass check. It's really just a round token which he gives to the woman he selects. She takes it from him after they are in her room and before anything happens. At the end of the evening, she cashes in her brass checks. That way no one gets cheated."

"So we wouldn't be handling any money at all," Corinne confirmed. "How about tips?"

"Those are yours to keep," answered Mrs. Woodley. "However, there is a share of your earnings that comes to me as payment for your room, board, and laundry."

"And how does that work?" asked Abigail, ready to do some rapid math in her head. *Felicia was right,* she thought. *She said Mrs. Woodley took her share.*

"I get 60 percent and you get 40," Mrs. Woodley said.

"60-40? Why do you get a larger percentage when we're doing all the work?" Abigail asked. "Shouldn't it be the other way around?"

Mrs. Woodley was ready with a well practiced explanation. It was a question that was always asked. She leaned forward in what she considered her frank and open pose.

"To answer your question, Abigail, I actually do a lot of work. I provide you with a safe place to live and work. You get decent food to eat. Your washing and ironing are done. Your room is cleaned. You do only one thing in return."

What a cavalier way to put it, thought Felicia. *There must be other jobs besides this one.*

She opened her purse and removed a handkerchief. The room was uncomfortably warm, and she dabbed at her forehead.

Mrs. Woodley drew back the heavy velvet drapes and cranked open a window.

"Is that better?" she asked.

"Thank you," said Felicia. "Maybe I'll just take off my jacket. I am feeling rather warm." *Hot under the collar is more like it, after listening to all this bogus sincerity.*

Abigail still couldn't summon up the courage to raise the only question she really wanted answered.

"How about clothing?" she asked instead, remembering what Felicia had said. "I don't have any dresses I could wear here."

"You can buy the evening dresses and accessories from me. Also, the rouges and powders you will need. Other things can be purchased at the mercantile store and charged to my account. That's not a problem."

Of course not, thought Felicia. *Wonder how much money you make on each purchase, Mrs. Woodley.*

"What kind of dresses would we wear?" asked Abigail. "I love velvet. It feels so soft against your skin. Not that I ever owned a velvet dress, but Mrs. Hale always looked beautiful when she wore her dark blue velvet gown."

Mrs. Woodley smiled indulgently at Abigail. Several of her regular customers would pay dearly to spend an evening with someone this fresh and innocent.

"You shall have one velvet dress, even a dark blue one, if you wish," Mrs. Woodley promised.

Abigail fidgeted with the edge of her jacket and shifted in her seat. She looked at Felicia and then at Corinne. *Neither one of them is going to ask because they already know.* She took a deep breath.

"What exactly is it that I'm expected to do?" she blurted out before she lost her nerve. "I've never done anything like this before."

Corinne was relieved to hear Abigail's question. "Yes, I'm curious about that, too."

Mrs. Woodley ordered a fresh pot of coffee and a berry pie served on her finest dishes to demonstrate the quality of her operation. The type of questions the two of them were asking indicated a growing interest. She didn't want them to leave.

She did, however, notice that Felicia sat silently. *She hasn't asked one question and there must be something she wants to know. It's obvious she comes from a wealthier background, but, if she runs out of money, I bet she'll be asking plenty of questions. For now, I'll settle for two out of three.*

"Basically, two things make you successful: being friendly and being willing. My establishment stresses quality not quantity, and that's why I can charge more. Men who come here know that, but they also know they are not your first. Your job is to convince them they are the best, they excite you and you are very satisfied. You act happy, you act carefree, you moan, you groan, and you make sure your pretense seems real."

"What happens if it *is* your first?" asked Abigail, turning bright red.

Mrs. Woodley, surprised, looked her over. "Are you telling me you are a virgin? You've never been with a man before?"

Abigail nodded, keeping her head down.

Trying to suppress her eagerness, Mrs. Woodley suggested in a controlled voice, "Well, Miss Abigail. I think we can make ourselves a lot of money if we hold a Virgin Auction for your first time. Some of the wealthier men, I'm sure, would pay well to be your initiator. What would you think about earning $100?"

Oh, this is going much better than I thought. Mrs. Woodley quickly ran through her list of clients who might be interested in a virgin. To truly be the first would be worth a lot of money to a few of them. And by having it an auction, she could profit handsomely.

Corinne and Felicia exchanged glances, hoping that

Abigail wouldn't accept the offer. Clearly, Mrs. Woodley anticipated a much higher figure for herself since she appreciated what a rarity a virgin was at a parlor house. But, Abigail proved they once again underestimated her.

"I'd rather keep 40% of the winning bid," said Abigail. "The first time is only the first time once and I want full value."

Abigail understood a lot more than any of them about being sold. Her parents, desperate for money to feed their other children, turned her over to the Hales as an indentured servant for seven years. This time it wouldn't be her parents. She would be selling herself, and she intended to get every cent she could.

Taken aback by Abigail's request, but anticipating the money to be made, Mrs. Woodley extended her hand.

Abigail looked at the outstretched palm. *If I shake her hand, I'll have more money than I've ever had in my life. How bad could doing it with a man be? Corinne's done it. Felicia's done it. If it's really bad, I just won't do it again. But, at least I'll have all that money.*

As she and Abigail shook hands, Mrs. Woodley thought, *So, it's Abigail, not Corinne, who's the first to accept.*

Chapter Seven: Decision

*Decision - something that is chosen after
considering the other choices*

"May I see what the upstairs rooms look like?" asked Corinne.

"Of course," Mrs. Woodley answered, as she stood and walked towards the stairs. "I'll show you the empty rooms and you can decide which one you would like."

She knew she could count on Abigail now and felt sure Corinne would follow. She hoped the other two would convince Felicia.

Corinne entered the room first and after a quick glance around, walked across the floor to look out the window. She couldn't find a way to open it.

"Is this window sealed closed?" she asked.

"Yes it," confirmed Mrs. Woodley. "The windows are always locked so no one can sneak men in and get around paying me."

Corinne had a momentary flash of Mrs. Corey keeping track of her every movement. She didn't want to find herself in that same situation again.

Seeing the expression on Corinne's face, Mrs. Woodley added, "It also keeps you safe, since no robbers can get in. Everyone knows there is a lot of money kept here in the evenings."

"But, what happens if there is an emergency and I need to get out?"

The closed windows made Corinne nervous. She imagined being trapped inside the room.

"You never lock your bedroom door," explained Mrs. Woodley. "That way, you can always leave the room. But, more importantly, if some client gets sick, or nasty, or even violent, one yell will get you help immediately. Henry is employed here for just that purpose."

The three women looked around. A brass and enamel bed, a chamber pot tucked inconspicuously beneath it, was piled high with pillows and quilts. It took up a great deal of the space. A carved oak dresser with matching mirror, a dry sink on which towels were neatly stacked, and two chairs placed on either side of a table comprised the rest of the furnishings. The whole room was tidy and spotlessly clean.

"All the rooms are basically the same, but I'm sure you'll be bringing some personal belongings with you. The first thing I would suggest is that you figure out where you are going to keep your money. You want to make sure it is well hidden."

Corinne nervously fingered the edge of her jabot. She looked around the room again. Her bravado was no match for the anxiety she suddenly felt. She couldn't make any promises yet.

"I'm not sure I can do this. Is it possible to give it a try, and if I can't, just leave?"

"As long as you don't owe me any money, of course you can leave," Mrs. Woodley readily agreed. She thought of the debt Corinne would run up after she purchased all her new gowns.

They retraced their way down the stairs and followed her back into the parlor.

It's time to tell them about the risky part of the job, she decided. Mrs. Woodley was scrupulous about keeping her girls healthy and working

"No one asked me about how to keep from getting pregnant, or what to do to prevent catching any sickness from the men."

The three waited for Mrs. Woodley, who knew exactly how much she could say without scaring them away.

"The first thing you must do is make sure you don't get pregnant. Before you see your first client, you will be required to get a health certificate from Dr. Meyers, who is our physician. When you are at his office, he will show you how to make a diaphragm from beeswax. I can help you with that also. Or, if you wish, he can set you up with a sponge to insert. A lot of the girls prefer the sponge because it has a silk string you can use to pull it out easily."

"Then, you want to avoid any of the illnesses you can get when the men aren't clean. You must insist they wash with quinine water before you even touch them. You want them to wash a large area, from their chest to their thighs, actually any part of their body that will touch yours. You'll find what you need on the commode next to the towels. Remember, before you do anything, they must wash themselves," she stated again, her voice underlining the importance of what she was saying.

Corinne listened carefully and tried to retain what she heard. If she worked here, there would be no mistakes.

One part of Felicia's mind pushed the information aside and the other tried to hold on to it. She didn't think she could bring herself to make money this way. Being a prostitute was sordid, and even though the parlor house looked respectable, there was nothing respectable about what went on there.

Abigail was still dealing with her agreement to sell herself. *I'm going to do exactly what my parents did. I was so angry at them. I couldn't believe they would do that to me, sell me into what was slavery masquerading by another name. Oh, how I hated them and cursed them. And now, I'm going to do the same thing.*

Images of her father, counting the money he received, flashed through her head. *No, it's not the same,* she reminded herself. *This time it's different. This time, I get to keep the money.*

When she tried to refocus, she realized the conversation had wound down and Mrs. Woodley was preparing to show them out.

When the women returned to the hotel, the debate resumed. Having made her commitment, Abigail hoped the other two would join her. She thought it grand to have real friends. She had associated with the other maids at the Hales, and, of course, Cook, but this was different. The three of them had already spent more time together than many people who were friends for years. Abigail wanted them with her at Mrs. Woodley's.

The conversation became a badminton match, with Corinne batting a reason to work at Mrs. Woodley's over the net, and Felicia volleying it back with a reason not to. Although Corinne put forth strong arguments and Felicia agreed with her logic, she said that she couldn't see herself having sex with strangers, leading "that kind of life."

Those last few words caused Corinne to sink down into a chair and sigh heavily. She began to talk about "that kind of life," a phrase her mother used to justify what she did. Then, she rose abruptly and started to pace. The words had reminded her of a time in her life she worked hard to forget. She walked back and forth as Abigail and Felicia watched in silence.

"When my mother died of pneumonia at 31, who do you think my father depended on then? Me! It was me!" she said, furiously jabbing her finger to her chest.

"He expected me to take over all the work she did. Can you imagine what it was like for a girl of thirteen to become a housekeeper and a mother and help run a business? I hated it and I hated him for making me do it. I was nothing more than a slave and President Lincoln freed them thirty years ago."

Corinne stopped to take a breath. Abigail watched her intently, disturbed to see her so distressed. This wasn't the strong Corinne who she depended on to get her across the country. This wasn't the flirtatious Corinne who charmed every man in the dining room. This wasn't the confident Corinne who asked questions of Mrs. Woodley. This was an extremely upset Corinne torturing herself with her past.

"Oh, Corinne. I'm so sorry. It sounds like you had a really bad time," said Felicia, reaching out to squeeze Corinne's hand. She thought of her comfortable life growing up, a treasured granddaughter in a wealthy household.

Corinne stopped walking and held on to the top of the chair. Her fingertips dug into its tufted high back as if to anchor her in place. She made a visible effort to cast off the ghost of her younger self. She didn't like to think about the past. No fond memories awaited her there.

"I left home as soon as I could and I swore I would never lead that kind of life. I don't ever want to be a wife. I don't ever want to be a mother. And I certainly don't ever want to take orders from a man again. I want to be free. And, the only way to make sure I am, is to be so rich I can do anything. I'm going to make that happen the fastest way I possibly can, even if it means doing something I don't want to do. If I could manage to get through those four awful years before I left home, I can manage to get through a few months at a parlor house."

Hearing her own words, Corinne realized she had made her decision. She would start at Mrs. Woodley's with Abigail.

Chapter Eight: Alternative

Alternative: a different option that may be chosen

When Felicia watched her friends leave the hotel, she felt an overwhelming sadness. With them around, she had companionship and encouragement. Now, she was alone.

Relying on Abigail's assessment of Vivian as a good source of information, Felicia went down to the lobby to talk to her. She was in her usual place behind the large mahogany counter. She stopped copying figures into a ledger, and asked how she could help.

"I'm desperate, Vivian," Felicia told her. "How can I make some money quickly?"

Without a moment's hesitation, Vivian said, "Try Big Swede's Saloon. He's a nice man and he's always interested in new girls."

"So is Mrs. Woodley."

Vivian pursed her lips in disapproval at the mention of the madam's name.

"No, it's not like that at all. The dance hall girls are only expected to dance, nothing else. One or two of them are even married women helping to support their families."

"Well, that sounds a little better. If I work at the saloon, at least I'll be around music. I guess I'll pay Big Swede's Saloon a visit."

After thanking Vivian, she started off. It was a bright, sunny day. The air felt crisp and fresh and it bolstered Felicia's courage. *Springtime*, she said to herself. *I've always thought of it as a time when anything is possible. I hope that's right today.*

She quickly covered the short distance to the saloon. When she stepped inside, it took a moment to adjust to the dim interior. Noise and activity stopped as all male eyes watched her movements.

Felicia headed for the bar, trying not to look self-conscious. The large, blonde man who stood behind it was aptly named. He was over six feet tall, and his blue eyes and fair complexion broadcast his Swedish stock.

Felicia carefully approached the wide wooden counter. She checked where she stepped because, although cuspidors were evenly spaced along the foot-rail, it was obvious the tobacco chewers' aim was highly inaccurate.

"Excuse me," she said, trying to maintain a semblance of composure. "Are you Big Swede?"

"Folks around here call me that, but my given name is Sven. How can I help you?"

He put down the glass he was wiping and gave her his full attention.

"My name is Felicia Welles, and I'm newly arrived in town. Vivian, at the hotel, told me you were hiring dance partners for the men. I've come to ask if you have a job available."

The crowd, which had quieted down when she entered, began to hoot and whistle. A few lewd proposals and offers to pay for another kind of job were called out to her.

Even though Felicia was dressed in a simple gray wool skirt and a black jacket buttoned to her neck, they could not miss her sensuality. No amount of modest clothing could hide her shapely figure. She was tall for a woman and her height was accentuated by excellent posture, a straight back and a head held high. Her dark brown hair was tucked under a small straw hat, but a few tendrils had escaped and framed her face.

When she heard the commotion, her eyes widened in fright. She gripped the rail tightly and waited for Sven to answer.

"Settle down, fellas and go about your business," Sven yelled at them. "The lady and I are having a private conversation."

Felicia mouthed the words "thank you."

Surprised such an attractive and obviously not down on her heels woman would need a job, he said, "Now, tell me, why is a nice young lady like you asking about being a dance hall girl?"

"A nice young lady like me has to feed herself and pay for her room."

He wasn't used to such a proper woman in his saloon, let alone one applying for a job. Since he opened the place four years ago, many women had come and gone, but no one looked like her. She belonged in a fine drawing room serving tea, not in a saloon hustling drinks.

"Well, I can always use a pretty face, but let me tell you exactly what you'll be doing and then you can decide if you want the job."

Although jobs were scarce in Crystal Creek, he couldn't imagine why she would chose to become a dance hall girl. *Because it's obvious she doesn't have a clue what the job entails,* he answered himself. *Bet she's never set foot in a saloon before today.*

"Come with me," he said. He motioned to a scrawny young man stacking bottles behind the bar. "Spike, take over for a few minutes."

He led her to a table in the back of the room and held out a chair. Then, he sat down across from her. One or two men moved towards them, but he waved them away. He clasped his hands on the table and leaned towards her.

"Let me explain how it works," he said. "There'll be a piano player coming in soon. When he starts to play, your job is to attract the customer to dance with you. He'll then pay me one dollar for a beer and a dance, twenty-five cents of which goes to you."

Felicia's quick intake of breath stopped him.

"Is something wrong?" he asked.

"No, I'm fine. Please go on. Let me hear the rest," she said. *Twenty-five cents. How will I ever earn enough money? What was Vivian thinking?*

"Don't worry, that's not how you make your money. Most of your money comes from tips and commissions if you get them drinking more than beer. You want them to buy themselves another drink and one for you. Drinks cost fifty cents a shot and you're not getting whiskey in your glass.

"What am I getting?"

"Watered down tea. Big profit in hustling drinks. If you're good at it, you can make as much as $40 a night."

That sounds a lot better, she thought. Felicia now felt calm enough to look around the saloon. The men had settled down and didn't seem as threatening. Some stood drinking at the bar in small groups of two or three. At a near-by table, cards were shuffled and cut. She heard periodic shouts from the small crowd watching two men compete in a dart game. Sven obviously maintained control here, which meant she would be safe. But, before she made up her mind, Felicia needed to ask one last question.

"Is there anything else expected of me besides dancing and selling liquor?"

"Do you mean entertaining men in a room out back or upstairs?"

She nodded her head.

"I leave that to the women in the bordellos and the parlor houses. I'm satisfied with the profit from the booze I sell."

Felicia liked Sven and felt comfortable talking to him. He was dressed like the other men in the room, in a plaid flannel shirt, but a cleaner version. She noticed his apron was starched and freshly laundered. When she first saw him, she made a judgment that he would be gruff and abrupt. But he proved her wrong with his simple explanations and attention to her concerns. She didn't think he would be a difficult man to work for.

"Then, I'm going to give it a try," she told him, relieved she managed to get herself a job. "Is there a special outfit I need to wear?"

He smiled, imagining how she would look in what she was going to wear. He expected to sell a lot of extra whiskey tonight.

"Come back at 7:00 tonight and I'll have Sally fix you up and go over the rules."

Felicia extended her slim hand across the table and it disappeared into his large ones. They smiled at each other, both pleased with the arrangement. As she walked out, the men who had been holding back looked at Sven. He nodded his head "yes" to their sounds of cheering, stomping and the clinking of whiskey glasses.

When she returned in the early evening, Sven introduced her to Sally Maddox. Sally, a married woman with a young child, was like a mother hen to the girls even though she was only twenty-four. A petite blue eyed, blonde, she worked at the saloon to help out her husband who was a miner.

Sally handed Felicia her outfit and kept up a steady stream of conversation.

"Since this is your first night, I'd suggest you watch the other girls. What we do isn't hard to learn. Mostly, you've got to remember to keep smiling."

Felicia nodded and took the outfit she was going to wear.

"Is that the whole thing?" she asked, looking at the short red satin dress.

Sally laughed and passed her a pair of fishnet stockings. "Here's something else for you."

"Oh, my," Felicia murmured, thinking about the amount of leg she would expose. The revealing outfit unnerved her and she avoided the mirror.

She thought of Grandmother Baxter who always told her to follow her instincts and do what she thought best. *What do you think, Gran? Am I doing what's best for me or am I making a big mess of things? I'm far away, alone and dressed in an embarrassing outfit. Maybe I should give it up and go home.*

No, no, she scolded herself. *Don't think that way. It's a job, not a life. I may be alone, but I'm doing the deciding for myself. And, under no circumstances, am I going home.*

Feeling a little better after her spirit boosting talk to herself, she walked to the dance floor.

The "professor," as the piano player was called, seated himself on the bench in front of the upright piano, cracked his knuckles, stretched his fingers and started to bang out a lively musical tune. A thin, wiry man, he looked as frenetic as the music he was playing. His hat, sitting at a rakish angle on his head of greased black hair, made him appear ready to leave when the last note was played. Felicia could hear the piano was out of tune. *But after all,* she told herself, *this isn't exactly Mozart I'm listening to.*

She and the five other girls clustered behind a rail to the right of the piano, waiting for the first customer to approach. Others followed, and within a few minutes, all of them were dancing.

This isn't too bad, she thought. It was almost impossible to dance and talk at the same time. The music was fast paced and when it stopped, Felicia was supposed to persuade the man to buy a drink. She wasn't quite sure how to do this and simply said, "Would you like to buy me a drink?"

She nodded to Sven and he put two drinks on the bar. After she downed her drink, she was dancing with a different man. This time, her partner started to rub up against her and when she pulled away, he yanked her back and whispered an obscenity in her ear. Sven started to move around the bar, but the music ended. The man staggered away drunk and oblivious to any wrong doing.

He's a harmless drunk, she told herself. *But I only got twenty-five cents for that dance. Hope the next one is better.*

She danced until her feet felt like weights she could not lift. She was sure the leather had worn off the soles of her shoes. It seemed to her the miners' clumsy feet, inside their heavy boots, unerringly found her toes. A throbbing started in her feet and as the night wore on, the pain extended way up her legs.

I can make it, she thought through gritted teeth when her muscles cried out for her to stop. She ran through a variety of responses to the men's apologies, and kept a smile plastered on her face. But, she was counting the minutes until she could change out of her dancing outfit and go to bed.

Finally, the music stopped and it was time for the piano player to leave. She was thankful the night was almost over. She had listened to comments she would have preferred not to hear, but thought she deflected most of the unwanted attention rather well. And, now, at last, she could leave. She hadn't kept track of how much money she was owed, but trusted Sven wouldn't cheat her.

When she walked over to collect her night's earnings, she saw a tall, thin, clean-shaven man with large dark eyes and a kind looking face sitting at the end of the bar. He obviously wasn't a miner because he wore a dark suit and a white shirt. And he had clean fingernails.

Clean fingernails, thought Felicia. *What an agreeable sight.*

He nodded at her as she stood there waiting for Sven, who slid an envelope across the counter to her.

"Doc, meet Felicia. She's new in town and started dancing here tonight."

The doctor rose and extended his hand.

"Felicia, this is Dr. Meyers. He takes care of the men who need tending to after they've fought with one another, or one of them takes a shot at a player whose poker game he didn't like."

Felicia, too tired for polite manners, gave the doctor a small smile. He offered her his seat, but she told him she was on her way back to the hotel. She left thinking he and Sven were a lot more civilized than most of her dance partners.

When Felicia opened the envelope, she was disappointed to see it contained only $15, a lot less than she expected. *But,* she told herself, *it was only my first night. I'll get a lot better at convincing the men to buy extra drinks. And I'll learn how to flirt with them so I get more tips.*

As she lay in bed, she couldn't escape the gnawing sense that something was not right about what she was doing. Wearing a skimpy costume and dancing so close was teasing, leading the men on. It made her feel cheap to do that.

I'll have to think about it in the morning.

And she fell into a deep sleep.

Chapter Nine: Questions

Question - a doubt or uncertainty about something

Across the street from the saloon, Abigail and Corinne moved into Mrs. Woodley's Parlor House.

It didn't take Abigail long to unpack. All she owned fit into one scuffed suitcase. Her underclothes were simple and well darned. She hung her few skirts and blouses, with one good suit, in the closet. She needed a new pair of boots, but they would have to wait. After she emptied the suitcase, she snapped the catch and shoved the empty bag under the bed.

She looked around. What was she supposed to do now? Restlessly, she moved from one piece of furniture to another. First, she fluffed the large down pillows and smoothed the satin quilt on the bed. She felt the softness of the towels stacked on top of the washstand. Moving to the dresser, she examined the blue and white painted ceramic pitcher and matching bowl, turning it over to see the stamp on the bottom. She noticed the slag glass lamp on the table was placed off center and moved it two inches to the right. The room was small and she quickly ran out of things to do.

Nothing was turning out the way she thought it would. She never considered the possibility she would auction off her body. So many questions floated around in her head. What would it be like to have men scrutinize her? How would she handle her first man? Could she stand having a stranger push his way inside her? Would it hurt? Would she bleed?

No one had ever talked to her about sex. She just prayed the winner would be gentle.

Her speculations were interrupted by Mrs. Woodley, who entered with an armload of dresses. A pair of ladies' soft kid boots topped the pile and ribboned undergarments dangled from her left hand.

"These are for you. Pick one to wear tonight," she said and thrust the pile at Abigail. "I want you to advertise what you've got, so be sure to wear this corset."

Abigail turned bright red and lowered her gaze. Mrs. Woodley cupped Abigail's chin in her hand and raised her face so she could look directly at her.

"Child, you have to do better than this. You are here to flaunt yourself and the more you show, the more money you'll earn."

Mrs. Woodley's tone was not unkind. She looked out for her girls and gave them all the necessary information to take care of themselves. But, she was running a business and expected it to be profitable.

Thoroughly embarrassed, Abigail nodded her head, hoping Mrs. Woodley would leave. *How will I ever do this?*

Mrs. Woodley tried to reassure her. "Tonight you'll see it's not so bad. Remember what I told you. Make sure you keep smiling, moan a little, act delighted, and it will be over before you know it. If you have to think, think about how much money you'll have at the end of the night."

Her mission completed, Mrs. Woodley left the room.

Abigail, her arms filled with new clothing, pushed the door closed with her hip.

Money was also on Corinne's mind. *I may start off at $5.00 a visit, but that's not going to last for long. I'll offer such good service, the men will ask for me by name. I want regular customers who I can charge extra to ensure my availability.*

She continued to scheme as she washed and toweled herself dry. She remembered the filthy rag she was expected to use on the train and happily buried her face in the fluffy towel that smelled of the outdoors.

I wonder how many customers I can handle in one night. She thought of Thomas. He was the first and only man she ever slept with. But, this was different. *I'm going to spend the night being a receptacle for more than one man. I have no idea how my body's going to react.*

Questions plagued her. *How sore will I be tomorrow? How many times can I douche before I irritate my insides? How can I be absolutely sure I don't catch any sickness from the men?*

She reviewed Mrs. Woodley's directions and promised herself she would scrupulously follow them. She would take no chances.

As Corinne hooked her petticoat, she wondered why she was putting it on. *Isn't the whole point to take it off? I'll only have to get dressed again and there's an awful lot to put on.* She decided wearing stockings and nothing else under her petticoats would be arousing to a man and convenient for her.

Corinne fastened the corset Mrs. Woodley insisted she wear. Her youthfully solid breasts were pushed up and greatly exposed. She anticipated how profitable men's reaction to her ample curves would be.

Next, she pulled the rust colored taffeta gown over

her head and let it drop to the floor. A former seamstress, Corinne recognized the quality of what she wore. *Mrs. Woodley does pay attention to details*, she thought, admiring the full sleeves and fancy ribbon sash. She adjusted the dress around her tightly cinched waist, and then carefully positioned the pleats until each fell into its proper place.

Her unruly strawberry curls were slicked back into a bun and she hoped they would stay in place. She added some feathers to her chignon to insure they did.

Her preparations complete, Corinne took a deep breath and proceeded down the stairs to begin her first night as a prostitute.

But, Abigail was the one who created a stir when she appeared in the archway. Conversation halted and heads turned in her direction. She hesitated, not knowing whether to enter the room and if she did, where to stand.

Corinne winked at her and resumed her dialogue with one of the guests. Perched on the broad arm of his chair, she spoke with great animation and waved her arms for emphasis. The gentleman, amused by her story, would periodically throw back his head and laugh with gusto.

The other five women expertly handled their conversations with clients. In their vivid gowns, they resembled a flock of brightly colored macaws as they fluttered and fussed over their customers. All were well practiced in knowing when to smile, when to laugh, and when to nod their heads in agreement. They appeared totally enchanted by their companions.

Mrs. Woodley spotted Abigail and motioned for her to approach. When she walked through the room, the two men leaning against the fireplace mantle stopped their exchange and looked her over. Her hair was carefully arranged in a topknot, with a few wispy curls strategically loose around her face. Her lip rouge was lightly applied and she had only the slightest color on her cheeks, all ploys to evoke innocence. From the dresses Mrs. Woodley gave her, she had selected a light lavender taffeta barely covering her bosom. Abigail was discomforted by the close inspection, but tried her best to look unperturbed.

One of the gentlemen pulled out his pocket watch and noticeably checked the time. He looked at Mrs. Woodley who was carefully staging the moment. A little anticipation would whet appetites and raise the bids accordingly. But, she didn't want to wait too long, and his gesture indicated impatience.

Judging the time had arrived, she called the group to attention.

"Gentlemen, you received a special invitation to attend this unique evening. As you know, Abigail recently arrived in Crystal Creek and will be joining us here at my Parlor. But, tonight, she needs someone to bring her upstairs and show her, for the first time, how her charms will be appreciated. This is her initial experience with a man and I'm sure any one of you can prove to her the delights of being a real woman."

She gestured for Abigail to turn around and show herself off. Abigail pivoted once trying to hide her embarrassment. Her arms dangled awkwardly at her sides, barely touching the skirts of her outfit. She tried her best to smile as she turned and surveyed the men. She wondered who it would be. Right now, she didn't care. She wanted it over, with herself upstairs and out of view.

"Shall we begin?" prompted Mrs. Woodley. "Who will open the bidding?"

Chapter 10: Auction

Auction – a sale where bidders compete for the prize

T.J. Hansen, the editor and owner of the *Crystal Creek Courier*, stepped forward and in a loud, clear voice offered $100. Tonight he was clean shaven and neatly dressed in his Sunday suit, and had made an effort to scrub off the black ink that stained his fingernails. He started the newspaper three years ago when there was not much news to cover. It grew with the town, and he now employed two typesetters and one other reporter besides himself. He recognized he would not be the highest bidder tonight, but was pleased to be included. At the very least, he would write an interesting story for the next edition.

Roland Hart chuckled when he heard the bid and said, "T.J., let's get more serious here. I'll bid $200."

Hart, the owner of one of the town's largest mines, was a regular customer at Mrs. Woodley's. He accumulated his massive wealth from the silver bullion taken out of his three mines. His six foot, two inch frame could easily intimidate anyone who didn't know him. He had a brusque manner but was an excellent businessman, always honest and fair in his dealings. When he heard about the "Virgin Auction," a rarity for sure, he made his intention to participate known. He brought enough money with him to go higher than his present bid. A few hundred dollars for this exceptional experience meant nothing to him.

Judd Cameron, a rancher with a 5,000 acre spread, spoke next. "Gentlemen, let's not insult the lady. I bid $300 and say the auction is over."

Cameron was a larger than life character who barreled through life at full speed. He could usually be found straddling his sleek, black stallion riding to the ends of his vast ranch. It was said he knew each of his cowhands personally and took care of their families if a need arose. With his rugged good looks and his cheerful personality, he was one of the most well-liked citizens in the town.

There were two other men invited to bid, but before they could do so, the price went too high. They would console themselves with the other new addition to the parlor house. With barely perceptible nods, they agreed who would be first, once the auction was over.

"I say continue," said Hart. "I'm offering $400."

Abigail watched one, then the other, of the two men still bidding. She was staggered by the price already offered, and wondered what they expected from her.

Was this only for the bragging rights of being the first? Would someone spend money for that? She didn't understand, but was excited by the growing amount. She stood quietly watching the men as they pondered their next offer. To her amazement, the bidding continued.

I'm going to use this money to transform myself. With all this cash, I can buy what I need. Corinne can tell me what real ladies wear, and about the latest styles and the best fabrics. And Felicia can teach me how to use words properly. When she speaks, she always sounds so refined.

A burst of applause interrupted her plans.

"$500," offered Cameron, raising the bid to what Abigail found an unthinkable amount.

Hart studied Cameron's face, and recognized he would continue bidding until he got what he wanted. It wasn't about Abigail any more. It was about being the winner. He signaled his withdrawal from the auction by raising two fingers to his forehead and walked over to the bar.

"Congratulations, Mr. Cameron," beamed Mrs. Woodley as she motioned to the bartender.

"Drinks all around. On the house!"

She gave Abigail a small shove in Mr. Cameron's direction.

Abigail gathered the courage and the resolution to do what she had to do. She walked over to Mr. Cameron and extended her hand.

"Yes, congratulations."

After a celebratory glass of champagne, Mr. Cameron offered his arm and escorted Abigail up the stairs to her room. He was a sympathetic man and earlier, when he saw the apprehension on Abigail's face, he resolved to outbid the others. He was curious why she allowed such an auction to take place, but decided against asking. Money was undoubtedly the answer. He wondered how she got reduced to selling herself. Where did she come from and how did she end up in Crystal Creek?

He watched with amusement as she carefully laid out the towel and soap. From experience, he knew she was following Mrs. Woodley's instructions, and he sat patiently on the bed until she indicated she was ready. He then rose, shrugged off his jacket and started to undo his large silver belt buckle. Abigail turned scarlet when she saw what he was doing.

"Abigail, try to relax. Believe me, I'll do my best not to hurt you," he said, attempting to put her at ease.

Abigail nodded and made an effort to relax. Mentally taking a deep breath, she went behind the screen in the corner of the room and removed her dress, petticoats, corset and stockings. She pulled down the pale pink dressing gown thrown over the top and tied it tightly around her waist. She crossed to the bed and slipped beneath the covers.

Waves of nausea made their way up to her throat. She swallowed several times and forced herself to look directly at Cameron. She was relieved he was handsome. She wasn't sure she could have done this if the winner was a fat, hairy man who smelled bad. She supposed she would have to put up with those men in the future. But, at least not tonight.

When he removed his shirt, his wide shoulders looked even larger. Although he was a big man, there wasn't any excess weight on his body. He slid into bed, pulling his long lean legs under the covers.

"Now, darlin', I want you to try to enjoy this. You're not experienced, but you're a woman and I know how to make a woman feel good. I'm going to take my time. We're going to do this thing right because I want you to know there are men like me who like to please our women."

He continued speaking in a soothing tone, trying to reassure her as he moved his hands over her body.

She tried to focus on the stroking of her arm, but the muscles in her body refused to cooperate. Every part of her was wary, anticipating what was to come. She tried to use tricks Corinne had told her to divert her mind, but none of them worked.

If only women could stay like this forever, Cameron thought. *Such smooth, silky skin and she smells so good.*

He enjoyed the feel of her body, although she was lying completely rigid, forgetting all her instructions. He could feel himself growing hard, but exercised control until he could get Abigail stimulated. He brushed her nipples with his fingertips and then cupped her breast in his hand. He could feel her nipples growing rigid.

"Good girl, Abigail," he whispered softly. "Let yourself experience how good this can be."

He continued to stroke her gently, running his hand down her arms and up her back. He turned her body towards his and pressed against her. He kissed her tenderly at first, and then, with more passion. He sensed her willingness, but understood apprehension eclipsed all her other emotions.

How long does this go on? Abigail wondered. *It hasn't been too bad so far. He's being gentle and I'm sure he's trying to make it easy for me.*

Then she felt how hard Cameron was and remembered when she learned what that meant. She allowed Frankie Johnson to push her against the kitchen wall and kiss her. When he pulled her close to him, she felt the same hardness and pulled away.

"What is that?" she had asked him. He laughed and said, "Don't you know anything?" When she shook her head, he explained what his hardness was. Feeling Cameron's now, she decided it would be over soon.

He moved his hands between her legs and felt for the place that would help her lose some of the control she was maintaining. As he ran his hand back and forth, back and forth, he could feel her tensing and when he finally felt some dampness, he mounted her, thrusting lightly.

Abigail flinched when she was entered. She braced herself for the pain she had been told to expect. But, it didn't hurt like it was supposed to. Cameron became more aroused and drove harder and harder. She let out a small cry when pain suddenly surged through her body. And then, felt only the emptiness as he pulled out.

That's it? We're done? That was worth $500?

He rolled off, and in order to give Abigail time to

compose herself, he lay still and looked up at the ceiling until she said, "Thank you. I know you tried to be gentle."

"Are you all right? Did I hurt you?"

She shook her head and looked down at the sheets. She saw only a few specks of blood. But, then a trickle of warmth oozed down her leg, and she reached for the towel next to the bed. She looked at the pink stain and started to get up for a washcloth.

He took her by the wrist before she could leave the bed and said, "Abigail, you were scared and tonight had to be difficult for you. But no customer wants a woman who lays there like a board. From now on, you've got to put on a show of enjoying yourself. I assume you are here for the money, and if you act like a willing partner, you'll get you what you want faster."

He let go of her wrist and she walked across the room. The smell of sex surprised her, a sweet, salty clinging smell. She rubbed herself vigorously with the washcloth and slipped on her robe.

He's right. Now I know what happens, she thought. *Why do men want this so much?*

She returned to the bed and sat on the edge facing him.

"You're right about how I should act. Those are the exact words Mrs. Woodley said to me. It won't be like this again. I will learn, and I will practice and I will get it right. Come back and visit me again and you'll see."

He let out a hearty full-throated laugh, and Abigail shyly smiled back at him.

"Why did you buy me?" she asked.

The question was unexpected, and Cameron leaned back against the pillows formulating his answer.

"Because I looked at you standing there like a deer when a hunter's snuck up on her. Frozen, but needing to run. I saw how uncomfortable you were, and I figured I could make it easier for you," he said.

"You did, and I thank you. But, can I ask you another question?"

He picked up a hairpin that had fallen onto the quilt and handed it to her.

"Of course, you can."

"You said I need to put on a show. How do I do that? What pleases a man?"

"Well, Abigail, I'm sure you will find that out as you work here, but I can start you off with a suggestion or two," he said.

But not too many, he thought. *A lot of men will find your innocence to their liking.*

She sat there, waiting, eager to learn.

"This is an expensive parlor house. The expectation is you offer yourself wholeheartedly. Try not to look like it's just a job to you. Act willing and eager. Be welcoming."

He was surprised by her naiveté. But, of course, Mrs. Woodley had hired her for exactly that reason.

"Act friendly, look like I'm enjoying myself. Then what?"

"I don't think it's going to be a problem. You are one pretty lady. And you know the old saying about how practice makes perfect."

"I'll try to do what you said. You are such a nice man."

She took Cameron's hand and brought it up to her lips. The simple gesture excited him.

He pulled her close and said, "Let's see how much attention you were paying."

When he left, Abigail listened until she heard Cameron's boots clatter down the stairs. Then she twirled around the room and hugged herself. She flopped into a chair and began to plan how to spend the incredible amount of money she would soon receive.

Chapter Eleven: Postmortems

Postmortems - an analysis carried out shortly after the conclusion of an event

Felicia was awake and dressed by 11:00am. She wasn't hungry, but Vivian insisted on placing a platter of food in front of her. She pushed the eggs around the plate until they were an unappetizing yellow jumble. She forced some coffee down and politely endured Vivian's endless questions. At last, she was able to escape and headed to Mrs. Woodley's to meet with Corinne and Abigail for a postmortem of the night before.

"Good morning. How are you today after all the dancing you did last night?" Mrs. Woodley asked as she stepped aside to allow Felicia to enter.

"Does everyone know everything in this town?"

"Dear, you must realize a new woman in town is big news, especially one who looks like you."

"It went well, thank you. Sven was very helpful and I'm grateful he gave me the chance."

Mrs. Woodley waited quietly, and Felicia didn't want her to get the wrong impression of why she was there.

"Are Abigail and Corinne awake yet? I've come to see them."

"I think Corinne is in Abigail's room. Go right on up."

As she watched Felicia climb the stairs, Mrs. Woodley wondered how many more nights it would take for her to realize she was dancing to the wrong tune.

Felicia hesitated when she reached the upstairs hallway. She forgot to ask Mrs. Woodley which room was Abigail's. She faced a long, narrow corridor with four doors on either side. She stood in front of the door on her right, and raised her hand to knock.

"Felicia, we're in here," called Corinne as she stuck her head out a door further down the hall. "Come on, we waited for you get here before we said a word."

"I didn't know which room it was," Felicia said and hastened towards Corinne. The red flocked wallpaper made the hall dark, and even this early in the day, the gas lamps beside each door were lit.

As soon as they were in the room, Corinne turned to Abigail.

"Felicia's here now. Let's hear it. You look absolutely pleased with yourself. I guess last night went well."

She adjusted a pillow behind her head and made herself comfortable on the bed.

"I'm ready. Don't leave out a single detail."

Abigail leaned against the dresser and cleared her throat.

"Well, to start, I have more money than I've ever seen in my life. Who would believe someone would pay that much to get so little? And, it was actually pretty easy. Mr. Cameron was so considerate and I didn't even have to moan and groan. But that was probably good because he's so nice, he would have thought he hurt me. Believe me, I didn't know what I was doing, and I got paid a fortune."

"How much did he pay for you?" asked Felicia.

"$500!" announced Abigail proudly.

"$500? That's wonderful," said Felicia, thinking about the $15 envelope for her night's work.

"And I made $50," preened Corinne. "I was only with two men, and they both gave me a huge tip. It wasn't really that bad. Both of them were gentlemen. They acted like I was a lady granting them my favor."

Corinne and Abigail turned expectantly towards Felicia. They were anxious to hear about her first night at the saloon.

"Sounds like you both did much better than I did. First of all, I had to wear this skimpy red satin dress that only came up to my knees. Also, some black fishnet stockings and red high heeled shoes. The finishing touch was a feather and some red rose nonsense in my hair. Can you just see what I looked like in that outfit?"

"Oh, Felicia, I can't imagine. It sounds awful," said Corinne.

"Wait, I'm not done," she said.

She unlaced her boots, then pulled them off and wiggled her toes. She started to massage the balls of her feet and continued.

"Then I danced and danced, if you can call getting stepped on repeatedly, dancing. My feet hurt so much this morning, I could barely get my boots on to walk over here. Oh, and I was supposed to sell liquor to get a commission, but I didn't do that very well. I hardly got any tips either and wound up with the grand sum of $15 for the night."

Corinne and Abigail could see how dejected Felicia was. After a minute, Corinne said, "Come and work here, Felicia. Look at the dresses Mrs. Woodley supplies. I can recognize quality and they are the latest styles. She doesn't stint on what we wear."

"Why should she? You're paying for it," said Felicia and began to point the toes on one foot up and down as she rubbed her calf.

"At least it's not red satin. My God, Felicia, you had to wear red satin!"

She ignored Corinne and continued her dismal recital.

"The men, with one or two exceptions, were raunchy, drunk, and dirty miners who only wanted to fondle me. Doesn't sound like the same class of men that come here."

"Mr. Cameron, who won the auction, is such a gentleman," said Abigail. "He told me he owns a huge ranch, with lots of cattle. He lives in a big house by himself, except for his housekeeper and the Mexican maids. He tries to learn Spanish, but he's not very good at it. So when he wants people to talk to, he likes to come to Mrs. Woodley's. He said he doesn't go to the saloon because he doesn't gamble and it's so noisy there. Besides, the whiskey is much better here."

When Abigail paused, Corinne said to Felicia, "Why are you so stubborn? If you worked here, you would get beautiful clothing, a comfortable bedroom, all your meals and you wouldn't have to associate with dirty, smelly drunks."

"Don't push me, Corinne. I still didn't have to 'entertain' any of those dirty, smelly drunks and that makes a big difference."

She sat up straighter and crossed one leg over the other. She began to rotate her foot in tight circles.

"Stop playing with your feet and listen to me!" pleaded Corinne. "You didn't make any money last night, and you still have to buy food and pay for your hotel room."

She squatted down in front of Felicia's chair. "Please, think about it. It's really not bad here."

"Corinne, you've only been here one night. How can you be so sure?"

"Because I saw the type of man who comes here. Because I had a lively conversation with an intelligent client. Because I danced to lovely music, not some off key saloon piano. Because I drank some good quality wine and because I made a lot of money. That's how I know."

Felicia said, "Give me time. Just give me time. I can't make such a drastic decision without a lot of consideration."

"Sounds like you have a hard time allowing yourself to make any decision," Abigail said.

They were interrupted by a knock on the door, and when Abigail opened it, Mrs. Woodley asked, "Abigail, do you have a minute. I need you to come with me to my office."

When they were gone, Felicia turned to Corinne, "Did you hear what Abigail just said about me?"

"Of course, I heard. I'm sitting right here," answered Corinne.

"You know what I mean. She acts totally oblivious and then, out of the blue, says something that makes you think she can read your mind."

"You mean like what she said on the train about the real reason Mrs. Hale gave the servants her old clothes?"

"Exactly. That it wasn't an act of charity, it was to make Mrs. Hale feel superior to them. I'm sure she was right about that and she's absolutely right about my decision-making problem," said Felicia.

"Well, my lovely friend, perhaps it's time for you to make the right one."

At the saloon that night, Felicia thought of the extravagant gowns Corinne showed her and grimaced as she slipped her dance-hall outfit off the hanger. She knew

Mrs. Woodley had kept her promise to Abigail, and a dark blue velvet evening dress now hung in her closet. *It's stupid to make a decision based on clothes,* she told herself and pulled the red satin dress over her hips. She fastened her stockings with a black lacy garter and attached the two ornaments in her hair.

Since she was ready early, Felicia strolled into the saloon. She made her way through the drunken laughter with a bright smile pasted on her face. One or two men looked up from their poker game, concentration broken by the flash of her legs. She playfully slapped their reaching hands and tried not to let her distaste show.

When she reached the bar, she climbed onto a bar stool and tugged at her skirt as it climbed above her knees. The gesture was met by loud whistles from the men who were watching her progress.

"I see you're back for another go at it," said Sven. He wiped the counter in front of her. "What are you doing out front so early?"

"I'm trying to act like I belong here," she answered.

You are never going to belong here, he thought. *You're a different breed.*

"It might help if you pick this up and belt it back."

He put a shot glass full of watered tea in front of her. One of the men at the bar chanted, "Drink, drink, drink." The others picked up his demand and a small crowd gathered around her.

Sven poured another one. He leaned over and whispered in her ear, "Try to smile, you look like a scared rabbit."

She threw back the drink and set the glass down on the counter so hard it almost broke.

"Now here's a shot of real whiskey because I see the professor coming and your night's about to begin."

She picked up the drink and saluted the men. Cheers

and whistles accompanied her as the men parted to let her pass.

Sven watched her swing open the rail and step up to the platform next to the piano. *Don't figure she'll last much longer. No matter how she tries, she's never going to be a dance-hall girl.*

Felicia's second night was worse than her first one. The crowd was more boisterous, and the men all over her, not caring that they were breaking the rules of the saloon. Her first customer smelled like he hadn't washed in a week, and she barely made it through the dance. She didn't even try to hustle a drink, she just wanted him gone.

Her next customer was so inebriated, he couldn't dance. He stayed propped up against her, grinning until the music stopped. No drink money there either. She breathed a sigh of relief when a stocky man with a pleasant smile took her hand. He was newly shaved and his clothes were brushed. But, his breath reeked of alcohol and when he laughed, expelling a mouthful of fumes, she almost gagged.

She continued to dance and smile and didn't complain as one after the other, clumsy, intoxicated men whirled her around.

After a while, Felicia could smell the stale beer and tobacco on her body. The shouts, the laughter and the curses of the carousers melded into a background of noise. The off-key piano offended her ears. She fought back an overwhelming desire to flee.

During the rests between dances, done to give the men more time to buy drinks, Sally told her it was pay day and always like this when the men got their money.

"The tips should be good tonight," she whispered and stepped down to join her next partner.

"They better be," said Felicia. "I don't know how much longer I can do this."

She was approached by a particularly obnoxious man, big bellied and smelling like a cigar. *He even looks like a cigar,* she thought as she glanced at his thick, squat body firmly packed into a brown suit. He put his chubby arms around her and held her much too closely. He invited her to his hotel room and when she politely declined for the third time, he accused her of being a snob.

The music ended but he didn't let go. He kept his pudgy fingers firmly wrapped around her arm. He began to call her names and insult her.

"Hey lady, don't pull that stuck up act on me. I'm the one with the bucks, remember? You're nothing but a dance-hall whore. What's the matter? Ain't I good enough for you, your majesty? Do you think you're better than me?"

"Don't you dare talk to me like that!" she said, pulling as far away from him as she could.

The man pulled her closer and whispered in her ear, "You're going to fuck me good for saying that. Come on bitch, we're leaving."

Felicia snapped. Memories of her husband's verbal abuse assailed her. She would not allow another man to denigrate her. She slapped the offender with every bit of strength she had. He became the target for all her frustration, all her indecision and all the drunks she'd tolerated the last two nights.

The man's hand went up to his face, and then he reached for his gun. Sven was all over him before he could get to it. He pulled the man's arms up behind his back and held them in a vise-like grip.

"I don't know what you just said to her, but out you go."

He pitched the man through the door and watched him stumble down the steps and into the street.

"Go spend your money somewhere else," Sven shouted over his shoulder and rushed back inside.

When he got there, Felicia was gone. He looked around the room but did not see her anywhere. It finally occurred to him to look in the back room. He found her there, buttoning her coat.

"Are you okay?" he asked.

He expected to find an hysterical woman, but she appeared completely composed, although there was an angry set to her mouth he hadn't seen before.

"It's obvious I don't belong here."

Her voice was too controlled, devoid of all emotion.

"If I have to put up with being treated like a commodity, I might as well go across the street and earn a lot more money."

"When you cross that street, you'll be crossing more than the road. The men on this side may be crude, even vulgar, and the men on the other side well-groomed and debonair, but be careful, Felicia. I've heard about some of the depraved requests they make of the girls. Remember, you don't have to do any of them. There'll always be someone else there who will."

Felicia stared at Sven. His little speech surprised her.

He walked over to where she had neatly stacked her dancing outfit. He let his fingers run over the smooth satin of the dress and then said, "Maybe you should go home. You don't look like you have to do this. I'm sure your family would welcome you back. If you need money, I'd be glad to help you out."

Touched, Felicia answered, "I have no family anymore."

Sven took her hand in his. "I wish you luck, Felicia. I really do. You seem like a nice woman, and I hope things turn out well for you."

Tears formed behind her eyes. *What is wrong with me?* she thought. *Can I only cry when someone is nice to me?*

She thanked him and let herself out the rear door, then continued down the alley until she reached the hotel. She slipped in the back way and went directly up to her room. Felicia looked out the window and down the street to Mrs. Woodley's Parlor House in time to see the light come on in Corinne's room.

Chapter Twelve: Start

Start - the first part or early stages of something

A triumphant Mrs. Woodley accepted Felicia as her newest "boarder." *Three out of three, exactly as I predicted.*

"I'll take these and put them in your room," she said, eyeing Felicia's well made cowhide cases. "You need to see Dr. Meyers for a medical examination and a choice of contraceptives. In your case, I'm sure it's a formality, but it's got to be done. My other instructions can wait until he certifies that you are healthy."

She watched Felicia walk down the street. *What a fine addition she's going to make. That girl has class written all over her. I wonder how many ballet lessons she's taken to get her back that straight.*

She recognized much of herself in Felicia. She, too, endured hours of music lessons, ballet classes and private tutoring from a long line of governesses. Then, marriage to a prominent lawyer, until he foolishly became smitten with one of his clients. In a fit of anger and humiliation, she took off to Colorado with Harold Woodley. The money he left enabled her to open the parlor house and make a pile of her own. *If he hadn't died, I wonder where I'd be today.* Mrs. Woodley shook her head and walked towards her office. She had a long list awaiting her attention.

Felicia appeared at the doctor's office and explained the purpose of her visit. After her examination, she sat in the chair beside his desk and watched him fill out the necessary forms. The room smelled of herbs and medicines. Large jars, with neatly affixed labels, filled the shelves. Her doctor, back East, had a library of thick medical volumes, not apothecary jars, in his office. She didn't see one book and wondered about Dr. Meyers' credentials.

He glanced at Felicia as he completed her papers. She reminded him of the porcelain dolls his sister collected as a child. They were beautiful to look at, but needed to be handled with care. She conveyed that same fragility and it brought out his protective instincts. He wanted to cry out, "No, don't do. You're too good for this."

Instead, he searched for a neutral subject.

"Sven told me what happened last night. He said the job didn't work out for you."

"No, it didn't," she said. "But I think Sven is a good, kind man. Meeting him made up for a whole lot of those awful men I danced with. How can he stand to be around them all the time?"

"It's not the same as it was for you. He doesn't have to dance with them."

Her spontaneous laugh aroused a sensation he believed long buried. Seeking a distraction, he busied himself cleaning the nib of his pen. He replaced it in the top drawer and then folded down the top of his glass inkwell. Nerves settled, he continued speaking.

"Most of the men are harmless. The miners do tough physical labor in dangerous places. At the end of the day, all they want is a place to drink and maybe gamble. The prospectors come in to throw enough liquor down their throats to forget they're not going to make their fortune out here. And, as you noticed, when any of these women-hungry men see a female, they react. To them, you are all gorgeous and desirable."

"But they have no manners. And their language," she protested.

He laughed and reminded her she lived in a mining town.

Dr. Meyers leaned back in his chair and formed a steeple with his fingertips. He wondered about the woman sitting at his desk. If two nights as a dance hall girl had discouraged her, why did she think working at Mrs. Woodley's would be any better? The men might not be as coarse, but did she have any idea what she was getting herself into.

"Are you and Sven good friends?" she asked. She remembered how comfortable the doctor looked sitting at the bar.

"Sven came to Crystal Creek five years ago to prospect for gold. After he lived here a year, he figured he could make more money selling liquor than waiting for gold nuggets to appear in his pan. He used what little funds he had left to open Big Swede's Saloon. I got here three years ago, stopped in for a drink, and we've been friends ever since."

"Then it appears there are two nice men in town, Dr. Meyers. Thank you for your help."

She folded the forms and put them in her purse. As she walked down his porch steps, she thought, *I just had a normal conversation with a normal man.* For the first time since she arrived in Crystal Creek, she felt encouraged.

Mrs. Woodley tried to keep smug satisfaction off her face as she took the doctor's certificate from Felicia.

"Why don't you get settled in? Your bags are in your

room. Up the stairs and two doors to your left. I've put you across from Corinne. We'll talk more later."

Felicia looked around at her new home. *Well, I'm certainly taking up less and less space,* she thought as she traced her trajectory from her grandmother's large home to her own modest, but comfortable house, to her room in a bordello. *Now, I'll try to start thinking like Corinne. This is an adventure. It's a way to make money fast. With enough money, I'll be independent. That's why I came out here, isn't it?*

She removed one item at a time from her suitcase and laid it on the bed. She neatly stacked her undergarments in the dresser and shook out her traveling suit. She was hanging it in the closet when she heard a knock on her door.

"We are the official welcoming committee," Abigail said, and presented Felicia with one red rose.

"But don't put it in your hair," warned Corinne. "We don't have any matching satin dresses."

Felicia was surprised by the sense of relief she felt when she saw her friends. They didn't stay long, but as she left, Corinne told Felicia she would stop by before she went to bed. For the next six months, they would end every night at Mrs. Woodley's that same way.

Once they were gone, Felicia stretched out on her new bed. She watched the reflection of the setting sun in her dresser mirror. The room was bathed in an orange glow. A feeling of optimism suffused her. *I did it. I made the decision. Right or wrong, from now on, I'm the one in charge.*

When it was time to get ready, she began what would become her nightly ritual. She twisted her long, straight brown hair into a knot and slipped in some pins to keep it in place. Next, she selected one of the gowns Mrs. Woodley hung in her closet. Felicia never wore such bright colors. *Yesterday red satin, and today I'm going to look like a peacock,* she thought as she sorted through the vivid outfits.

She chose a green velvet gown which went nicely with the emerald earrings she intended to wear. They were one of the few things Stewart gave her that she took with her. The jewelry was her insurance in case she ran out of money.

She laid the dress on the bed and put on the corset Mrs. Woodley supplied. After she pulled and tied all the laces, she slipped the dress over her head. She walked over to the floor mirror and turned to view herself from all angles. The Felicia she was used to seeing had disappeared into the bright green gown. *Except for the color, I could have worn this dress to any of the fancy balls I went to. Bet if I looked like this then, my dance card would have filled up more quickly.*

As she imagined what the night would be like, she reminded herself of how easily she could drift away mentally and still look engaged.

How ironic. Who would have thought I would do that again. Whenever her husband began one of his tirades, she would sit passively and pretend to listen. But, in her head, she went far away. One of her favorite techniques was to see how high she could count before he stopped his rant. She once reached 1,020. She smiled to herself. *Tonight I'll count again, but instead of numbers it will be dollars.*

Fully dressed, she walked to the vanity table. The few containers Mrs. Woodley supplied were arranged on top. She reached for the powder first. Since she never wore make-up, she would guess her way through the process. She patted the powder on lightly and then picked up the rouge. She dipped her finger into the small round pot and rubbed some onto her cheeks. Then she applied the darker red lip rouge to her lips.

My goodness, I've become a "painted lady." It was a derogatory term used for prostitutes and she now realized its origin. *Look at me, Gran. I followed the rules and what did I get? A marriage of misery and despair. A life with no happiness and no joy.*

She scrutinized her new self. *Let's see what happens when I don't follow the rules.*

She took a deep breath, and with her head held high, made her way downstairs to the parlor. The other women were already there, chatting as they awaited the arrival of their first clients. A silence fell when Felicia entered the room. No one made any attempt to hide her curiosity. A woman in a deep red gown, the exact color of the divan on which she sat, unabashedly looked her up and down. Felicia could read derision well, having seen it so many times on Stewart's face.

Corinne came to her rescue. She put her arm around Felicia's waist and said, "This is my dear friend Felicia. I'm sure Mrs. Woodley told you all about her."

A tiny, sweet-faced young woman jumped up from the large, overstuffed chair which dwarfed her, an effect she undoubtedly fostered, and kissed Felicia lightly on both cheeks.

"Welcome to Mrs. Woodley's, Felicia. I'm Livvy and if you have any questions, come and talk to me."

The ice broken, the other women introduced themselves. Apparently, a number of them used working pseudonyms. No mother would name her daughter Prairie Rose, Texas Queen or Maybe Minnie. Felicia was especially tickled by Lulu Lee, who said she added Lee to her name, hoping the former Confederate soldiers would think she was related to General Robert E. Lee.

Mrs. Woodley bustled into the room to confirm they were ready. One by one, she inspected the women and when she was satisfied, left to let in the first customers.

Felicia wandered over to the piano and envisioned herself

playing as she hummed a Chopin melody. Mrs. Woodley, with a client in tow, appeared at her side and cleared her throat meaningfully.

"Felicia, this is John Hutchins, the new manager of the Crystal Creek Opera House."

Felicia followed her instructions and smiled warmly. As he looked her over, Hutchins smoothed the sides of his moustache and goatee. They were a few shades redder than his thick auburn hair. Of medium height, he was slimly built and impeccably dressed in a well-tailored suit. Felicia knew what a custom fitted suit like that cost. She looked down and noticed his shoes were shined to a mirror finish. His tie was knotted with precision, and his Adam's apple bobbed when he said, "I don't think I've seen you here before. I'm certain I would have noticed you."

"Why, thank you. You're right. This is my first night here."

"Shall we drink to that?" he asked as he signaled the bartender.

No need to hustle here, she thought as she accepted the glass of wine he handed her.

"I assumed you'd prefer wine to bourbon," he said and raised his glass. "To beginnings." His deep baritone voice made the toast sound significant.

She took a sip of wine. *Corinne was right. This was excellent.*

"Mrs. Woodley introduced you as the new manager of the Crystal Creek Opera House. Do you make the arrangements for all the acts?"

"I do. We have an excellent selection of artists lined up. Are you familiar with classical music?"

"I play the piano."

"A string quartet arrives in two days. They will be followed by the Great Western Opera Company making

94

their debut at our theater. I expect it will be a grand social event for Crystal Creek."

"Sounds lovely. I always attended the opera back home."

It struck Felicia that this identical conversation could have taken place in someone's drawing room, and she had to remind herself where she was and what she shortly would do.

"Shall we dance?" Mr. Hutchins held out his hand.

Drink and dance, not unlike the saloon, she thought as she stepped into his arms. But, tonight she enjoyed the music and found their dialog engaging. She wasn't sure how she would enjoy what would happen next, but right now, she was waltzing to the pleasing sound of a well-tuned piano.

When the music stopped, he looked at his watch and said, "Shall we retire to your room?"

She watched as Mr. Hutchins carefully hung his suit and shirt on the gentleman's valet at the foot of the bed and precisely lined up his shoes. When he was satisfied all was just as he wanted it, he climbed into bed.

She undressed as he indicated he wished her to do. She was later to find out this was not always necessary, but depended on the client's wishes. She felt self-conscious as no man but Stewart had ever seen her naked and she quickly slipped beneath the covers.

He performed like he had memorized an instruction manual. First he kissed her neck and then he fondled her breasts. He moved his hands down her back to caress her buttocks, all the while pulling her closer and closer to him. When he found himself hard enough, he reached for the rubbers he brought with him. It was not a common occurrence for men to bring "English gentlemen."

Fastidious to the smallest detail, she thought.

"Shall I help you?" she asked, to which he readily agreed.

He mounted her and finished quickly. The moment he was done, he hastened out of bed and back into his clothes. Fully clad, he checked his watch again, thanked her and left.

She lay there and compared him to her husband. *Not much different. It's all about them. But, there's no reason to expect it wouldn't be.*

She greeted her next client, a young, tall, impossibly thin man with the saddest eyes she ever saw. Ethan Anderson was obviously ill at ease and although he tried to make small talk, he didn't do it well. He seemed relieved when they left to go to her room.

Once there, he headed not to the bed, but instead to one of the chairs. As he dropped into it, he announced he paid to just talk. He needed someone to talk to, but only a woman. He didn't think any man would understand how he felt.

Felicia sat down opposite him and waited. He was overwrought and would begin when he was ready.

"You look like her, you know."

"Like who?"

"My wife. She died two months ago, and it's all my fault."

"I'm so sorry," Felicia said. "Please, tell me about it."

"She didn't want to come out here. I made her come, and now she's dead because of me."

"What happened?"

He stared vacantly at the windows as he tried to compose himself. He repeatedly clenched and unclenched his fists. He gulped a few times and then drew in a deep breath which rattled around in his bony chest. He put a fist up to his mouth but he couldn't hold back his loud sobs. With his head in his hands, he broke down and wept. Felicia sat motionless until he was able to begin his story.

"I'm an architect, but I wasn't too successful where we lived. I thought with the money pouring into towns like Crystal Creek, and all the buildings going up as fast as they could be hammered together, there would be a better chance of doing well out here. Ella, that's my wife, tried and tried to talk me out of it, but I was determined to test my idea."

He paused and braced himself for what he would say next.

"We were only out here a month when Ella got some kind of fever and in two days she was, she was…gone. If we were back home, the doctor could have given her some medicine. But, out here, there's only one doctor, and when Ella got sick he was away tending to someone else. By the time he came to us, it was too late. So you see, if I didn't drag her out here, she'd still be alive."

His story done, he studied the battered felt hat on his lap.

"I'm so sorry," Felicia said again. Faced with such grief, she couldn't think what else to say.

"Did I tell you, you look like her?" he asked.

Felicia reached out her hand to comfort him and he flinched.

"Don't touch me. It would be disloyal to Ella."

He jumped up and said, "I gotta go. I could only afford to pay for a short time."

He jammed his hat on his head and strode to the door. She imagined his step appeared a little lighter as if telling his story had lifted some of the weight of his sorrow.

"Thanks for listening."

She sat there and stared at the closed door. *How sad. But, he's young. Time will pass and he'll be able to get on with his life.*

Wanting to believe it was true, Felicia slowly walked down the stairs to continue her evening.

At the exact time Mr. Hutchins checked his watch, Dr. Philip Meyers hoisted himself onto his usual stool at the end of the bar. Sven immediately poured a beer and slid the mug down the counter. Philip raised it to his lips and drank it halfway down.

"What's bothering you, Doc?" asked Sven when he saw the beer disappear so rapidly.

"I can't help thinking about what's going on at Mrs. Woodley's."

"Same thing that always goes on there. Why the interest tonight?"

"Felicia."

"You don't even know her. What? You saw her here once?"

"And she came to my office this morning."

"And?"

"I don't know, Sven. There's something about her."

"There sure is. I offered her money to get home."

"And what did she say?"

"She had no home to go to."

Philip took out a small pouch of tobacco and reached into his pocket for a piece of rolling paper. He gently tapped some tobacco onto the paper and licked it closed. Sven struck a match on his heel and lit the cigarette.

"Look," said Philip, pointing across the street. "Isn't that Bennett going in there? How such a bully stays in the Mayor's office is beyond me."

"You know, I heard talk a while ago he tied up one of the girls and roughed her up pretty badly."

"The talk is true. I took care of her. Lots of abrasions and contusions on her wrists where she struggled against the rope. Mrs. Woodley hushed it up fast. She didn't want to mess with Bennett."

He threw the cigarette on the floor and crushed the butt with his boot. He drank the rest of his beer and pointed at the mug. Sven picked it up to refill.

"And you know, he'll head right to Felicia. He likes to check out the new girls."

"If you're so worried, go play Sir Galahad."

"I don't ever go, and even if I went tonight, what good would it do? I can't keep watch over her every night."

"Then drink up and forget about it. There's nothing you can do."

Sven put another beer down in front of the doctor and then, as the music stopped, busied himself pouring drinks for the thirsty crowd. He kept an eye on one of the poker games and hoped there wouldn't be any trouble. So far, the night had been uneventful.

Philip couldn't stop his vigilant watch of the parlor house. He pointed again.

"Look. There's Hutchins coming out. Thinks he's such a fancy dude, cozying up to his well-heeled customers. He should hear what they really think of him."

Sven burst out laughing, tickled at the doctor's latest comment.

"Am I going to listen to you badmouthing every person who walks in or out of Mrs. Woodley's tonight?"

"Nope. I'm going to shut up right now."

He drained his mug and held it out. "Pour me another cold one."

When he left Big Swede's Saloon, the doctor was drunk for the first time in his life.

Chapter Thirteen: Origin

Origin - the event through which something comes into being

Her mind registered that someone was knocking, but her eyes refused to open. It felt like she had just fallen asleep. The knocks persisted, and Felicia slowly rolled herself out of bed. She opened the door to Abigail's raised fist, ready to knock again. She tried to focus. The form hurrying across the hall turned into Corinne tying the sash on her robe. It was too much movement so early in the morning.

"Go away," Felicia mumbled and returned to bed, burying her head beneath the pillow.

"Time to wake up sleepyhead," Abigail said brightly. "No breakfast after 11:00."

"I'll miss breakfast. I'm not ready to get up."

"Oh, yes, you are," said Corinne pulling the covers back. Then she mercilessly jerked up the pillow covering Felicia's head.

Felicia opened one eye and said, "If I could sleep for a few more hours I would feel a lot better."

Corinne handed her a dressing gown and said, "Up, up. Get moving."

Felicia slowly put on the robe Corinne held out to her.

"How did last night go?" asked Abigail, unable to contain her curiosity any longer.

"Not too badly. It wasn't much different than tolerating my husband. But I did listen to such a sad story. A young man just wanted to cry his eyes out over his dead wife."

She walked over to the commode and poured some water into the basin. She splashed a great deal of it onto her face. It didn't help. Felicia was not an early riser.

"Well, I had a great night," said Abigail, handing Felicia a large white towel. "I'm not too good at this but the men seem to like me asking them what I should do. It's usually the same request each time, but I ask them all anyway because it makes them very generous before they leave."

Felicia walked to her bed and attempted to crawl back in. But, Corinne held the edges of the cover together.

"You have to get up," she said. "Come on, up, up. Time to greet the day."

"Start by looking at all my money," Abigail demanded.

She held up the bundle and then fanned the bills into the shape of a feather duster. She flitted around Felicia's room, lightly brushing the tops of anything she passed. She started with the dresser, which she industriously cleaned with her imaginary duster, then the commode, and then the table. She moved the lamp, looking very thorough, and finally, took three long swipes at the window sill.

She returned to the table and made a great pretense of studying it. Then she wagged her finger at an imaginary spot and said in a perfect imitation of Mrs. Hale, "Oh, Abigail. You missed a spot, right over there. You really must be more careful, dear."

She turned and faced the imaginary matron. Switching

to her own voice, she said, "Mrs. Hale, why don't you go dust yourself!"

She burst into peals of laughter, delighted with herself, delighted with her money and delighted with her sass.

Abigail's merriment was contagious, and both Felicia and Corinne joined in the laughter.

Felicia managed to tuck her feet under the covers and leaned back on the pillows. "You are such a perfect mimic, Abigail. I can actually hear Mrs. Hale saying that to you!"

Corinne asked for another. "Do Vivian from the hotel," she urged. "Tell us what bad, bad women we are!"

She perched on the edge of the bed as if she was in a theater.

Abigail put her hand on her waist, shifted her weight to one side and thrust out her right hip. With Vivian's nasal twang she scolded, "Now, ladies, there will be no gentlemen brought upstairs. We have our standards here at the Crystal Creek Hotel."

"You are so good, Abigail," said Felicia, now wide awake. "How do you do that?"

But, Corinne didn't care how she did it, she just wanted more.

"Can you do Felicia?" she asked.

Abigail thought for a moment. Then she primly folded her hands in front of her, opened her eyes wide and lectured in her best schoolmarm voice, carefully enunciating each word, "Well, ladies if gorgeous means full of gorge, then…"

She paused to blink her eyes coquettishly, place her hand lightly to her throat and continued, "…flirtatious means full of flirt."

This bit of nonsense set them giggling again.

"Oh, no, you don't. You're not getting away so easy," Felicia declared, wagging her finger at Corinne.

She turned to Abigail and said, "You've got to do Corinne now. After all, fair is fair."

"Oh, Corinne is easy."

Without any hesitation, Abigail rubbed her hands together greedily. "Men, men, men. Money, money, money. I want pots and pots of money."

"Am I that obvious?" Corinne asked and grinned wickedly at her two friends.

"Mrs. Woodley, you have to do Mrs. Woodley."

Abigail mimed a large application of lip rouge and opened an imaginary parasol. She strolled leisurely past the bed, saying with mock sincerity, "Ladies, welcome to my boarding house or should I say, bawdy house? You get a room and you get bored."

She formed a circle with the thumb and finger of her left hand through which she moved the pointer finger of her right hand in an obscene gesture.

"Abigail, you are full of surprises," laughed Corinne.

Delighted to be the center of attention, Abigail continued her performance. She strutted across the room, sashaying her hips and twirling a lasso as if roping a cow.

"Texas Rose," they called out.

Then she switched to a mincing walk, carefully holding up her nightgown and tottered across the room.

"Who am I now?"

"Maybe Minnie," Corinne said instantly. "Do you think she ties her legs together so she can practice her walk?"

The possibility elicited a round of speculation and the three of them merrily pranced around the room exaggerating the small, dainty steps Minnie affected.

Next, Abigail curled a strand of hair around her finger and said in a whispery voice, "Welcome to Mrs. Woodley's Crystal Creek Parlor House."

"Livvy!'" they both shouted.

She crossed the room and picked up a towel which she waved in the air as she marched back and forth singing "Dixie."

"Too easy," said Felicia. "That's our southern belle, Lula Lee."

Having imitated everyone she could think of, Abigail took a deep bow and threw kisses to her appreciative audience who applauded her enthusiastically. With a flourish, Corinne presented her with an imaginary bouquet.

Felicia jumped up and headed towards the door. "Okay, laughing ladies, I'm ready for breakfast now."

"Laughing Ladies," repeated Corinne slowly. "I like it. That's who we are from now on. The Laughing Ladies."

"Well, this Laughing Lady is more than ready for breakfast," repeated Felicia. And suddenly, she was very, very hungry.

Chapter Fourteen: Tribulations

Tribulation — something that causes great difficulty or distress

Six months after their arrival in Crystal Creek, all Mrs. Woodley's clients knew who they were. The name "Laughing Ladies" had stuck. Ironic, because if you looked closely at a Laughing Lady, you would see that her inviting smile never quite reached her eyes.

Felicia stripped the sheet off her bed and threw it in the bin she kept in the far corner of the room. She closed the lid on the dirty towels and soiled linens and walked to her dresser. After selecting a freshly washed nightgown, she sat on the edge of her bed and began to braid her hair.

"It's about time!" she murmured when she heard the tentative knock.

Ever since they began working at Mrs. Woodley's Parlor House, she and Corinne ended the evening together. Their talks made Felicia feel needed, something long missing from her life, and Corinne got a confidante whose opinion she trusted.

A disheveled Corinne practically fell into the room.

"Good grief, that last guy was rambunctious."

As she re-pinned her curly red hair, the look on her face made Felicia ask, "What? Why do you look like the cat that swallowed the canary?"

Corinne smirked and said, "Because I have an announcement to make."

She held her skirt out and curtsied with exaggerated fanfare.

"Tomorrow morning, I am going to look at a house in town that's for sale."

"How did you hear about it? Nothing's ever for sale in town," said Felicia, moving over on the bed to make room for Corinne.

"I told T.J. to put his ear to the ground and hinted that I would be most appreciative if I could get first crack at any house that was for sale."

"Corinne, you are a sly one. If anyone would know, he would. The editor of the town newspaper must hear all the news first."

"He told me the Griffin's son is in Crystal Creek. He's here to sell their house. How perfect does that sound? It's such a big house and right in town. With a few changes, I bet I can make it into the most luxurious parlor house in Crystal Creek."

"Oh, Corinne, that's wonderful. I am so happy for you," Felicia said and gave her friend a big hug.

Then, her practical side edged itself into the conversation.

"If you like it, can you actually buy the house now?"

"I am ready. If I have to look at one more overweight, pompous, grasping fool and act like I am thrilled with him, I'll let out a scream that will be heard all the way back East."

A terrifying scream broke into the room. Startled, Felicia looked at Corinne. Corinne stared back, shaking her head.

"It's not me."

They ran into the hallway. Animated chatter filled the narrow space as doors burst open and women raced towards the sound. Abigail, whose room was closest, reached the door first.

"It's Livvy," she called out to the gathering group.

Anxious faces looked into the room at the woman keening on the blood-soaked sheets. She was still wearing her brightly colored pink evening dress which was now awry and covered with darkening stains. Her usually well coiffed hair was undone, falling onto her shoulders and partially covering her tear-streaked face which was devoid of any color. She was writhing in pain, doubled over as she rocked.

Corinne gathered her into her arms. "Livvy, what is it? What happened?"

"She promised me it would work," Livvy moaned.

"What would work? What have you done to yourself?" Corinne demanded.

"Someone get the doctor," Felicia ordered as she grabbed towels and water from the nightstand.

Abigail stood frozen to the spot. She knew what was wrong.

"Livvy tried to get rid of her baby," she said softly.

Corinne and Felicia stared at her.

"How do you know that?" Corinne asked.

As Livvy continued to sob, Abigail told them what she thought had happened.

"Livvy missed her monthlies twice and was sure she was pregnant. She went to see Chipela, you know who I mean, the Ute medicine woman. She makes a blend of herbs that she says will end a pregnancy. But something must have gone wrong."

All the women who worked at the parlor house knew

the consequences of getting pregnant. It was the first thing Mrs. Woodley cautioned against when they were hired. She even showed them how to shape a small cup out of beeswax and insert it before any physical contact. She also insisted they douche themselves thoroughly with vinegar and water between visitors. Had Livvy been careless?

As she listened to Abigail's explanation, Felicia continued to wipe Livvy's face with a warm cloth. *Please, please*, she prayed silently. *Don't let Livvy die. Please don't let her die.*

Then, she whispered, "Livvy, Dr. Meyers is on his way. Hang on, sweetheart. We're all here. We'll take care of you."

Felicia hoped she was right but it didn't look good. *Poor Livvy. She's never had any luck.*

Livvy's usual sunny face was now contorted with pain. *What a life,* Felicia thought. *A father who deserted the family. An alcoholic mother who couldn't take care of her children.*

The doctor's arrival interrupted her thoughts. Felicia looked up from the bed and thought once again how much the tall, lanky doctor reminded her of President Lincoln. He was clean shaven, but with the same deep-set eyes and hollow cheekbones of the former president.

"What happened here?" he asked.

He looked at the now silent Livvy and took in the bloody sheets and the frightened women.

Abigail told him what she suspected.

"Okay, let's have a look at you," he sighed as he motioned the others to leave.

Livvy started to cry again. Between sobs, she managed to describe what the medicine woman had given her.

"It was a little bag full of dried roots. She said to brew it into a tea and drink it all down."

While Livvy spoke, the doctor examined her and then reached into the black bag where he carried his medicines.

As he unscrewed a bottle, Livvy clutched at her stomach and begged, "Oh my God, please help me, Dr. Meyers."

Another pain seized her. Blood flowed onto the bed and a large clot appeared on the sheet. Livvy saw it and panicked. She grabbed the doctor's arm and pleaded, "Please don't let me die, Dr. Meyers. You've got to help me. I don't want to die."

He removed her hand and laid it across her chest.

"I think the worst is over now, but I want you to listen carefully to what I am about to say."

Dr. Meyers paused to collect his thoughts.

"I have no idea what you took, but it appears you've lost the baby. Your bleeding should ease up now. I'm going to give you medicine to help you sleep, and I'll be back in the morning. Before I leave, I'll send one of the women in to help you clean up."

From all the times he had seen this happen, he knew how the scenario played out. He was familiar with the difficulties an unwanted child caused, and was scrupulous in his instructions to the women at the bordello. As the doctor who signed their health certificates, tended to their illnesses, and kept them in condition to work, he understood their fears and anxieties. He only wished he could do more.

When he came west, he never intended to take care of women. He planned to only minister to men's needs. He could handle gunshot wounds, broken bones and black eyes and not get involved. Unfortunately, he was the only doctor in town. It hadn't worked out the way he expected.

He nodded to the women who waited in the hallway. One at a time they filed back into the room to say goodnight to the now sedated Livvy.

Too upset and anxious to go to bed, the three friends sat together in Felicia's room.

As soon as the door shut, Corinne smacked the table in anger.

"Why would Livvy go to that medicine woman? Chipela isn't a doctor. Why didn't she go to Dr. Meyers for help?"

"She probably didn't want Mrs. Woodley to find out," Abigail said.

She rocked back and forth in the chair, her arms wrapped around her body.

"Dr. Meyers would never say anything," Corinne insisted.

"Who else could she turn to for help?" asked Felicia. "She couldn't go to her brothers, they disowned her. We're the only family she has."

She looked down and noticed a blood stain on the front of her nightgown. She wet a cloth and began to dab at it, but the water made it spread out even more.

"What do you think Mrs. Woodley will do?" Abigail wondered. "Can you imagine how angry she's going to be when Dr. Meyers tells her what Livvy did?"

"I guess she'll let her stay after she recovers. I certainly hope so. I like Livvy," Felicia answered as she rubbed at the stain without success.

"Livvy was really nice to me when I first came," said Abigail. "I was completely naïve six months ago, and she taught me so much."

"She was kind to me also," Felicia added. "I remember my first night here. She was the only one who said hello when I came downstairs."

"Well, ladies, we can sit here and tell each other good things about Livvy all night. But, that's not going to help. I think I'll try to get some sleep."

Corinne blew a kiss to each of them and headed for the door.

"Felicia, try some borax on that. Or, better yet, leave it for Mary to wash."

The events of the evening left Abigail feeling unsettled. What if it was Corinne or Felicia lying on that bed instead of Livvy? For six months, they were each other's support and solace. She couldn't bear the thought of losing either of her two friends.

Chapter Fifteen: Funeral

Funeral - ceremony for somebody who has died

Just as it started to get light, Abigail awoke with a start. She slipped on her bathrobe and padded down the hall. Livvy lay on her back, motionless. Abigail tiptoed over to the bed, not wanting to disturb her in case she was asleep, but as she got closer she realized Livvy would never be disturbed again.

Abigail raced out of the room.

"Wake up, wake up," she yelled as she pounded on Felicia's door. Then she crossed the hall to Corinne's door. Both women responded immediately and one look at Abigail told them what happened.

"Oh, no," wailed Felicia. "She's too young to die."

She looked at Corinne who clenched and unclenched her fists.

"Let's get Dr. Meyers back, although there's nothing he can do now."

As the other women awoke, they were told the news of Livvy's death. They looked at each other, sharing the fear this could happen as easily to any of them. If you had the baby, you lost your income and if you didn't, you might lose your life.

The next day, dispirited and with great sadness, the women prepared for the hastily arranged funeral. They dressed simply in everyday clothing, their extravagant finery left behind in their closets.

Dr. Meyers and the Reverend made the necessary arrangements, and the small band of women wended their way to the tiny cemetery in back of the church. Ten crosses were already placed on a small plot of land which sloped away from the building. A white picket fence surrounded the area.

One of Mrs. Woodley's regular customers saw the group and asked what had happened. When he heard, the businessman briefly checked the watch fob dangling from his vest and with great solemnity joined the procession.

As they continued down the main street, another client decided to walk with them. He undid his chaps and hung the leather leggings over a nearby porch rail. With his hat clutched in his hands, he fell into the line.

Just as they reached the church, a mining engineer, after a hasty conversation and still gripping his long, rolled maps, caught up with the slowly moving assemblage.

The men added a sense of dignity, something Livvy never was able to find in her lifetime.

The dark clouds threatened rain and intensified the already dreary morning. The humid air, which made each breath an effort, stifled any conversation. The dismal day enveloped them as they gathered around the gaping hole and the Reverend began the service.

"Oh Lord, hear our prayers for this woman who has been removed from us way too soon."

Felicia stopped listening and gazed up at her Snow

Angel. The figure of the Snow Angel formed each spring when the melting snow disappeared in all but the deeper crevasses. And when it melted, it seemed to leave behind a wraith of a woman with her arms outstretched to the heavens.

For six months, Felicia had looked up at the long white form depicted against the rocky slope of the mountainside. She came to envision the likeness as a personal guardian watching over her, more real than those supposedly in heaven.

But, you weren't watching over poor Livvy, she silently chastised the Snow Angel.

Abigail held on tightly to Corinne, fearing if she let go, she would disintegrate.

"Livvy was the same age as I am," she whispered to Corinne. "It's scary to think someone that young can die."

She wondered if she had made a mistake when she ran away from a safe, warm house, all her needs taken care of, and come to this place where death could swoop down and carry her away. Who would protect her from Livvy's fate?

Corinne managed to look calm, but the flush on her cheeks gave away her anger. *What was Livvy thinking? To go to a medicine woman, when she had such a capable doctor to turn to. I wish I could grab her and shake some sense into her. But it's too late now.*

The simple pine box was lowered into the ground. One by one, the women stepped forward to throw a handful of dirt onto the coffin. Tears slipped down their cheeks as they approached the grave. They wrapped their shawls more tightly around their shoulders as if they could protect themselves from Livvy's fate.

When the last handful of dirt was thrown and the service completed, Felicia, Corinne and Abigail, as they did so many times before, remained silently standing as one, gaining support from each other's presence.

Dr. Meyers glanced over at the three women huddled together. The air was chilly, yet not one of them seemed to notice. Silhouetted against the sky, like three statues frozen in place, they stood at the top of the gently sloping mound, their long skirts falling to the ground, their arms wrapped around each other and their heads bent forward. Once again, he wondered what happened in their lives to bring them here.

He walked over to the three women who were still not moving. *The Greek Muses,* suddenly occurred to him. *Yes, that's who they remind me of, the Greek Muses.* But they were flesh and blood, not myth, and the cold, damp weather surrounded them.

"Ladies, I think you should get inside where it is warmer," he suggested.

The three turned at the sound of his voice. Felicia spoke first, "Yes, you're right, Dr. Meyers. Let's go."

Abigail, still clinging to Corinne, was pulled along quickly as they started down the path to the front of the church. Dr. Meyers walked alongside Felicia, worried about the way she looked.

"Felicia, come with me and let me make you a cup of coffee. You look like you could use a drink, and I don't think alcohol is the best choice."

Felicia turned her head until she was facing him and said in an emotionless voice, "Yes, perhaps you're right."

She recognized this familiar numb place, a place she went to when her husband started to berate her. This place she created, where his fury couldn't reach her. It was her armor against the harsh words he hurled at her in his anger, a retreat removed from the sickness in her stomach and the twisting of her gut as she tried not to react. Now, it provided a sanctuary from the shock of Livvy's death.

Corinne and Abigail looked back, and Felicia hastened down the path to tell them she was going with Dr. Meyers. A light drizzle continued to fall, and she pulled her shawl over her head. She shivered slightly.

"I hate drizzle," she said with too much vehemence. "It's much worse than real rain. The dampness goes right through you."

Drizzle always reminded her of the bleak mornings she spent crying after her husband left the house.

Dr. Meyers put his hand under her elbow and hurried her along. He felt a need to take care of her. Her vulnerability made him want to soothe her, to tell her not to worry, to listen to her concerns.

The embers in the fireplace were still glowing. He picked up a poker and adjusted the wood until the flame caught beneath it. Felicia watched the sparks rise up the flue and tried to shake off the gloom consuming her.

Dr. Meyers returned, carrying a tray laden with two mugs, a coffee pot and a large plate covered with a cloth.

"My housekeeper left some cake, and I thought you might like it with your coffee," he offered with a shy smile.

"Dr. Meyers…" Felicia began.

"Please call me Philip," he said. "I've been meaning to ask you that for a while. I think we know each other long enough to use Christian names."

Felicia smiled for the first time in hours.

"I didn't know you were a Christian. I've never seen you at church."

He laughed, then asked, "Now what were you going to say when I interrupted you?"

"Just thank you. Thank you so much."

Philip settled himself into a seat next to Felicia and poured the coffee. She accepted the steaming cup and wrapped her hands around it, enjoying its warmth.

"Cake?" he offered again. "My housekeeper is a really good baker."

"No, thank you. I'm not ready to eat anything, but the coffee is wonderful."

Felicia sipped slowly and thought what a fine man he was.

"I understand how difficult this must be for you," he began. As a doctor he recognized the look of shock when someone faced the reality of a death. "It's a high price to pay for carelessness."

"Followed by foolishness to go to a medicine woman," added Felicia. "Why didn't she go to you?"

"Because she knew I would never give her what she got from the medicine woman," he said in a tone which caused Felicia to feel chilled again.

"I suspect there's more to your answer than Livvy. Am I right?" she asked.

Taken aback by her question, Philip stalled for time. "Can I heat your coffee for you?"

He picked up the coffee pot ready to pour.

She was right, of course. He liked this intelligent woman. He didn't know why, but he was drawn to her from the first time they spoke. He assumed she did what she did because she needed money, but from the way she comported herself, he was sure she came from a well-off background. It was hard to grasp who she was since she revealed nothing. It intrigued him.

"Philip, I'm sorry. You don't have to answer my rather impertinent question," she said. "As a matter of fact, I think I should be going."

With the necessary thank-yous made, she walked the

short distance to the Crystal Creek Parlor House where she found the main parlor deserted.

She looked around the room and her eyes went right to the piano. Sentry-like, it stood in front of the mirror, upright and stoic. Men came and went, but the piano remained standing guard. Felicia yearned to sit in front of the keyboard, press her hands to the keys and play with abandon. The music would allow her to escape. She once asked Mrs. Woodley if she could do so and the response had been that Felicia was employed to make money not music. So her talent remained hidden.

Felicia looked down at her long, slender fingers. She didn't want to think about how many times she raised her hands to her face to protect it from her husband's verbal onslaughts. He never struck her, but it seemed necessary to physically ward off his taunting and degrading remarks as if they could somehow indelibly mark her. Sometimes she wished he would just hit her and get it over with.

When they married, she never once supposed she would become the target for all his anger, for his determination to make her pay for his mistake. She was tall for a woman and able to look directly into his eyes. But, never courageous for long, she invariably flinched and held up her hands for protection.

Now, she thought, *I use these same hands to please my customers.*

Since coming to Mrs. Woodley's, she had gained a few pounds, but liked the softening effect on her austere patrician features. She learned how to apply make-up to accentuate her large dark eyes and porcelain complexion and mastered the art of curling her straight brown hair. She looked nothing like the proper matron who stepped off the train six months earlier.

She hummed softly as she thought about Corinne's

plans. She decided it was time to make a move of her own. She pulled out the piano bench, positioned herself in front of the keyboard and began to play.

Hearing the music, one by one, the women slipped into the parlor to listen to the soothing sounds of Mendelssohn. They silently seated themselves and listened with rapt attention as she continued.

Mrs. Woodley hurried to the parlor to see who was playing her piano and stopped in the doorway as she looked around the room. She remained still until Felicia finished playing.

"That was beautiful, Felicia. I had no idea you could play so well," she said as she entered the room.

"Of course you didn't," snapped Felicia. "You wouldn't let me play."

Mrs. Woodley had never heard her use such a sharp tone before. She realized all the women were waiting to see how she would respond.

"It has been a most unpleasant day, and I realize we are all on edge. I'm sorry."

She walked over to Felicia and put her hand on her shoulder.

"Please, dear, play some more."

Chapter Sixteen: Negotiation

*Negotiation - reaching an agreement
through discussion and compromise*

Yesterday's stormy front passed, leaving a day filled with sunshine. The sky was a brilliant blue, the bright swath of color broken only by a solitary cloud. The air was crisp, with a hint of the cold to come. Sunlight poked through branches and filigreed the leaves, turning them into dabs of light and shadow. Corinne found it difficult to reconcile her feelings of sadness about Livvy with the beauty of the day.

She looked around at the countryside she had come to love. The sharply defined jagged edges of the mountain and the vast mesa filled with scrub created a hard masculine terrain. She much preferred it to the lush green rolling hills of the Northeast which she thought soft and feminine. Maples and oaks were traded for the piñon pines and blue spruce, the daffodils and tulips for the delicate columbines and the wild scarlet paintbrush.

She learned to horseback ride and explored the countryside whenever she could. A compass was always tucked in her pack as the surroundings, once she left town, stretched out in an endless, unmarked vista. She blessed the female rancher who created the divided riding skirt so women could ride astride, instead of the unsafe side-saddle position inflicted on them by their cumbersome attire. The women out here wouldn't put up with that and one of them figured out how to avoid it.

I can't believe I'm living here six months already. Where did the time go? The hours move so slowly and yet, the weeks and months just disappeared.

As the months passed, word got around about Corinne. Wealthy men knew, for a substantial extra payment, she offered "special services." Word also got around that you never overpaid for what you received. She never lacked for takers and her money accumulated faster than anticipated. So much so, she was now on her way to view a house that was for sale.

Halfway down the street, she found the lane. When she turned in, she saw a solitary house a short distance away. She liked the location because it was close to the center of town, but at a discrete enough distance to make it possible to enter and leave without being seen.

The front door was centered and flanked on each side by two windows with dark green shutters. The second floor had four windows perfectly lined up with those below. She approached slowly, taking in the tall cottonwood trees which framed the house.

A garden, badly in need of attention, ran down the left side of the house. She smelled lavender and thought about sachets for the dresser drawers.

Corinne walked up the three steps to the front porch. She turned and had an unobstructed view to the street. Only trees defined the sides of the lane. *Perfect,* she thought and crossed to use the brass doorknocker.

Almost immediately, she heard footsteps approach. A

serious looking young man pulled open the door. He was not dressed for the West. With his three piece suit, stiff white collar and carefully knotted tie, he looked like he belonged in a big city office. His shoes had recently been polished.

Guess he hasn't been walking around town taking in the sights, was her first thought.

"Miss Sullivan?" he asked as he stepped aside.

She extended a gloved hand and said, "You must be Mr. Griffin."

"Please call me James."

As she entered the house, he took in her good looks. After much deliberation, she selected a russet colored suit with matching hat. A simple gold brooch was pinned to the collar. She added only a hint of rouge to her lips, since she wanted to look businesslike for this transaction.

Someone has loved this place, she thought as she followed him through the house. The spacious front room led into the dining room. Corinne noted the immense dining table surrounded by twelve chairs.

"We are a big family," commented James when he noticed her counting the chairs.

In addition to the enormous table, the room contained a matching mahogany buffet against one wall and a rounded-front china cabinet, its shelves filled with a large collection of paperweights.

Next, they went into the kitchen. Although all the dishes, pots and pans were in perfect order, the room had a look of abandonment. This was confirmed when she lifted a canister and saw the clean circle it left on the counter.

From the kitchen, they walked down a wide hall to the two bedrooms in the rear of the house.

"This is where Mr. and Mrs. Roberts lived when they

worked for my parents. She did the housekeeping and he did the grounds. Their son slept in the other room."

"That explains the lovely garden I noticed as I walked up the lane," Corinne said.

"Yes, Mr. Roberts loved his garden and my mother always put bouquets of freshly cut flowers all over the house."

As she followed him up to the second floor, she asked why the house was for sale.

"My parents were killed in an accident. Their horse was spooked and the carriage overturned. And now, no one in my family wants this big house. I'm only here until I can sell it, and then I'll go back to San Francisco."

He led her through the bedrooms and continued to talk as he opened each door.

"I have seven brothers and sisters, and my parents always hoped a few of us would settle here. They loved Colorado and wanted us to come out here and be with them. But, none of us wanted to live so far away from everything."

Her mind was calculating. The house was perfect.

It's obvious the family isn't interested in it, and he's made it clear all he wants to do is sell it and leave. I wonder how much he'll compromise on the price.

"I think I might be interested in buying the house. But, it will be another two months until I could pay you the full price. If you need to sell it immediately, I'm afraid it's not possible for me just yet."

She paused and waited for his response, hard pressed to keep from smiling when a look of eagerness appeared on his face.

"Well, a price is always negotiable," he said. *Buy it. Please buy it.*

"Does an all cash payment make it more negotiable?"

asked Corinne. *Oh, thank goodness. Let's see what kind of a deal I can manage.*

"Give me a number," he suggested. *Cash! I could get out of this God forsaken town right away.*

"If I buy it now, I could pay you $2,400," offered Corinne. *I'll pay more, but he's such a kid. Maybe, he'll go for it.*

"I would prefer to sell it with all of the furniture. Can we agree on $2,900 for everything?" *Let's see if I can get more if I throw in the furniture. I sure don't want to fool with getting rid of all this stuff.*

He made his offer so quickly, Corinne wondered if she should have started with a lesser figure. But, she knew she could manage the price.

I'll keep some of the furniture, especially in the bedrooms, sell the rest and use the money to help with my other costs. That way, I'll still have enough money left to make a few changes to the house and get it exactly the way I want it.

"Agreed!" she answered. "Of course, subject to the approval of my lawyer who I will ask to draw up the contract."

Mr. Lewisohn, an attorney, as well as a favored client of hers, could be trusted to do all the necessary legal work.

"Where and when shall we meet to complete the transaction?" he asked.

He gave her his card and expected her to complete the exchange with hers.

"I live at Mrs. Woodley's Parlor House if you need to find me."

A bright red flush crept up his neck and spread across his face as he realized what was planned for his parents' house. Corinne stood quietly, watching him and waiting. She was aware of what was going through his mind and hoped his desire to sell would overcome any moral objections he might have.

His first impulse was to cancel their agreement. But, then, he weighed the advantages of a quick sale and reconsidered. The price was more than he expected to get, he'd return home to praise from his siblings, and he didn't have to deal with the problem of emptying the house. Besides, none of his brothers or sisters would care how the house was used.

He extended his hand and shook on the sale.

Ten days later, Corinne unlatched the gate and danced up the walk to her new house. Enthusiastically waving the deed over her head, she unlocked the front door. Abigail and Felicia followed right behind into the huge front room.

As soon as they were in the house, Corinne began to dash from place to place, speaking faster and faster. Words crowded each other, as she shared her plans.

"Over there will be the sofas and some chairs, and I think I'll put the bar along the far wall."

She moved excitedly about the room, explaining how it would look.

"Silk drapes in front of the windows, tied back with matching tassels. I adore tassels."

She whirled and pointed to a spot facing the stairs.

"Right there," she said. "That's where your piano will go, Felicia."

"What kind of piano will you get?" asked Felicia.

"You tell me, you're the expert. I expect you to fill the room with glorious music. And I will make sure the girls indicate the large tip bowl which we will place on the piano," said Corinne.

"And even drop in a fake tip so her client won't want to appear cheap and will match it," said Abigail. "Remember how good I got at doing that?"

Corinne headed off down the hall and fidgeted impatiently, waiting for them to catch up.

"Come and see the kitchen," she called. "I'm going to order a cast iron stove and build shelves on this wall. Maybe put a nice long work table right in the middle. I want my cook to have lots of space to prepare fabulous meals."

They returned to the main room and Corinne veered off to the right.

"Come on, come on."

She hustled up the stairs and checked to see if she was being followed. When she reached the landing, she threw open one bedroom door after another.

"Can you believe all these rooms?" she asked and returned from the end of the hall.

Without giving them time for a good look, Corinne picked up her skirts and started back down.

She continued to talk non-stop as she moved towards the rear of the house.

"Now, follow me through here and you'll see where Abigail's office will be."

She stepped aside so they could look into the room.

"We'll get you a lovely desk to work at, Abigail. This window has an open view of the mountains, so I would put the desk right in front of it if I were you. What do you think?"

Abigail rushed to embrace Corinne.

"Thank you, Corinne. I can't thank you enough."

"Don't thank me. It's going to work out well for both of us. You have a good head for figures and are so methodical. And most importantly, I can trust you."

"When do we start?" asked Abigail, hoping it would be soon.

"Whenever you are ready," answered Corinne. "I'd like

you with me from the second I start to spend money, and I can hardly wait to begin."

Felicia hugged Corinne. "You made it happen, Corinne. I'm so happy for you."

"I did it! I really did it! Wait until you see this place when I'm done with it. It will be gorgeous, and those rich men will want to come here and spend, spend, spend their money. I want to make so much money I can't count it fast enough."

"What are you going to name it?" asked Felicia.

Without the slightest hesitation, Corinne answered, "The Laughing Ladies, of course."

They bought a bottle of champagne on the way back to Corinne's room and had just poured out three glasses when the door burst open and Mrs. Woodley charged in.

"So, it is true!" she cried when she saw the champagne flutes in their hands, and the guilty looks on their faces.

Her topknot of curls quivered furiously. The looks she shot at each of them were like bullets from a repeating rifle, and Corinne resisted the impulse to raise her hands above her head.

Mrs. Woodley's substantial chest heaved as she angrily asked, "Are you all planning to walk out on me? How could you do this to me when I took you in? When I taught you everything."

"Mrs. Woodley, please sit down and let me explain," Corinne said in what she hoped was a placating voice.

"No need. I know exactly what is happening. You bought the Griffins' house and you are going into competition with me."

"Yes," admitted Corinne. "I did buy the house, and I do plan to establish a business."

Mrs. Woodley reached into her pocket and pulled out a

cigar which she expertly lit. Corinne rushed to the window to pull it open before she remembered it was sealed shut. She opened the door, but thought better of antagonizing Mrs. Woodley further by asking her not to smoke.

"I didn't know you smoked cigars," said Abigail, dumbfounded at the sight of a woman with a large cigar in her hand.

"There's a lot you don't know. So, I suggest you just sit and listen," snapped Mrs. Woodley.

She turned back to Corinne and demanded, "When did you plan to tell me all this?"

"I only signed the papers this morning. But, I know the way news spreads in this town. I should have told you before you heard it from someone else. I do apologize," Corinne said in an attempt to mollify her. "But, how did you find out so quickly?"

"Mr. Lewisohn, of course. He's been a regular customer here for three years. Did you think he wouldn't tell me?"

"I think he could have waited until the ink was dry on the deed before he ran to you with the news. And don't you think he should have let me be the one to tell you?"

"You want to tell me. Here's your chance. Tell me."

She pulled on the cigar and blew out a long stream of smoke.

Corinne fanned the air. She hated the smell of cigars. They brought back memories of her father who liked nothing better than a good stogie.

Suppressing a cough, Corinne decided flattery was the best approach. In her most conciliatory voice, she said, "As Mr. Lewisohn has already told you, I bought the Griffin place. I've watched the way you run your establishment and I hope I can do as well. I'm planning a very expensive, luxurious place and intend to offer fine dining as well as what you offer here. I'm aiming for the most exclusive clientele and will charge considerably more than you do, so I don't think we will be in competition."

"Of course, we'll be in competition," Mrs. Woodley retorted.

"But, Mrs. Woodley, this town shows no sign of slowing down. There's an endless supply of men to support businesses like ours. Look at how many parlor houses are here already."

Trying to calm herself, Mrs. Woodley walked over to the window and looked down at the busy street. She watched as Sven unloaded his whiskey order. She could tell it had just arrived because the driver was giving his horses water.

A long, low whistle announced the train's departure from the station, and she saw the businessmen it brought carrying their smart leather bags into the hotel. People were in constant motion. Men, and even a few women, entered and left the stores, intent on their chores. *Corinne is absolutely right, the town is booming.*

Feeling more under control, Mrs. Woodley turned around to face Felicia and Abigail.

"I suppose it's too much to hope you two will be sticking around," she said as she sank into a chair and looked for somewhere to drop the cigar ash. Corinne rushed forward with a tin basin.

Abigail hung her head, embarrassed, unable to speak. Felicia answered for both of them.

"We're going as soon as Corinne is ready for us."

"And will you continue as employees of Corinne's?"

"Yes, but in a different capacity," explained Felicia. "Abigail will be Corinne's bookkeeper and manage the finances, and I'll be playing the piano for the guests."

"Well, you three have got it all figured out, don't you?"

She turned to Corinne. "It's not as easy as you think. You have a lot of responsibility when you own the business."

"I hope my girls will have as much respect for me as yours do for you," said Corinne.

"Yes, Mrs. Woodley," said Abigail finally finding her voice. "You've been kind to me and I won't forget it. But this is not what I want to do. The money from the auction was wonderful and I thought I could keep doing this, but I really want to stop."

"And how about you, Felicia?" Mrs. Woodley asked.

"I'm ready to stop, too. Especially since I'll be playing the piano, which I love to do. I see what kind of money the professor makes here, so I think I'll be all right."

"Well, I can't say I'm happy about this, but I can't stop you," Mrs. Woodley said.

She picked herself up and exited with as much dignity as she could muster.

"I think she took it rather well," said Corinne as she closed the door. "After all, she is losing three good money makers."

"Too well. Something else is going on we don't know about," said Felicia.

Abigail hesitated, then said, "I did hear something yesterday, but I don't know if it's true."

"What?" they both asked.

"Maybe Minnie told me she heard from a customer, who knows a woman, whose brother works in Mr. Lewisohn's office, that he's getting married. And he told her Mr. Lewisohn is marrying Mrs. Woodley. He's seen her in Mr. Lewisohn's office a lot, and Mr. Lewisohn did run over here to tell her about your house."

"Abigail, you might be right. Mr. Lewisohn was a regular customer of mine for while, but he just stopped coming," Corinne said. "Can you believe she's getting married again? She's been married twice, you'd think she'd have learned by now."

"Corinne, you're impossible," laughed Felicia. "But it makes sense now. I heard Mr. Lewisohn was opening an office in Denver. I bet she's going with him."

"And if she does, what will happen to this place?" asked Abigail. "Do you think she'll sell it?"

"I'm sure Mrs. Woodley can handle her own problems quite well," Corinne said.

She reached for her untouched champagne glass.

"Now, where were we? Oh, yes. To the Laughing Ladies Parlor House."

Chapter Seventeen: Preparations

*Preparations - the work or planning involved
in making something happen*

For the next few weeks, Corinne basked in the sounds of banging, hammering and sawing. She meticulously supervised the work to ensure it was done to her exact specifications. Abigail and Felicia were an enormous help, completely engaged by their new jobs.

Corinne was relieved she didn't have to deal with any of the account keeping because she found looking at all those numbers tedious. Felicia had ordered the piano and was now tackling the selection of music, another job Corinne would have found onerous.

As work on the house neared completion, she sat on the newly hung porch swing, flipping the pages of a thick Montgomery Ward catalog. She had already gone through the Sears Roebuck catalog beside her, reveling in page after page of items to buy. When something caught her eye, she folded down the corner to make it easier to find again. She looked in dismay at the number of turned down edges.

The next page featured illustrations of appropriate

mourning dresses. They reminded her of how far she had come. *No more long days of managing the funeral parlor for my father. No more dressing bodies. No more funeral cards. No more hushed, somber place of death like the last time I ran a house.*

She chuckled as a thought occurred to her. *The only stiff member allowed in my house will be the kind you don't stick in a coffin.*

Footsteps broke into her reverie. She pulled her woolen cape more tightly around her as she greeted Felicia.

"Which catalog is it today?" asked Felicia as she climbed the three steps to the porch.

"It's the Montgomery Ward and you can stay and help me find more things to buy."

She moved over and patted the space beside her.

"What's left to buy?" asked Felicia, thinking about the already full house.

"There's always something left to buy," said Corinne and adjusted the catalog so they could look together.

She had unpacked crates of oak furniture which arrived from Ohio. It took longer than she expected, and Corinne was relieved to have all her furniture in place. One piece at a time, she arranged it. Then arranged it again, and again, until she got the room exactly the way she wanted it.

Furniture and draperies, dishes and glassware, paintings and lamps, a whole household had been transported from places across the country to become part of The Laughing Ladies Parlor House.

She shuddered remembering the trouble the cast iron stove caused. It took four men to maneuver it into the kitchen. The stove was expensive, but since she had splurged on fine china and cut glass stemware, she wanted delicious meals served on them.

The problem of a cook still frustrated her. She needed

someone in the kitchen who knew what she was doing, and who did it well. *Not well*, she amended, *I want the best.*

Unable to sit still, Corinne jumped up so quickly the catalog slid to the floor. She didn't even notice.

"I don't know what else to do about finding a cook."

Felicia reached for the catalog and set it on the swing.

"Don't worry, Corinne. You'll think of something."

"I've run out of ideas. I placed advertisements in all the area newspapers and hardly got any responses. And the women I interviewed just didn't have the expertise I want."

She moved to the edge of the porch and leaned over the railing. She watched two of the men carry a stack of piled boards to the back of the house.

"I even tried a few Eastern newspapers hoping to attract someone who wanted to move out West. The men searching for wives place advertisements in them all the time. I thought maybe an offer of a job would be an incentive. But, no one answered."

"Cheer up. Things will work out," Felicia said.

Hoping to provide a distraction, she suggested they take a walk to see who was coming to the Opera House.

"The new signs get posted on Wednesdays."

"Thanks, but go on without me. I've got to stay and wait for my liquor order. Sven's bringing it over sometime today."

Corinne walked into the house and headed towards the kitchen.

For inspiration, she told herself as she touched all the new equipment and appliances. She adjusted a few copper pots not perfectly aligned, then double-checked the running water in the sink. It had cost her most of her remaining money to bring water into the house, but she thought it a good investment. The two necessaries on the second floor would be greatly appreciated, especially during the fast approaching cold weather.

I don't want to open until I can offer meals. What am I going to do? No one is going to knock on my door and say "Your new cook has arrived."

At precisely that moment, she heard a knock at the front door.

She went to answer, smiling at the coincidence. She expected to see Sven, but instead found a small woman, with two battered suitcases, standing on the porch. Her clothing looked slightly too large as if she had recently lost weight. She wore her dark hair parted in the center and pulled straight back into a bun. Almost black eyes stared at Corinne as she groped for words.

"I see advertisement. I come here to cook for you," she said with a heavy foreign accent.

It took Corinne a minute to understand.

"Please come in."

She led the way into the parlor and indicated the settee. The woman followed and began to speak as soon as they were seated.

"My name Lili Marchand and I read advertisement in newspaper. I am good French chef."

Corinne's mind raced. *A French chef. What a coup! I could advertise how The Laughing Ladies' meals are prepared by a chef all the way from France. Oh, I hope she can really cook. No sense asking for her references. I probably couldn't read them anyway.*

She studied the woman sitting in front of her. *Guess there's only one way to find out.*

"Well, Lili Marchand, let's see if you are the answer to my prayers. Suppose we go shopping for enough ingredients to prepare a dinner for three. If we like what you make, the job is yours."

"*Oui, Madame.* Your idea is pleasing to me. You shall see, when you are finished with the meal, you shall put me in the kitchen."

"Come with me. I will put you in the kitchen right now."

Lili placed her belongings on the counter and proceeded to open all the closet doors to check their contents. To her dismay, she found nothing on hand. She stood behind the large work space in the middle of the kitchen and looked up at the hanging array of pots and pans.

She walked to the pantry and discovered it, too, was empty. She checked the stove and found it in pristine condition.

When she completed her inspection, she told Corinne, in her broken English, she was ready to go shopping.

Corinne brought Lili into Wilson's General Store and introduced her to the shop owner. As Lili gazed in admiration at the heavily stocked shelves, Corinne said, "Mr. Wilson, give Lili whatever she asks for. She's preparing dinner for me tonight."

Then she asked Lili, "Can you find your way back to the house if I leave you here?"

Lili nodded she could, and Corinne hurried off to find Felicia and Abigail.

They were both at home, at the house they shared since leaving Mrs. Woodley's. Corinne burst into the front room without even knocking.

"Exciting news. I may have found a cook."

"But I left you only an hour ago. When did this all happen?" asked Felicia.

"I was sitting in the kitchen, trying to figure out how I would ever find a cook, when Lili knocked on my door looking for the job. She's French, and I told her to make dinner for the three of us. So, I need you both as my official tasters. If we all agree it's good, I'll have my new chef."

Abigail clapped her hands in delight. "I'd love to come."

"Has she bought anything yet? *Boeuf bourguignon* is a great test for a French chef," said Felicia. "Of course, you'll have to give her some of your better red wine. She'll also need some good quality meat for stewing. It's not hard to make, but the seasonings are crucial. Tell her to do some browned potatoes and garden peas with it."

Corinne listened, growing more surprised as Felicia continued.

"You've been holding out on me," Corinne scolded. "You sound like you know your way around the kitchen. Are you sure you'd rather play in the parlor than in the kitchen?"

"Absolutely!" Felicia laughed.

"She's at Wilson's store right now," said Corinne, racing out the door with Felicia in tow.

They caught Lili still making her purchases, and Felicia made her request. The scents now emanating from Corinne's kitchen brought hope that her search was over. The air was filled with aromas of spices, wine and simmering beef.

Precisely at 6:00, Corinne began to set the table. *Finally, finally. I get to use all my beautiful things.*

She shook out an embroidered tablecloth onto the round oak table. Then, she circled it, adding the opaque white china dishes. She remembered how nervous she was when she unpacked the crate. But, much to her relief, nothing was broken.

Next came the silverware with its ornate scrollwork design and then, the crystal stemware. She held a glass up to the light and admired the rainbow of colors reflected by the pattern cut into its surface. Tall white candles in the center finished the setting.

She stepped back to admire her work. *Simple, but stylish,* she thought, pleased with herself.

Corinne went into the kitchen to see if the wine had been opened yet. Lili was stirring the contents of a large cast iron pot, but pointed to the decanter on the far counter.

"Dinner is almost ready," she said and lifted the lid off another pot. The aromas were irresistible, and Corinne didn't think she could possibly wait until dinner time. Her stomach now commanded her brain. She edged over and asked for a taste.

"*Mais, non,*" huffed Lili. "You must wait until dinner, when I serve you."

She shook her head and shooed Corinne out of the kitchen.

When Felicia and Abigail arrived a few minutes later, Corinne rushed them into the dining room.

"I am so glad to see you. Let's eat. The smells coming out of the kitchen are driving me crazy."

Corinne took off to tell Lili they were ready, and returned with the wine decanter in hand.

"Here's to Lili…fingers crossed," toasted Felicia and the three touched glasses across the table.

Dinner was excellent. They all agreed the *boeuf bourguignon* was perfection. The empty bread basket was testimony, as they had used the last piece to wipe their plates clean. The meal ended with what Lili called *café au lait* and a delectable custard pudding she pronounced as *crème brulee.*

"Another toast," proposed Felicia. "Here's to Lili… fingers uncrossed."

"I shall joyfully drink to that," beamed Corinne.

She raced into the kitchen and returned, dragging Lili

with her. She poured another glass of wine and handed it to Lili.

"Please help us toast the new chef at The Laughing Ladies."

It took Lili a moment to understand what Corinne said, and when she did, a glorious smile appeared. Her eyes sparkled and she looked radiant. Her entire appearance changed dramatically. The transformation was astonishing.

"I drink to that," Lili said and took a sip. "French wine, I see. *Très bon.*

"Please sit with us," invited Corinne, bringing over a chair. "This is Abigail, my bookkeeper, and Felicia, my pianist. They're also my dearest friends."

"Corinne told us you just appeared at her door this morning. What made you decide to come to Crystal Creek?" asked Felicia, curious to find out more about this incredibly good cook.

"I come with my brother, he…." She paused, trying to find the words in English.

"*Je parle francaise,*" said Felicia. "*Que voulez-vous dire?*"

She turned to Corinne and Abigail. "I told her I speak French and asked her what she wanted to say."

"Felicia!" said Corinne, falling back in her chair in mock consternation. "First it was cooking, and now you know French. What else are you hiding in your beautiful brain?"

With Felicia's help, Lili related her story.

She was born in Marseilles, a French seaport, and had lived there all her life. Her mother owned a tiny bistro near the waterfront, where she served meals to the lonely fisherman and occasional tourists who found their way to that disreputable part of the city.

Lili helped her mother, first serving food, and then, little by little, she took over the cooking. When her mother became ill, Lili nursed her for months and continued to run the restaurant after her death. If not for her brother Claude, it would never have occurred to her that she could have a different life.

Unlike Lili, he was a restless spirit and not willing to spend his life waiting on their shabby customers. He had big dreams and found a way to make them come true when he read about the American West.

Untold wealth was available to men who were daring. He made up his mind to go there. Claude followed his dream, and Lili followed her brother across the ocean and the American continent. He was her only family and she did not want to be without him.

It was only after she arrived in Crystal Creek that she realized what she had done. When Claude saddled up a horse to go prospecting, she would be alone. She didn't feel very daring any more. But, she knew how to cook and had read Corinne's advertisement.

Another bottle of wine vanished as the three of them listened to Lili's story. Corinne yawned and said, "Before I fall asleep, let me show you the bedroom you can have if you want to live here. It's in the back of the house, right across from Abigail's office."

Lili, slightly tipsy herself, gratefully accepted Corinne's offer. *Somewhere to live and somewhere to work,* she thought. *Claude will be so relieved I found a place to stay. Now, he can go off and not worry about me.*

She felt incredibly blessed.

The next morning, as she fluffed a few throw pillows, Corinne heard a commotion outside. She opened the door to see a buckboard driven by Judd Cameron being guided down the lane. One of his men walked ahead, pulling back overhanging branches to allow him to pass with the oversize load which hung over the sides.

"What in the world are you doing, Cameron?" she called as she walked down the steps to greet him.

He tied up the reins and jumped off the wagon. "Hello, little lady. I'm here to make a special delivery to my favorite gal."

Judd Cameron was the first of Corinne's regular customers. With his good looks and his out-going personality, he could have chosen any of the ladies, but he wanted Corinne. During the time she worked at Mrs. Woodley's, they became good friends. Many evenings he stayed for the companionship and conversation she provided and left without a trip upstairs.

He admired her spunk and her intelligence, but even more he admired her courage and her ambition. He even thought of asking her to marry him, but knew she was totally focused on her goal of becoming an independent businesswoman. She made it clear, on several occasions, she thought marriage a form of slavery or, at the very least, another form of prostitution. Not too good a prospect for a wife.

"And leave it to you to bring something huge," Corinne was saying. "You do love grand gestures, don't you, Cameron!"

She walked around to the back of the wagon, and could immediately tell by the long rolled shape, he was bringing her a rug.

"What are we waiting for?" he shouted to his helper. "Let's get this into the house."

The two of them pulled the rug out of the wagon and hoisted it onto their shoulders. They carried it into the hallway. Corinne followed, eager see what he brought.

"Don't you touch that rug until you get your new cook

out here with some of her delicious coffee and a slice of whatever she's baking," Cameron said as he sniffed the air and wiped his forehead with a large checkered bandana.

"Cameron, how do you know about my new cook? I just hired her last night."

"She shopped for all her ingredients at Wilson's store didn't she?"

She laughed and said, "Okay, Mr. Sherlock Holmes, I'll do what you ask."

She left for the kitchen, only to return a few minutes later to relay Lili's answer.

"Lili, that's her name, said she'll be out with something for you as soon as you show me the rug."

He threw back his head and roared.

"Women! Should've known you'd get your way. Laughing Lady, you know you can get me to do whatever you want."

He cut the ropes holding the roll in place and yanked on the edge to uncurl it. Corinne watched a beautiful Aubusson rug unfold, its magnificent floral design created with pale greens and pinks on a beige background. The subdued colors were woven into an intricate pattern. Corinne recognized the quality of what Cameron was giving her.

"Cameron," she whispered. "This is magnificent. I don't know what to say or how to thank you."

"I heard tell you were out of the thanking business," he smiled. "So, if you will just tell Lili to bring out my coffee, I would most appreciate it."

After Cameron left, she stood in the large front room and looked around one more time.

Yes, she thought. *It's perfect now.*

She wandered over to the window and pulled the drapes back so she could see down the lane. She watched the wagon's progress until it turned the corner onto the street.

Chapter Eighteen: Readiness

Readiness - finished and prepared for something to happen

Corinne pulled the curtains back from the window that faced the garden. No matter how late she went to bed, she was awake by seven and at her desk soon afterwards. She had partitioned off part of the huge dining room and made it into her office.

The first piece of furniture she ordered was a slant top lady's desk. The heavily carved lid folded down to provide a writing surface. Four pigeonholes and two small drawers were now filled with notes and bottles of ink. She kept a heavy ledger in the wide front drawer and planned to enter the names of her clients and any information about them that might prove useful. It was a small space, but the early morning sun flooded the room with light.

She hired eight girls, her plan being to add more as business warranted. The first two selections were easy, as Maybe Minnie and Lulu Lee expressed interest in joining her. The secret was out, Mrs. Woodley planned to re-marry and leave Crystal Creek. As soon as they heard, the two women contacted Corinne.

Other women appeared as word got around Corinne was launching a new parlor house. For many women, it was standard procedure to move from town to town, staying in one place for only six months. Business fell off as they became "old hat." By moving to a new location, they became fresh and exciting. But Corinne's standards were too high for many of the woman who spoke with her.

She was distracted by the sound of coffee beans being spilled into the grinder and listened as it whirred into action. That meant Lili was up and beginning her morning routine. Corinne knew she would shortly smell freshly brewed coffee, and her stomach rumbled with anticipation.

By the time Corinne got to the kitchen, the coffee was ready. She again blessed the kitchen gods who sent her Lili. The storekeepers and the purveyors already loved her. Lili enjoyed nothing more than a good haggle over price and always sealed the deal with a thick slice of cake and a mug of hot coffee. Corinne never realized the variety of choices people offered until they started to find their way to Lili.

"Only two more days until we open. Do you have all the supplies you need?" Corinne asked as she pulled out a stool from beneath the wooden block in the center of the room.

"*Mais oui*. Mr. Wilson, he saves me the fresh vegetables. And from Mr. Hoskins, milk and cream and butter and cheese."

Lili's face lit up as she described the lamb, beef and venison that were brought to her.

"And the trout. *C'est magnifique.*"

She was offered only freshly caught fish. Word had gotten out that when Lili looked a fish in the eye, she could tell exactly what time it had been caught.

"Now, if I can only convince you that California wines are as drinkable as French wines, you could order those as well."

The comparative merit of various wines was a continuing discussion, with Lili refusing to believe that any wine could measure up to her beloved French vineyards.

Corinne returned to her desk, but couldn't focus on what needed to be done. Her mind kept going over how she would run her business. She checked her mental list one more time.

She would cater only to the most wealthy and powerful of the community. From experience, she knew a mine owner could spend in one night what one of his miners earned in five months.

She had already made clear to the women she accepted that they were to look and speak like high class ladies at all times. She would not tolerate drugs, and foul language was absolutely forbidden.

In anticipation of opening night, she primed them on local events and especially, local politics. She informed them who owned what and who ran what. She knew the men's opinions on many different topics and also knew their likes and dislikes. She wanted her women to hold their own in conversations, be skilled in the art of entertaining and willing to indulge eccentric requests.

Corinne leaned back in the chair and tapped her pencil impatiently.

I hate making lists, but if I don't write down exactly what I still need to do, I know I'm going to forget something. How in the world can Abigail be so happy going over endless numbers and placing them into those neat little columns she makes? But, thank goodness she keeps such good records of my expenditures. I'll even put up with those lectures she gives me about spending money. What Abigail doesn't understand is you can't put a price on making a dream come true.

She made another effort to get organized. She jotted

down a few notes and when she checked her calendar, saw today was her meeting with the sheriff and the mayor.

Over breakfast, they were to reach an agreement on the amount of her fines for running an "illegal establishment." From working at Mrs. Woodley's, she knew her girls would pay a fine as well. She hoped Lili's wonderful food would make the arrangements as palatable as the breakfast being served.

She tossed the pencil onto her desk, telling herself she absolutely must check up on those preparations.

Her visit to the kitchen was met with raised eyebrows.

"Corinne, you do not need to manage my kitchen. Go find something else to do and let me continue my work."

Corinne went back to the dining room and checked the table. It was set with the morning dishes, brightly painted yellow and blue French Quimper ware. The dishes were an extravagance, but Corinne coveted them from the first time one of Mrs. Corey's customers had brought a plate into the shop to show it off. They were used only for breakfast, replaced by the elegant Limoges china at dinner time.

Precisely at 9:30 am, her two guests arrived. After a last minute check in the hall mirror, Corinne opened the door. She thought what an odd couple the sheriff and the mayor made as they stood on her front porch. Their physical differences were striking.

Sheriff Tremont was of medium height and very slim. His slight build fooled many a drunk who thought he could easily knock the sheriff down with one punch. However, once the sheriff got his hands on you, there was no escape from his iron grip. He had never been known to fire his gun because the intransigent look in his eyes could turn people to stone. Many a bully, twice his size, meekly holstered his gun when ordered by the sheriff to do so.

Mayor Charles Bennett was a taller man with a slight

paunch covered by a well tailored suit. "Too much fine living," he'd brag as he patted his belly. He was first elected mayor when the town incorporated and remained unchallenged ever since. A cunning politician, his carefully cultivated connections served him well.

He was a regular customer at Mrs. Woodley's. He'd slip in and out unobtrusively, and never settled on one girl as he was a greedy man and wanted to sample all women within reach. Tales of his physical demands abounded, and Corinne tried to avoid him as much as possible.

She stepped aside and invited them in. They glanced around the room, taking note of the expensive furnishings. With its muted tones and fine silk drapes, the room was ready to welcome refined company. No flocked wallpaper and red velvet curtains for Corinne. The two men followed her past the well stocked bar, through the parlor, and into the dining room.

"Help yourselves gentlemen. Lili's put breakfast on the buffet."

Sheriff Tremont poured himself some coffee and looked around.

"You've done a beautiful job with the place, Corinne. Wouldn't recognize it, even though my wife and I were here quite a few times when the Griffins owned it."

Mayor Bennett walked over to the buffet and lifted all the lids before he heaped a platter with eggs, sausage and grits. He stacked up a few slices of bread, added butter and came back to the table.

"You know you are lucky to have found Lili. I hear tell she is one mighty fine cook," he said as he started to scoff up his food.

"You must come for dinner one night, Mayor," she said and gave him one of her well-practiced social smiles. "And after dinner, as well."

The sheriff continued to drink only black coffee, but the mayor, after a second visit to the buffet, leaned back in his chair with hands folded over his full stomach and said, "Let's get down to business now that I can testify to Lili's fine cooking."

Corinne planned carefully for this meeting. She wore a dark navy, conservative two piece suit with starched white collar and cuffs. She slicked her hair back into a simple chignon and applied only the faintest trace of make-up. These men knew her as a prostitute, and she wanted to face them as a businesswoman. It would have been easier if the sheriff hadn't come. With a witness to the transaction, the mayor was bound to be more intractable. He needed to appear as an astute official.

"You do know we have an ordinance here in Crystal Creek against running a house of prostitution," he began. "But, you also know we have only the one sheriff and he is a mighty busy man. Can we all agree to let you run your business without interference? Let's call it your license fee."

"Sounds fair to me," Corinne agreed. "And what is the suggested fee?"

"We'll start with an initiation fee of $300. Then, set the fine at $50.00 a month for breaking the law. Each of your girls will have to pay $5.00 a month as well," he stated. "Since we use part of these license fees to pay the sheriff's salary, I'm sure he'll be conscientious in his collection."

"And why so much?" asked Corinne, struggling not to sound hostile although she felt her temper rise. "$50.00 a month sounds like a lot of money to me."

"Why, Corinne. You plan to sell whiskey here, don't you?"

"Yes, I do," she answered.

"Then, there's your answer," the mayor said.

The sheriff sat quietly through their interchange. But,

when he saw Corinne about to object, he said, "Whisky can lead to trouble."

"Not usually," she refuted. "After a few drinks, my girls will have the men upstairs and they'll quiet down real fast."

"The price is $50," the Mayor insisted, a hard edge creeping into his voice. He wasn't used to being questioned, and especially by a woman like Corinne.

She might be surrounded by finery now, but it wasn't so long ago she was only too glad to comply with my requests. I'm not going to sit here and argue about a $50 a month fee. I can imagine what she plans to charge her customers. She'll probably pull in more money than I do pretty soon.

"Well, *Miss* Sullivan," he said. "Perhaps, if that amount is not agreeable to you, you can find another use for this place. Sheriff, don't you think it would make a fine boarding house? At the rate people arrive in this town, I'm sure Miss Sullivan would have no trouble keeping all her bedrooms occupied."

He turned and gave her a look filled with such animosity that Corinne found it difficult not to squirm. She stared back and knew if she wanted to open for business, she would have to agree to the amount he dictated. It didn't pay to antagonize the mayor, and if she continued any further dissent, she would make him look bad in front of the sheriff.

Not good business to start out with an enemy. Might as well do it graciously, she thought. She extended her hand to the mayor and as he shook it, she said, "Help yourselves to more coffee. I'll be right back with my first payment."

She climbed the stairs to her room at the end of the corridor and locked the door behind her. Corinne anticipated the mayor's demands and money was put away in a safe hidden behind a large oil painting. She carefully removed the painting from the wall opposite her bed and laid it on the quilt, then opened the safe and counted out the initiation fee. She added her first two months fines and the fines for the eight women. *Almost $500 in cash. He's not making it easy.*

When Corinne returned, she placed the money on the table in front of Mayor Bennett, who pushed it over to the sheriff as if touching it might dirty his hands.

"Don't you want to count it?" Corinne asked.

"We trust you, don't we, sheriff?" Bennett asked in his most officious voice.

Sheriff Tremont rose to leave as soon as he pocketed the money. He appeared uncomfortable with the transaction and ready to make his exit, unlike the mayor, who made no attempt to hide his enjoyment.

Corinne, with as much graciousness as she could muster, escorted them out. She leaned against the closed door and muttered an obscenity under her breath. But the triumph of her accomplishment quickly dispelled her foul mood. She looked around. She had done it, after months of planning and hard work, she had created this elegant establishment.

The next time the mayor visited, he would be paying her.

Chapter Nineteen: Opening

*Opening - the occasion on which
something is formally presented*

Corinne lifted the dark green taffeta gown from the hanger and placed it on her bed. She had used her expert dressmaking skills to design a dress with a low cut bodice trimmed in black lace and bordered by velvet ribbons. The same lace cascaded from beneath the wrists. She returned to the closet and removed the French kid opera toe shoes from their satin lined box. They were an extravagance, but, tonight, Corinne wanted only quality.

A gardenia was tucked into her upswept hairdo. She had tamed her bright red curls with numerous pins and added the flower to keep it in place.

Felicia arrived early and went upstairs to Corinne's room. She was barely in the room when Corinne pirouetted to show off her gown.

"What do you think?" Corinne asked, expecting an affirmation of her accomplishment.

Felicia tilted her head to the side and said, "I'm not sure. Something is missing."

Corinne's face dropped and in a voice filled with apprehension asked, "What? What? Tell me. What's missing?"

Felicia undid her drawstring purse and reached inside for a small blue box. She removed the lid and took out her emerald earrings.

"Darling, Corinne. These are what are missing. Wear them tonight, and each time they brush your cheek, remember your friend loves you and wishes you success."

Not bothering to hold back tears, Corinne reached out for the earrings and put them on. "Felicia, I don't know what to say."

"Don't say anything," she answered. "They look magnificent and so do you."

Now, Felicia stood quietly as she was looked up and down with a critical eye. Corinne insisted on designing the dress Felicia wore. She wanted complete control over every detail of her opening night, and Felicia's piano playing was an important part of the evening.

Corinne looked proudly at her creation and thought how well its simplicity suited Felicia. The wine colored velvet dress, with its low scooped neckline, devoid of decorations, showed off her long neck. The tight, fitted bodice came to a vee below her waist. The sleeves were narrow and tapered at the wrist so they would not interfere with her piano playing.

"I am so envious of your height," Corinne said. "Whatever you wear looks elegant because of your great proportions. I always feel like I am sweeping the floor with my dress, but yours just drapes perfectly.

"Lot of good it does me when I am going to spend the evening sitting down at the piano," said Felicia.

"Better than lying down," laughed Corinne.

She grabbed her friend's hands and held her at arm's length. "Oh, Felicia, I'm so happy tonight. And even happier you and Abigail will be here to share it with me. When she arrives, I think I'll hang an 'unavailable' sign on her."

Felicia grinned. "Remember her first night at Mrs. Woodley's and the auction? Quite a difference tonight."

Not only Abigail's life had changed. They were all financially independent now and looking forward to their futures. Mrs. Woodley's had been a means, not one they enjoyed, but a way to get what they came west looking for. Corinne was the only one who had arrived with a definite purpose. Tonight she was about to show off the results.

Felicia's piano playing was an important part of the evening, and it would be the first time Philip heard her perform. She invited him to come for dinner and stay afterwards to hear her play. He normally did not go to a parlor house unless he was tending to one of the girls, but tonight he was making an exception. She was glad she had asked him to come.

He's so kind and considerate and he listens when I express an opinion. He really listens and mulls over what I say before he responds to me as his equal. She felt a warm flush as she thought about Philip.

Corinne noticed the rapid coloring of Felicia's cheeks. She also noticed the happy look in her eyes.

"I'm so glad Philip is joining us," she said.

"Remind me never to play poker with you," smiled Felicia.

Corinne hugged her and said, "He's such a good man, isn't he?"

Not willing to reveal her feelings further, Felicia suggested it was time to go downstairs and wait for Abigail.

"I'll be right down. I just want to make a final check of the ladies."

Felicia reached the bottom of the stairs just as Abigail came into the hall. Together, they walked to the front room to wait for Corinne. She joined them shortly and looked approvingly at Abigail who wore the third dress she designed for the evening.

She kept in mind Abigail's unwavering desire to look like a lady and created accordingly. The dress was made of shimmering pale peach satin. A tulle rosette with a crystal beaded center was placed in the exact center of the modest neckline. The same tulle peeked out from beneath the short puffed sleeves. Thin velvet ribbons hung gracefully down her arm. The dress had a full flowing skirt with a small bustle.

Corinne turned to Felicia and said, "I think she's done it. Our friend has turned herself into a beautiful lady."

"I couldn't agree more," Felicia answered. "Turn around, so I can see the back."

"It's only because you both helped me so much," protested Abigail. "You're the ones who showed me what to wear and how to speak. I never could have done it without you."

"Nonsense," said Corinne. "You're the one who did the work to transform yourself."

Abigail was a quick study with her native intelligence and gift of mimicry. She learned to dress smartly and to eliminate vocabulary and expressions which revealed her lower class origins. She now looked and sounded respectable. She barely recognized herself when she looked in the mirror.

Corinne left them to see if Lili needed anything. She knew how unnecessary it was, but couldn't stay still. Lili was a miracle, even if Corinne did not believe in miracles.

She rejoined them just as Philip entered the room. He carried a large bouquet of flowers which he presented to Felicia with a small bow.

"I thought these would look nice on the piano."

Felicia gave him a radiant smile and left to get a vase. His eyes followed her across the room, and when she disappeared into the hallway, he turned his attention to the other two women.

"You both look magnificent."

He leaned towards them and whispered, "I have nothing in my little black bag to mend all the hearts you two are going to break tonight."

He was dressed in a dark gray cutaway suit. He had struggled to fasten his tie correctly and even if it was slightly askew, he was proud of his appearance. Getting this dressed up was unusual for him, and he enjoyed wearing the elegant outfit.

Philip hoped Felicia's invitation was an indication she thought of him as more than a doctor. He didn't want to reveal his true feelings too soon, afraid she would end any further contact. There had been a few dinner dates and a buggy ride to admire the autumn show of the aspens. It was a start and he wanted it to continue.

Animated chatter and the rustle of skirts meant the ladies were about to enter the parlor. Corinne had paired each of them with a specifically invited guest, and spent a great deal of time with her decisions. She knew how lasting first impressions could be.

With a final look around, Corinne went to usher in the first arrival. When she opened the door, she found Cameron standing in front of her.

"I'm so glad you could make it," she said, genuinely happy to see him. "You look particularly striking tonight. Formal attire suits you."

His broad, muscular frame was contained in a dark suit with silk lapels. He smelled of cologne and even managed to slick back the hair which normally fell onto his forehead.

"I know how much you dislike fussing and I appreciate your effort," she said. She linked arms and walked with him into the parlor.

He looked around the room and said, "Well, I see you haven't moved any furniture since I left last Thursday. Is it some kind of a record for you?"

He made Corinne laugh as he always did. *You can't be around Judd Cameron and not enjoy life,* she thought.

"The arrangement shows your rug off perfectly, don't you think?"

"Lovely lady, I think it shows you off perfectly. Don't you look a sight in that dress? And emerald earrings to match."

He spun her around to admire her from all angles.

"And, now, point me to the bar and some of that imported champagne you told me about."

It was much more difficult to greet the next guest with a show of hospitality. Mayor Bennett said hello in his perfunctory manner and immediately started to survey the women in the parlor.

I can almost wipe the drool off his chin, thought Corinne as she presented him around. It was with reluctance she included him on opening night, but to not give him bragging rights was a recipe for trouble. She paired him with Sweet Betsy, a vivacious blonde with a quick wit, because Betsy could handle any difficult situation which might arise.

Roland Hart, owner of the largest silver producing mine, and T.J. Hansen, the newspaper editor, were the next arrivals.

"Welcome, gentlemen. Come with me. Let's get your evening started. The bar is this way."

She saw their eyes widen as they walked into the room and took in its expensive furnishings. Their reaction pleased her. She understood the seduction of sumptuous surroundings. She beckoned to Annie and Dusty Rose to join them.

Annie, a willowy brunette with sky blue eyes, took

Hart's arm and led him to a seat in front of the fire. She was the picture of femininity tonight, perfect for Hart, who saw himself as a gentleman, irresistible to the ladies. He was actually quite dull, but Annie would pretend otherwise.

Corinne matched Dusty Rose with T.J. When Dusty Rose first expressed interest in working for her, Corinne was curious about her dusky complexion and dark, ebony eyes. It wasn't unheard of for former slaves to pass themselves off as white. Corinne decided to hire her anyway because of her arresting looks and obvious intelligence.

The remainder of the invited guests arrived and she looked around the room, proud of her achievement. Drinks were being poured, laughter was heard and a gay atmosphere filled the room. She knew the geniality would continue when she announced dinner was served.

Felicia had invited Philip, but Abigail came unescorted, reluctant to ask anyone. The table was set for five, and Abigail and Felicia wondered who would sit in the fifth chair. Corinne's choice was a subject of much speculation between them, and they finally culled the list down to two names: Cameron, because she liked him and Mayor Bennett, because it was political. They were both relieved to see Cameron approaching.

Corinne joined her friends at the large round table. The rest of the room was organized into tables for two, with name cards arranged at each place. She waited until all were seated and then rose to welcome them.

"Gentlemen, in the spirit of the holiday season, I carefully selected a special gift for each of you. She's a gift I'm sure you will delight in unwrapping, but I do ask you to wait until after dinner."

When the laughter subsided, she continued, "I'd like to welcome you, my first guests, to The Laughing Ladies. I hope you enjoy the evening and return again and again."

Her short speech was greeted by raised glasses and a few congratulatory remarks. Corinne acknowledged their good wishes and signaled the waiters to serve dinner.

After the first course, Corinne made a tour of the room, briefly stopping at each table.

As she neared T.J.'s table, she heard Dusty Rose ask, "What made you choose to do it?"

Before he could answer, T.J. saw Corinne approach and rose to greet her.

"Congratulations, Corinne. You've done an excellent job. I'm sure everyone is as pleased as I am."

Dusty Rose looked up at Corinne, "I'm getting quite an education on linotype and printing presses."

"T.J., this must be a first. There isn't much she doesn't know," commented Corinne as she winked at Dusty Rose. She made a bit more small talk and moved on.

His loud laughter made it evident Betsy was holding the mayor's interest. *Good girl, Betsy*, she thought and after a few polite remarks, kept circulating.

Annie was listening to some dry facts about the variety of ores found at the mine camp, and Corinne marveled she could keep such an interested look on her face. Hart rose as she approached their table.

"Corinne, I want to personally compliment your efforts. You can be sure I will pass the word about what you've done here."

"Why, thank you. I'm glad you're pleased."

Corinne floated away, relieved to have the backing of one of the town's most influential businessmen.

She noticed Lulu signal the bartender for another bottle of wine. With Lulu working for her, she would end the night with a nice profit from liquor sales. Lulu's client, Andrew Clovis, hotel proprietor and entrepreneur, owned half the buildings on Main Street. A prosperous businessman, he lived mostly on the income from his properties. He was a wine connoisseur and it was well known he backed a few vineyards in California. Corinne made sure to order a few cases from each of them.

As she neared the next table, she saw Maybe Minnie wrapped in a black lace mantilla and wearing a fluted tortoiseshell comb in her hair. *She reminds me of Goya's Duchess of Alba, but I bet she plans to play Carmen tonight.* Her client was Ivan Kozlov, a Russian impresario who made his fortune by opening a string of opera houses in mining towns. He correctly sensed there would be a hunger for culture and capitalized on that desire. By all accounts, The Crystal Creek Opera House was quite successful.

"Corinne, perhaps you would like to design some scenery for me," Kozlov said as his eyes swept across the room.

"Why thank you, Mr. Kozlov. But, I think I'll stick to what I know best."

"Ah, my lovely Miss Sullivan, if all my artistes were as wise as you."

She hadn't fully completed the circuit of the room when Abigail beckoned.

"Lili is asking if you are ready to have the main course served."

As she rejoined her table, Cameron leaned over and nodded at the rest of the room.

"Looks like you've got everything the way you like it, completely under control."

"Cameron, I swear sometimes you can read my mind."

"Tonight, it's pretty apparent what you're thinking. But, you can relax," he said as he took her hand and gave it a reassuring squeeze.

"Thank you, Cameron. You know how much I respect your opinion."

"Especially when it agrees with yours."

"Am I that obvious?" she asked.

He brought her hand up to his lips and kissed it lightly.

"What's obvious is that you are beautiful, intelligent and accomplished."

He put her hand down and sat back in his chair with his arms across his chest.

"You know what else you are good at?" he asked.

"What?"

"You've managed to assemble quite a strong little community here. And how many people do you think are aware of how much money you pour back into the town? Too bad you're not appreciated as much as you should be."

"By the townswomen you mean?" said Corinne. "Why should I care what those women think?"

"My mind-reading ability tells me you do care, but don't want anyone to know. I think recognition means a lot to you."

"My bank account gives me all the recognition I need," she answered with more emotion than she intended.

She was glad to see the main course being brought to the table.

"Now, don't go sulky on me, Corinne. I apologize if I stepped over the line."

She reined in her temper and smiled at him. "Don't worry, I'm fine."

Relieved he was off the hook, he sampled his food.

"Looks like Lili's done you proud," he said, cutting into the thick slab of tenderloin.

After dinner, they adjourned to the parlor where Felicia would play for them. Corinne told her to include some lively dance music which would make the men thirsty. It was the fastest way to increase liquor sales before everyone disappeared upstairs.

At Corinne's signal, Felicia began her first night as "the professor" with a waltz. Cameron extended his hand and led Corinne to the end of the parlor where a space had been cleared for dancing.

She stepped into Cameron's arms and they started across the floor. For a large man, he was very agile and moved gracefully. With his black hair and dark eyes, he was a perfect foil for her brightness. Corinne felt light-headed and was grateful for his firm grip.

It must be the wine, she thought. But more likely, she was intoxicated by success.

"Corinne, honey…" whispered Cameron.

"If anyone, it would be you, but I don't go upstairs anymore," she answered before he could continue. It was what he expected her to say, but disappointing nevertheless.

When the music ended, he decided he would make his exit.

"It's been quite an evening. And now that The Laughing Ladies is successfully launched, I'll say good night."

As he called for his coat, he saw Abigail ready to leave and insisted on taking her home. He couldn't resist saying, "Quite a bit different from the first time we took a walk together."

"Things changed, Cameron. I followed your advice and got quite good at pretending. But, I never got used to it. I always hated what I was doing."

He thought back to the innocent young girl he successfully bid for many months ago. She looked and sounded nothing like that person.

"Well, it's over now and you've started your new life. I'm really happy for you."

He helped her up to the wagon seat and with a small whip of the reins, the horse started down the lane towards town.

Chapter Twenty: Revelation

*Revelation - disclosure of something
previously hidden or secret*

Each night, Philip arrived to walk Felicia home.

"Too many drunks and who knows what else," he used as his excuse. They both knew that was not the reason.

Tonight, as they slowly strolled through the quiet streets, Philip complimented both her playing and her selections.

"I particularly liked the Mozart concertos," he said. "They're not easy to play and they created exactly the right mood to end the evening."

Felicia thanked him, liking how he singled out one piece to compliment. She couldn't remember any conversation when he didn't notice small details. She supposed it was because he was a doctor and had to pay close attention to symptoms in order to make the correct diagnosis. Still, she liked being the recipient of his interest.

A full moon, shining through the tree branches, lit the street and created shadows on the ground. The night was so still they could hear their footsteps crunching as they walked. Everything changed when they came to the main street. The hushed loveliness was shattered by the bright lights of the saloons and dance halls. Drunken laughter and loud shouts engulfed them as they hurried through the endless activity. Neither of them spoke until they turned onto the street which led to Felicia's house.

She and Abigail agreed to share a house when they left Mrs. Woodley's. Although Abigail worked during the day and Felicia at night, they were able to find time to spend together. They "played Corinne" as Abigail called it, searching through catalogs and ordering furniture. Abigail had never lived in a place of her own, and endlessly chattered about what would look good and where. Felicia was just glad to have a normal life in a peaceful household.

The early winter air was cold and when she shivered, Philip removed his jacket and placed it around her shoulders.

"Philip…" she began, but could not continue because he placed one finger over her lips.

"Don't say anything unless it's thank you. No protests allowed."

"Philip," she started again. "Kindness is a remarkable quality and you give it so generously. I really do appreciate that. I also appreciate you."

A shot of adrenalin surged through him. Determined to tread carefully, he simply answered, "Felicia, what you said means a lot to me."

Then, he changed his mind. *Now or never*, he thought as he stopped at the porch steps and faced her.

"And you mean a lot to me. You must know how I feel about you."

"There's something I need to tell you before we continue this conversation," Felicia said and broke free to race up the steps. Her hands shook as she unlocked the door.

The fire had gone out and the house was chilly. Normally,

it didn't matter, but tonight she was not going directly to bed. She had something to say to Philip. It was time she told him the reason she hesitated about encouraging his interest.

"Why don't you get a fire going while I run upstairs for my shawl?" she asked and left the room.

He placed his jacket on the couch and stacked the logs. He wondered what she could possibly need to tell him. *No sense speculating, she'll be down in a minute.*

He lit the kindling and watched the sparks jump from one sliver to another until one of the larger logs began to smolder and finally ignite.

He couldn't stop himself. *I wonder if she's going to tell me the reason she came out here. Not that anything in her past would matter to me. I wonder if my reason for being here would matter to her.*

She came through the door clutching a large woolen shawl around her shoulders. He sensed that more than cool air motivated her to hold herself so tightly.

She sat down next to him and without any preamble, blurted out, "I'm married, Philip."

He was stunned. Felicia married. Not what he expected to hear. He waited for her to continue.

"I ran away from my husband. One day I decided I wouldn't take his verbal abuse any more. I packed up and left. I met Corinne and Abigail on the train coming west. And the rest you know."

"Aren't you going to add anything else?" Philip asked. "That's a pretty startling piece of information you just told me."

Felicia lifted an andiron and pushed at the pyramid of wood. As the top log fell, a whoosh of orange and red erupted. Satisfied, she returned to her seat beside Philip.

"Did he ever hit you?"

"No, he didn't. But, sometimes I think what he did was worse. He found fault with everything I did. He would yell at me, criticize me and make me feel like a stupid, untalented person."

As she talked about Stewart, emotions buried for months began to resurface. Fighting for control, she made herself continue.

"At first, I would answer back and argue with him. But I realized pretty quickly I was better off not speaking. If I did, he would punish me by not talking to me. He wouldn't answer, he wouldn't speak, and I had to wait until he decided he'd punished me long enough. It would be fine for a day or two, and then would start all over again. I always felt like I was walking on eggshells. I was slowly losing myself, who I was, and becoming more and more submissive."

Does he understand? She tried to gauge Philip's reaction, but he wouldn't look at her. *I need him to understand why I left.*

She sat up straighter and pulled her shawl tighter, wearing it like protective armor. She had to push the words out, no matter how painful.

"Wives don't leave their husbands. Society shuns them if they do. I was a good girl, Philip. I followed all the rules. But then one day, I made up my mind. I wasn't going to follow them anymore. I walked out the door. And before you say anything, I want you to know that I have never regretted doing it."

Philip leaned forward, his clasped hands between his knees, and stared at the fire. He focused all his attention on the flames being drawn up the flue. An explosion of sparks flared, and a log fell off the burning pile. Although a great deal of heat radiated from the hearth, he felt chilled.

Finally, he asked, "How long have you been married?"

"Five years."

She couldn't stop the tears. She wiped her eyes with the back of her hand.

Relating all this was harder than she thought it would be. Felicia wanted Philip to know about her life before Crystal Creek, the mistake she had made, how desperate she had been. But she didn't want him to think she was an awful person. She sat there, miserable, not knowing what else to say.

Time passed in silence. Then, Philip reached out and pulled her towards him. He tightened his arms around her.

"It's only a piece of paper," he said. "I don't care that you're married. I only care that you are here, next to me. Nothing else matters."

"I'm sorry. I didn't mean to fall apart," she said, slipping out of his embrace.

He debated whether to tell his story, but decided one confession a night was enough. They sat together in the reflected light of the fire and kept the conversation neutral.

But his feelings weren't neutral and he wanted Felicia to be clear about how he felt.

"I think having the courage to leave an intolerable situation is admirable. If you'll let me, I'd like to keep on showing you my admiration."

Felicia understood what he was asking and was ready to take the chance.

"Don't go," she whispered.

She laughed softly as she locked the bedroom door. "I'm like a schoolgirl, sneaking you up to my bedroom, being quiet so no one will hear us."

"Why are we whispering?" he asked.

"Because Abigail is sleeping in the next bedroom."

"And Abigail doesn't know what happens behind a bedroom door?" he laughed.

She tapped his chest lightly, and then looked steadily at him.

"She'll know what this means. Are we ready to announce it to everyone?"

"Hell, yes. I want the whole world to know."

He turned her face up to his and put an end to all further conversation.

He's not Stewart, she told herself. *Philip isn't pretending. He wants me, not my money. Tonight, I don't have to escape into a world of my own. I can connect in every sense of the word.*

As she snuggled against him, he groaned with pleasure.

Afterwards, they lay on the bed, side by side holding hands. Felicia was shaken by a joy bubbling up inside her and spreading to every part of her body. She had allowed Philip into her private world, and he brought nothing but pleasure with him. She traced his profile with her index finger.

He propped himself up on his elbow and smoothed back her hair.

"I love you, Felicia," he said softly.

She looked at his face. Happiness surged through her.

"I love you too," she murmured and moved her body closer to his.

Philip had visits scheduled in the morning, so he was up early. He insisted on preparing breakfast, and Felicia busied herself setting the table.

All domesticity, she reached into the ice box for the milk and butter. They'd had the cooler for a few months now, and she couldn't count how many trips she and Abigail had saved to the cold storage in the cellar.

When Abigail arrived downstairs, she heard voices in the kitchen.

Company at this hour? Felicia is never up early in the morning. Who would be coming for breakfast?

She pushed open the kitchen door and saw Philip at the stove scrambling eggs. One look at the two of them and Abigail was across the room hugging Felicia.

"Ladies, please sit down," ordered Philip, carrying the cast iron pan to the table. "I am serving breakfast and you want to eat your eggs while they're hot."

When the three of them were seated, Abigail asked, "Does anyone else know besides me?"

"No, actually we didn't know ourselves until last night," Felicia said.

She sliced some bread and passed it to the others.

"Can I tell Corinne when I see her?" Abigail asked. "Please let me tell her. She'll be so happy for the two of you."

Felicia and Philip exchanged glances, and he deferred to her.

"Yes, you may," said Felicia. "You might as well. I won't be there until tonight, and I wouldn't be so cruel to make you keep the news to yourself the entire day."

Abigail stopped eating and said, "It's so exciting. Can, I mean, *may* I tell Lili also?"

She had caught Felicia's slight emphasis on the *may*.

"Corinne isn't much of a romantic is she?" asked Philip, imagining her reaction to their news.

"What do you mean?" asked Felicia.

"Precisely what I said," he answered. "She strikes me as a no-nonsense person."

"But, she'll be happy for you both, she will," Abigail said, feeling the necessity to defend Corinne.

Felicia put her fork down, suddenly nervous about anyone hearing about her and Philip.

"Maybe I don't want this news out yet. After all, I am still legally married."

"But what difference could it possibly make?" asked Abigail. "You were married when you worked at Mrs. Woodley's. So why should anyone care now?"

"I don't know," said Felicia.

I've done it again, she thought. *Acted before I considered the consequences.* She remembered how hastily she left Saratoga Springs, with no train ticket, no food and no plan for her future. *But everything worked out for me then and it will now, too.*

"You're being ridiculous. Who is going to find out?" asked Abigail. "If you didn't remind me just now, I wouldn't have even remembered. And Corinne certainly won't say anything."

Felicia looked at Philip. "But, what happens if someone does find out?

"Felicia, you told me you're married and I don't care. Who cares what anyone else thinks? It's time to end this fruitless conversation."

He cast about for a way to divert their interest and settled on the obvious.

"So, ladies, tell me, how do you think last night went?"

"I thought it was a great success. The opening went exactly as Corinne hoped it would," said Abigail.

She walked over to the stove and brought the coffee pot back to the table. "Anyone else need more?" she asked.

Felicia pointed to her empty cup.

"I agree. For me, it was an absolutely perfect evening."

She looked over at Philip. Abigail caught her glance and felt like a third wheel.

"Well, I'm off to work," she said pushing back from the table. "Thank you, Philip. Breakfast was lovely."

She took a final sip from her cup and placed it back in the saucer.

"I expect it will be a busy day for me today. There'll be lots of reckoning of accounts to do. Did you see all those empty bottles?"

When the door closed, Philip reached over and took Felicia's hand. He raised it to his lips and said, "Did I tell you yet this morning that I love you?"

She smiled at him. "Why Dr. Meyers, I believe you did."

Chapter Twenty-one: Additions

Addition - somebody or something that increases the intensity

Abigail's day had begun in a small bedroom at the back of the house she shared with Felicia. Mrs. Lucy Fairchild, daughter of the bank president, refused his bribe of a newly built house and followed her husband to Denver. Her father was more than eager to sell his error in judgment to the two women.

Before she got out of bed in the morning, the first thing Abigail did was to pull up the window shade and look at the Sawatch mountain range. Its imposing presence confirmed she no longer slept in a small airless room at the top of a house in Albany. Now, she awoke in her own home, not at Mrs. Woodley's dreading the thought of welcoming strangers to her bed.

After breakfast, she set out to The Laughing Ladies with a short stop at the newspaper office. A catch-up with T.J. was now part of her morning routine. He was an inveterate gossip and a good source of the latest news.

The tinkling of the bell announced her entrance, and T.J. looked up from his typesetting to greet her.

"Good morning, T.J."

She reached for the folded copy of the newspaper he left on the counter for her.

"Just a minute, Abigail," he said and pushed aside the tray full of small letter blocks. He rummaged on the shelf where he kept his papers and gathered up a handful of grey and cream colored cards.

"Look at these," he said and handed them over to her.

"What are they?" she asked and began to sort through them. Photographs of women in various stages of undress were on the fronts of the cards.

"They're called cabinet cards," T.J. said. "I thought you might like to show one to Corinne. They'd make nice advertising for her."

She turned over one of the cards and saw the name and location of a business written on the reverse side. They reminded her of the funeral cards Corinne once described.

"They're called cabinet cards because they're the perfect size to stand on the shelves of a cabinet," Abigail explained to Corinne when she handed the card to her a few minutes later. "T.J. thought you might be able to use them."

"It's not a bad idea. Might be an interesting way to show off the ladies," Corinne said as she studied the scantily clad woman in the photograph.

"You can put The Laughing Ladies advertisement on the other side," Abigail suggested. "If some new businessman arrives in town, you could send him a set of cards and he could make his selection beforehand. He'd be committed to you before he even found out about any of the other parlor houses."

"Abigail, you are quite the salesman. I believe you've talked me into it."

The two women walked into the dining room. Corinne stood back and studied the oak cabinet with its curved glass panels. She had kept the cabinet because she recognized the quality of the craftsmanship. Two lion heads were carved into the wood which separated the middle panel from the ones on either side. Brass covers, shaped like claws protected both front feet.

"I never took Mrs. Griffin's paperweights out of here. It would be the perfect place to display the photographs. Maybe put a few cards on each shelf. What do you think?"

Abigail agreed, pleased Corinne liked her suggestion.

Later in the day, Corinne walked over to the newspaper office. Many itinerant photographers passed through the town, and she wondered if T.J. could find the one who made the cards.

One month later, Oscar Hill arrived with camera equipment and props.

Abigail and Lili joined the eight ladies and Corinne in the parlor. The room filled with pleasant anticipation as the women watched, fascinated by the photographer and his equipment.

Mr. Hill carefully opened his camera to reveal the dark brown fabric bellows which looked like an accordion. He mounted the camera onto a tripod and next unrolled a heavy black cloth which he placed over the camera stand. Then he reached into his satchel and removed a long black rubber tube with a bulb at the end. Finally, he stacked up a pile of glass plates next to the tripod.

He turned to Corinne and said, "I think we're ready. Who's first?"

Corinne had decided to pose each of the women wearing a white satin garment and holding a single rose in her hand. She thought picturing what was beneath the clinging fabric would be more provocative than actually seeing what was there.

"I'll go first," volunteered Sweet Betsy.

Corinne made up her mind to hire Betsy the minute she walked into the room. With a big smile on her face and an eager step, she exuded such energy and vitality that Corinne found her irresistible. When she heard the story Sweet Betsy related about her background, it seemed impossible such a vibrant, happy soul could have had such an appalling past.

Betsy looked expectantly at the photographer. He had arranged a folding screen, draped in white, to act as a backdrop. A few long-stemmed red roses waited in a vase.

Mr. Hill handed her the white satin fabric and said, "Wrap this around you and then drape it over one shoulder."

She left the room and returned a few minutes later.

Great laughter broke out when Betsy re-appeared. She was short, and the fabric pooled in folds on the floor. Even though she gathered much of it in her hand, it kept coming loose and tripping her as she came into the room.

"Sexy wench, aren't I?" she asked and joined in the laughter. "Someone do something before the fabric takes over and I slowly disappear into its folds, never to be heard from again."

Madeline jumped up and started to rearrange the satin. After a few yanks and pulls, she stepped back and shook her head.

"I give up," Madeline said, and she threw her hands up in frustration.

The two women looked at Mr. Hill. He searched through his bags and found some large clips. With a few practiced movements, he successfully arranged the fabric.

"How do you want my hair?" Betsy asked Corinne.

"Let it down," Corinne answered, and Betsy pulled out the pins which kept it in place.

Her blonde hair fell loosely below her shoulders. Corinne nodded with approval.

"Leave it natural. We want you to look like you just got out of bed."

The other women watched how the photographer carefully positioned Betsy. He returned to his camera, inserted one of the rectangular glass plates and picked up the rubber tube. He placed his head beneath the cloth and called to Betsy, "Don't move!"

He pressed the rubber bulb at the end of the tube and a bright light flashed. The little gathering gasped. Mr. Hill emerged, giving Betsy new directions as he set up for another shot.

The women followed his every move, mesmerized by the process. Now that they saw exactly what was expected, they were all eager to volunteer. When Betsy left the room, Madeline jumped up and followed her.

"I'm next," she called out merrily and hastened across the room.

Corinne watched the long, straight backed Madeline trail after Betsy. The two women were complete opposites in both appearance and manner. Madeline was tall and dark with a naturally reticent manner. Betsy could barely keep her exuberance under control.

Corinne remembered how she hesitated before she hired Madeline. But, her poised look and her fine education impressed Corinne, and she decided to take a chance even though she preferred more experienced girls.

Madeline stood posed in the doorway, a vision in black and white. The long satin folds hung gracefully over her curves and her raven colored hair, unpinned and loose, contrasted sharply with the starkness of the white fabric. She knew she looked good and twisted slowly to give the full effect.

Corinne was elated. She wanted style and understatement. Madeline personified both.

When he finished with the remaining six ladies, Mr. Hill turned to Corinne.

"How do you want to pose for your picture?" he asked.

She hadn't thought to include herself, but after an afternoon of observation, she wanted a photograph.

"Give me a few minutes to change into a more suitable dress." She had the emerald green gown she wore to her opening night in mind.

"I won't be but a few minutes," she assured him. "Take a few shots of Abigail while I get ready."

As Corinne hurried up the stairs, she blessed all the practice she had in getting in and out of clothing in a hurry.

When she returned, Mr. Hill seated her at a table and chair positioned in front of the screen. He had removed the satin draped over it to reveal an intricately cut wooden pattern. He placed the stained glass lamp from the hall on the table and moved a tall areca palm next to it to make an appealing tableau.

When he looked through the lens, he regretted he could not reproduce the fiery red of her hair or those remarkable green eyes. The black and white print would not do justice to her colorful image.

When they finished, Corinne walked across the room to Lili.

"Mr. Hill, I'd like you to take a photograph of my French chef, Lili, and then we shall all partake of her wonderful cooking."

The photographer beckoned to Lili.

"I believe you are next," he said and indicated the chair Corinne had just vacated.

"Oh, no, no, *mais no*," protested Lili, ready to make a dash to the kitchen door.

"Oh, but you must," Corinne insisted and blocked her path. "And smile, Lili. You are so beautiful when you smile."

Lili walked to the chair as if on a death march. She sat ramrod straight, her hands tightly clasped in her lap. But, the photographer was adept at getting people to relax.

"You know, Lili, a Frenchman named Louis Daguerre invented portrait photography."

He was rewarded with a big smile. "But, of course, we French are a very intelligent people."

"Look at the camera and keep your smile," he said, as he ducked beneath the cloth.

He quickly put another glass plate in the camera and continued talking.

"His photographs, called *daguerreotypes*, were extremely popular for a while in the United States," Mr. Hill told her, warming to the subject.

"Are your pictures daguerreotypes?" asked Lili, proud to take part in a Frenchman's invention.

"No, what I do is completely different," he answered. "You can't make copies of daguerreotypes, so most people favor this method of photography instead."

By the time Mr. Hill took three shots of her, Lili was giving directions and arranging her own poses. Abigail would later swear she heard Mr. Hill chuckle as he took Lili's last picture.

Two weeks later, when the finished photographs were delivered, Corinne was well satisfied. She looked at the portrait of herself and decided to have an oil painting of the photo made. She would give the cabinet card to the artist and avoid the endless time posing.

Oh my, she thought. *I'm getting like those stuffy old aristocrats who fill their homes with portraits of their ancestors.* But, the idea of an oil greatly appealed to her.

It was a late winter morning and absolutely quiet outside. No sound of brooms as shopkeeper's swept the wooden walkway that ran down the main street of town. No fragments of conversation floated through the air. No rhythmic clop of horses walking by. Only silence, broken by the occasional call of a bird and the answer of its mate.

Corinne leaned back in her chair and looked out at the aspen trees. She could detect a haze of chartreuse on their branches. The rough white bark reminded her of birch trees, so plentiful back East. It was almost spring again and close to a year since she arrived in Colorado.

A staccato knock on the front door interrupted her thoughts. She slid the photographs into the top drawer of her desk and rose to answer. She wondered who could be here this early in the day. Lili's purveyors usually used the back door.

She faced a well-dressed man of about thirty. Instinctively, she eyed him up and down. He carried his clothing well, or perhaps it was the confident way he carried himself. Tall, perhaps 5'11", stocky, but well-proportioned. A full head of light brown hair was combed straight back from his forehead and his moustache was neatly trimmed. Dark brown eyes caught hers as he inquired about arrangements.

"How is this usually done?" he asked.

Corinne suppressed a smile, and invited her guest inside. He wore a light brown duster which brushed the tops of his dark leather boots as he followed her to her office. It fell open when he reached up to remove his wide brimmed hat. She could see a neatly ironed red flannel shirt tucked into canvas trousers.

He chose an upright chair and sat forward with both hands on his knees. A sheepish smile momentarily crossed his face as he confessed, "I've never done this before and I thought I better check it out beforehand, rather than just stop in tonight."

"Well, Mr..." she paused and waited for him to supply his name.

"Gibson, Daniel Gibson."

"Well, Mr. Gibson, I can certainly reserve a room for you, but it is usually used after dinner, which I assure you is the best you will find in town."

Corinne couldn't imagine why, but this man's presence was making her pulse race. Disconcerted, and finding it difficult to think, she coughed to cover her discomfort. She pulled out the ledger she kept in her desk and made a show of writing in his name.

"I assume you are new in town. I don't recall having seen you before."

"Yes, we...that is, my wife and boys...arrived about two weeks ago."

"How old are your boys?"

He looked ill at ease and asking about the familiar was a well used tactic.

"John is four and Joshua is eight months old."

"I pride myself on knowing everything that goes on in Crystal Creek, and I haven't heard one word about a new family in town," she said.

"We're out at the old Widener place until our house is finished. We managed to get here a bit sooner than expected, but the carpenters are doing their best."

As an afterthought, he added, "I'm the new engineer at the Terrance Mine."

The new engineer. I wonder when Old Henley left. Henley had many disagreements with the management, but she hadn't heard he actually quit. She stored this piece of information and then asked, "Shall I put you down for tonight?"

Daniel Gibson studied the stunning woman facing him. She wore a simple pale green blouse and dark wool skirt, but he could easily imagine the soft curves beneath the fabric. Not accustomed to doing business with a woman, he was impressed by the way she handled herself. *As well as any man*, he thought and shifted in his seat. She looked directly at him, waiting for his answer.

Corinne was appraising Mr. Gibson with her professional eye. She knew the signs. Obviously well-off, although he wore work clothes. His boots were quality leather, and when he reached into his pocket, he pulled out a heavy gold watch fob. Well cut hair and hands that were not scarred or calloused, all clues that told Corinne he would pay well for his evening.

"At what time should I return?" he asked as he rose to leave.

"Dinner will be served at 6:00pm."

She mentally ran through her ladies, deciding who would best suit him. Surprised by a yearning she had forgotten was possible, she wanted to be the one to spend time with him.

I must get control of myself. The last time I felt like this was when I met Thomas, and look how that turned out, Corinne lectured herself. *Rule number one…the most important rule …don't get involved with a client.*

Her admonitions tumbled over each other. *I no longer see clients. I eat dinner in the kitchen, alone. I own the business now, I only supervise the evening. I sleep unaccompanied. For God's sake, I don't do this anymore.*

But no matter what she told herself, it did no good. With a swish of her skirts, she got up and walked down the hall to the kitchen.

"Lili, there will be one more for dinner tonight and I'll be joining Mr. Gibson at his table."

Chapter Twenty-two: Gratification

Gratification - the feeling of pleasure that comes when a need or desire is fulfilled

Corinne approached the table where Daniel was seated. She saw surprise and then approval register as she crossed the room. He rose to pull out a chair for her.

She usually would have greeted him at the door and shown him to his table, but tonight a series of mishaps delayed her.

After pulling dress after dress from her wardrobe, she chose the peach taffeta gown with the fitted bodice. Corinne liked how it complemented her red hair which decided to be particularly unmanageable as she rushed to get ready. She spent frustrating minutes pushing and pulling it into place. The rubber bulb at the end of her sprayer broke off, and she had to remove the whole atomizer to get to her perfume. By the time she returned all the rejected gowns to the closet, she was late coming downstairs to greet her clients. When she entered the front room, she saw Betsy had stepped in to help and all was under control.

Corinne adjusted her skirts as she sat down, deciding

she had pulled her corset too tight. She moved a bit forward to alleviate the strain on her ribs. Daniel mistook her action and leaned forward as well. In a soft voice, almost a whisper he said, "Does this mean we'll be spending the entire evening together?"

She pushed her wineglass towards him.

"If you are agreeable."

"I assure you, I am," and he began to fill her glass.

Again, she admired how well he wore clothes. A black frock coat, with silk-faced lapels, sported the newly fashionable chest pocket with a handkerchief folded into it. The tight-fitting cut accented his broad shoulders. Beneath the jacket, she could see a double breasted waistcoat with his gold watch fob dangling from the front. A dark cravat, tied with a Ruche knot, completed his outfit.

"In expectation of a lovely evening," he said as he touched his glass to hers.

Corinne felt the heat of anticipation rise. *I wonder if he's experiencing the same reaction I am. Or, am I just someone to pass the time with?*

She looked over the rim of her wineglass and asked, "Has your family settled in yet?" *How banal. I can do better.*

"We're all fine."

His brief answer indicated this was not a conversation he wished to continue. Corinne, acutely attuned to men's moods, switched to a different subject.

"And your job? Do you like it?" she tried. *Another tiresome question. What is the matter with me tonight?*

Daniel shrugged and said, "I know all about myself. Let's talk about you. When did you come to Crystal Creek?"

"I arrived a little over a year ago," Corinne began, deciding how much to reveal. She chose a shaded version of the truth. "I was able to save enough money to set myself up in business more quickly than I expected, and here I am."

"I think I just heard the condensed version of your story. Anything else you want to tell me?"

"You don't really want all the details of how a woman came to settle in the West, do you?" Corinne asked, glad to see the first course being served.

The two remained silent while their dinner was placed on the table. Without a glance at the food, Daniel answered.

"I'm actually amazed at how an unmarried woman could cross the country by herself, manage to find a job which paid enough to save a sizeable amount of money and then start and run her own business."

"Let's call it my spirit of adventure. Life back East didn't offer me the opportunity to do any of those things. As you will soon find out, if you haven't already done so, attitudes here are not the same as those in other places."

And thank goodness for that! she thought as she sampled her steak. *I must tell Lili how good this bordelaise sauce tastes. What a gem that woman is.*

Daniel gestured towards his plate. "You were right when you said this was the best dinner in town. It's delicious."

"Yes, I'm fortunate to have Lili. Now that the town has grown, you'll find many niceties here. Fine dining is just one of them."

"I wish my wife could appreciate them. She's not at all happy here. Suzannah misses her friends and her family, and she finds life here much too primitive. I don't know what will happen if she can't adjust."

"If it's of any help to you, that's a familiar story. She may come around after you move into town and she meets more people. There are a number of families living here. We're really quite civilized. We have a newspaper and there's our Opera House. Harry Houdini, the great magician, is scheduled to perform there this summer. I'm sure she'll adjust."

"I wish she could think more like you," said Daniel as he finished his dinner.

"Women like your wife don't hold much stock with women like me."

Corinne finished the last of her wine.

"Shall we?" she asked and pushed her chair back from the table.

They walked into the parlor where Felicia was playing the piano. Daniel apologized before he started to dance.

"I'm not much of a dancer. Just never could get the hang of it. But, I'll try one dance just so you don't think I'm a coward."

Corinne moved closer to him, and when he took her hand and put his arm around her waist, she didn't care how graceful he was.

While they were dancing, Cameron came into the parlor. He looked around, searching for Corinne, and found her in Daniel's arms. He arranged his features into a neutral expression and hoped the stab of jealousy wasn't obvious. *What is going on? She told me she didn't do this anymore.*

He had dropped by, expecting to spend a few hours with Corinne. He came to The Laughing Ladies twice a week and looked forward to their regular conversation. He would probably propose again and she would laugh it off, treating it as a running joke between them. He was prepared to wait, as long as it took, for her to realize he was serious.

But there would not be conversation tonight. He watched Corinne smile at her partner. *Who is he?* he wondered. *And how did he get her to change her mind?*

He saw Felicia watching him and tilted his head in Corinne's direction. Felicia followed his gaze and shrugged her shoulders.

Disheartened, he turned and left. Corinne never noticed him.

"Shall we sit by the fire?" she asked and led Daniel towards the sofa.

It was a chilly night, and she added a few more pieces of wood. Daniel ordered sherry and they sipped as they stared into the flames.

"You certainly have created a lovely room. As nice as any..." and then he stopped, because he realized how belittling his intended compliment would sound.

Corinne smiled. "Don't be embarrassed. I'm well aware this is not a 'respectable' citizen's drawing room. But I agree, it is a lovely room."

"Not too many drawing rooms have an Aubusson rug on the floor," he said.

"It is beautiful, isn't it?

Outwardly, she seemed composed but she was perplexed by her behavior. *What is going on? Why am I so tongue-tied around him?* she asked herself. *I'm so nervous I'll say the wrong thing. I've got to remember who I am and what I do well.*

"Have we had enough conversation?" Daniel asked. "Can we go upstairs now? I don't know how much longer I can continue to look at you and not touch you."

Without a word, Corinne stood and walked towards the stairs. Felicia watched, surprised to see Daniel follow her.

When they reached her bedroom, she started to undress, but he reached out and caught her hand.

"Let me," he said. "I find it seductive to remove a woman's clothing."

Corinne stood motionless. Daniel slowly undid her gown and pulled it down from her shoulders. As his fingers unbuttoned, unhooked and unlaced, she cursed the many petticoats and crinolines she had on.

His eyes never left hers as he stepped back and took off his jacket and then, his shirt.

"You are so beautiful," he said, as he sat at the edge of the bed and looked at her.

She ran her hand across the thick thatch of hair on his chest and was seized with a craving to touch every part of him.

He drew her close and began to kiss her. She was surprised at how much pleasure she took in kissing him. It was as if she'd been in hibernation, hiding from physical sensations, tamping them down, and now they came bursting forth. She did not intend to stop them.

He moved his hand down her arm and pulled her closer to him. The kisses became more intense. She felt him grow hard and shifted her body to align with his. The move elicited a moan, and he again kissed her passionately. She slowly moved her hand across his back, down his side, lower and lower.

"Please don't touch me yet," he gasped. "I want this to last awhile."

She was glad to comply. She felt her desire rising. It was wonderful to feel so alive and full of sexual need.

Later, Daniel murmured into her ear. "Thank you, Corinne. It's been such a long time."

"But, you're married."

"Yes, I am."

"But, surely…." She started, but decided not to continue. This was not a conversation she was entitled to have with a customer. *What an awful thought! A customer. It seemed like so much more.*

"Suzannah is so afraid of childbirth, she won't even sleep in the same bed with me."

"You don't mean she's done forever?"

"Apparently so. She sleeps in another room."

Corinne couldn't imagine how his wife wouldn't want

to get into his bed at night and be enclosed in his arms. *What am I thinking?* she wondered. *I'm in bed with a paying customer.*

Daniel sat up and faced her.

"Corinne, I'd like to come here on a regular basis. With you, I mean. Do you do that?"

"To tell you the truth, I don't," she answered. She crossed the room, pulled her dressing gown down from the screen in the corner and belted it around her waist. She returned to the bed with a moistened wash cloth in her hand.

She's so casual about this, he thought. *Completely unlike Suzannah who always acted as if she deserved a reward because she indulged my repugnant actions.*

He watched Corinne and then said, "Maybe I didn't ask you what I really wanted to before. What I meant was, would you continue to see me? Tonight felt like more than a business transaction between us."

"Are you sure it's not just relief that your dry spell ended?"

Daniel insisted, "I think I can tell the difference between pretending to enjoy yourself and a genuine response. Can you deny you felt something?"

"No, I can't. But, Daniel, think about what you are suggesting. Men come and go here and their wives put up with it, just as your wife might if she knew. Like her, they're usually so afraid of childbirth they don't mind their men finding sexual satisfaction in another woman's arms. But, it's not allowed to mean anything. If you turn up here on a regular basis, Suzannah might get concerned."

"I'll have to make sure she doesn't find out. There can be lots of business dinners, meetings go on into the night. Leave it to me."

Corinne stood there, not answering.

"I'm a strong, healthy man who's been denied too long.

I refuse to give up what I found again tonight. And, I want you, Corinne, not anyone else."

He reached for his trousers and pulled out a billfold from one of the pockets.

"Don't worry. I'll pay you," he said.

She slapped the money away. Bills scattered across the bed. He looked surprised at her reaction.

"Isn't this what you do?"

Embarrassed that she had let her temper get the better of her, she tried to explain.

"No, I don't do this anymore. I'm with you because I want to be, not because I'm getting paid. What you said before was right. I was attracted to you this morning, and that's why I'm here tonight."

He ran the back of his hand down her cheek. "Corinne, I want you. I need to feel like a man again."

She knew she shouldn't agree, but also knew she couldn't stop herself.

"Let's try it and see what happens."

He pulled her to him and kissed her. Then, he got up to dress.

"I'll be in touch again as soon as I can."

And he was gone.

Corinne walked to the window and stood in the deep shadows. She watched him walk up the lane and disappear into the night.

To Corinne, the week that followed was much longer than seven days. Each night as she opened the door, she hoped to see Daniel in front of her. Each morning as she ran errands in town, she hoped to catch a glimpse of him on the street. As time passed, she started to believe she had fooled herself, spinning a fantasy about what happened.

And then, he was there.

Before he walked in, he stomped his feet, knocking the snow off his boots. He removed his hat and shook it, creating a flurry of white.

"Quite a night," Daniel said, handing her his hat and coat.

Corinne wanted to fling herself into his arms and suppressed a smile at the thought of her guests' faces if she did.

"Let me bring you a drink. Go and sit by the fire and warm up. Your hands are frozen."

As she walked to the bar, she felt a rush of anticipation at the thought of another night in his company. Drinks in hand, she joined him on the couch. He bent forward to wipe the melted snow off his boots and returned the handkerchief to his pocket. He straightened up and took the bourbon she offered.

"I know it's been almost a week, but this is the first time I could reasonably disappear for a few hours."

"I heard about the trouble at the mine. Did they get it all straightened out?" she asked as she sipped the new wine Clovis had sent.

"How did you find out?" he asked, amazed she knew such privileged information.

"Remember? I told you I hear all the news about what goes on in this town. After a drink or two, the men relax and talk about themselves and their problems. But, don't worry, we're discrete."

"Yes, the situation got settled, but it did make more work for me. That's what kept me away so long. But, I don't want to talk about the mine. I'd rather hear about you."

Desire grew as they sat in front of the fireplace. He obviously felt the same way since although he made small talk as he sipped his bourbon, his mind was already upstairs.

It didn't take them long to finish their drinks.

Felicia, seated at the piano, watched Corinne walk up the stairs with Daniel close behind her. There was no doubt what it meant.

When did Corinne change her mind? she wondered as her fingers automatically found the right keys. *And why him? I always hoped Cameron would be the one.*

This became the pattern of their time together. He would come to the house when he could. Sometimes he could get word to her beforehand, and sometimes he would just appear. They would share a drink, idle conversation and then, they would share themselves.

It was satisfactory, up to a point. For days, Corinne, would wait to see him. Then, too brief a time spent together followed by her longing to be with him again. She told herself this was all he could offer, it would never change, and even if he wanted to change circumstances, she didn't trust he could. She tried to convince herself that it was a good arrangement for her. She got pleasure from a man, but still maintained her freedom and the financial control of her assets.

How long can this go on? She smiled as she recalled a recent conversation in which Daniel had asked, "Do you think when we're sixty, we can still do this?"

She looked at his strong, firm body next to hers and tried to imagine it with wrinkles and sagging skin.

"You sure wouldn't be as sexy as you are now," she answered. "But, I'll keep you."

He gazed up at the ceiling, his hands folded behind his head. Suddenly serious, he said, "Corinne, if I ever don't show up, you'll know I'm dead."

Chapter Twenty-three: Adjustment

Adjustment: to make slight changes in something

A few nights later, when all was quiet, Felicia cornered Corinne. She was merely curious at first, but then became insistent.

"Corinne, you made it very clear you no longer accept clients, yet I keep seeing you take one particular man upstairs with you."

"Since when do you keep tabs on me?"

"I don't. But when I play, I can't help but see the stairs since they are directly in my line of vision."

When Corinne didn't respond, Felicia turned away and began to sort her sheet music. With unnecessary concentration, she divided it into two stacks. The larger one she put back into the piano bench.

"Well, he pays me quite well," Corinne lied. "No sense alienating anyone."

Felicia would have no part of it.

"It's more than money, Corinne. I see how you are when he's here. But, even more, I see your disappointment when he's not. I know you too well. What's going on?"

She looked intently at Corinne, waiting for an answer. When none came, Felicia gathered up the second pile of music and stuffed it into her bag with such force that the top sheet ripped in half.

Corinne walked to the piano and played a few notes.

"Do you think we need to have this tuned?" she asked.

Felicia continued packing without looking up. Corinne closed the piano lid and turned towards the hallway.

"I'll just go say good-night to Lili."

What Corinne really wanted to do was sing out to the world about Daniel. To tell Felicia, to tell anyone who would listen, how he filled her every thought and how she wanted to be with him every minute of the day. But, she held back.

I'm afraid to share him with anyone, that's what it is. If I talk about him, I would destroy the fantasy I've created for myself. Instead of the great love affair I have built up in my head, reality would show it for what it is, a madam and her married client. I don't want to see us that way. And if either Felicia or Abigail knew how I really felt, what would they think? I'm the one who always protested I wasn't interested in marriage or even another romance, and now I would have to admit I've fallen madly in love with someone I can never have.

Abigail was not any easier to hold off. Felicia, unable to pry information out of Corinne, told Abigail her suspicions and one morning, out of the blue, Abigail asked, "Who is this man you're so interested in?"

Corinne knew why Abigail asked. Felicia had been talking about her.

"Why does it matter so much to the two of you?" she asked.

"Because we're your friends and friends don't keep secrets from one another. We feel shut out," Abigail answered. "I've seen him, by the way, and I can certainly understand your interest."

"When did you see Daniel?" asked Corinne.

"Daniel Gibson, the new engineer at the Terrance Mine? Is that who he is?"

"How do you know about him?" asked Corinne.

"You forget, I read the newspaper in the morning. There was an article about him the other day. His house was finally finished, and he and his family moved into town."

The mention of Daniel's family felt like a vise gripping her, an ache inside her which swelled into physical pain. Corinne was excluded from that part of his world. Daniel had been honest from the start. He told her he had no intention of leaving his wife, and Corinne believed him. Even though Suzannah had moved out of his bed, they shared two young sons and a substantial amount of money. Divorce was a stigma he did not wish to settle upon her.

It took considerable effort not to confess how Abigail's piece of news affected her. Instead she said, "He comes here like all the other men, for the good conversation."

"Oh, stop it Corinne! You're talking to me. If you like him, what's wrong with admitting it? You're human. You're allowed to have feelings for a man."

"Okay, I admit it. I do like him."

Corinne slumped into the leather chair in front of Abigail's desk.

"He's good looking, he's smart, he's witty and he's married!"

Abigail leaned against the edge of the desk and asked, "What will you do? Sounds like you've got it bad.

Corinne shook her head and looked down at her lap. It was a question she asked herself many times.

Daniel managed to come to The Laughing Ladies on a regular basis, but their arrangement would have to change. Suzannah lived in town now and was more apt to hear rumors. It had become risky to meet so often.

"Well, if you and Felicia noticed Daniel, then someone else will too. We'll have to do a better job of hiding or other men will demand the same privileges from me."

After her conversation with Abigail, Corinne decided to share her concerns with Daniel. Her first opportunity came the following afternoon. She had just returned from the dressmaker's shop when he stopped by. He walked into her office and caught her admiring herself in front of the mirror.

"I like your new jacket," he said. "The color suits you."

Her face grew warm, embarrassed to have her vanity exposed.

"I came by to say I'll be back later tonight."

She put the black, fur trimmed shrug back into its box. She gave him a quick hug and decided she might as well say something now. It was no use putting it off. Even though she didn't want to limit the little time they managed to find, it had to be done.

She steeled herself and said, "Daniel, I don't think you can keep coming to The Laughing Ladies so frequently."

"Why? I don't understand. Can't you pass me off as a regular customer?" Daniel asked.

"It won't work. I've made it very clear I no longer accept clients. How long will the regulars believe you are here for only conversation and drinks? Pretty soon, there will be talk, which will reach their wives' ears, and then your wife will hear it as well."

He started to pace up and down her small office. He stopped at the window and banged his hand on the sill. Then he turned and asked, "Are you saying you want to stop seeing me?"

"That's not what I meant at all," she replied and dropped her gaze.

She refused to allow him to see how much he meant

to her. She couldn't imagine her world without him. The tightness in her chest was sometimes unbearable when she thought about him and wanted to speak to him and couldn't.

"Then we'll figure out a way to see each other and not have anyone know," he insisted. "And, we'll do it right now."

Corinne made the only suggestion she could think of.

"I have to mingle with the guests until they all go upstairs. Then, no one cares where I am. Can you possibly manage to come here that late?"

"It's not perfect, but I'll take what I can get. There can be lots of reasons for me to be out late. Don't worry, leave it to me."

Corinne walked around her desk and smoothed back his hair.

"Oh, Daniel, I wish we didn't have to do this, but one of us has to be realistic."

He lowered her hand and pulled her close.

"Corinne, I'll do whatever you say. I have no right to make demands on you. I'm here only at your pleasure. If someone comes along and wants to marry you, there's no reason you can't simply say good-by to me."

"What are you talking about? I don't want to get married. I've got the life I arranged for myself, and I find it most satisfactory. Why would I want to ruin it by getting married?"

He tilted her head up and smiled his endearing little boy smile before he kissed her, not a bit like a little boy.

"I've got to get back to the mine office, but I'll see you later tonight," he said.

She heard him whistling as he walked down the lane.

Chapter Twenty-four: Contrast

*Contrast - a marked difference between
two things when compared*

It was almost 9:00pm when Corinne heard his light tap at the back door. She rushed to open it thinking, *How could Suzannah not suspect? Or maybe she does, and is relieved Daniel doesn't make any demands on her.*

Corinne often wondered how Suzannah would react if she found out her husband was a regular visitor, and their relationship had become more than a brief stop at a bordello for quick relief.

"Good evening, Laughing Lady," said Daniel as he shook the snow from the brim of his hat and tossed it across the room.

"You're getting good at that," commented Corinne, as his hat landed precisely on the hook of the coat tree.

He laughed and said, "And at some other things as well."

Corinne smirked her agreement.

"Come outside with me for a minute," he said. "It's snowing, and it's a beautiful night."

Corinne pulled on her coat. Arm and arm they stepped out into the gently falling snow. The night was clear and stars dotted the sky. The moonlight turned the suspended snowflakes into luminous crystals. The air was aglow with their patterns of brightness. It was indeed beautiful.

"This reminds me of those paperweight globes I have. They look exactly like this when you shake them," said Corinne. She leaned against his shoulder, lost in the moment.

"I wouldn't want to share this with anyone but you," he said.

His words gratified her, but they also caused an anguish she tried to suppress. *I only have him for this little time we spend together. Are these short times really worth the long hours I miss him and want him and know he will never be my own?*

Sadness engulfed her and she tried to rationalize the melancholy away. *Maybe this is better. It's easier to maintain an illusion if we're not together all the time. When we do see each other, we look our best, we act our best and we don't deal with the mundane responsibilities of life.*

Corinne ran her hand down Daniel's cheek. "So good to see you," she said and burrowed even closer to him.

He picked her chin up and kissed her softly.

"Are you ready to go in?" he asked, and they moved together out of the cold.

Later, he propped himself on his elbow and gazed at Corinne. He absentmindedly twirled a strand of her hair and thought how well the color suited her. Her eyes were closed and when she opened them, they had a look of pleasure he had never seen on Suzannah's face. It made him feel strong and potent.

Seeing him look so smug, she rubbed her foot slowly up

and down his leg. He leaned over her and reached out to the nightstand. He turned his watch to see the time.

"You better stop," he said. "I have to go. It's later than I thought."

Never again will I deny my needs, he promised himself as he began to dress. *Suzannah may not want me, but Corinne does.*

"Sometimes I think you look better dressed than undressed," she said, as he started to pull on his clothes.

The expression on his face made her quickly backtrack.

"Although, maybe not. Especially when I see that lovely part of you that's usually hidden."

He stopped buttoning his shirt and glanced downward.

"Mind tells me I have to go, but looks like the body isn't so willing."

"I'll be good," she laughed and nestled into the covers.

He reached for his belt and slipped it through the loops of his pants. As he buckled it, he asked, "Do you think if I gave Suzannah the house, the money and the boys, she would let me go?"

Corinne knew what her only answer could be. She didn't need to think about his question.

"You would never leave John and Joshua, Daniel. Why even talk about it?"

He pushed her legs out of the way and sat down in front of her.

"You don't understand what you mean to me, Corinne. You want me for me. You don't see me as the provider for your children, the paycheck at the end of the week, someone who makes your life comfortable. You welcome me to your bed and make me feel you're glad I'm here."

"Daniel, don't talk about leaving. Don't even dream you

could. You may think you can, but you can't. If you walked out the door, you would feel so guilty you would be on your way back in before you even got off your porch."

"But, I feel guilty about what I do to you. I have nothing to offer the way it is now. I don't know if you should go on seeing me."

Oh, no, thought Corinne. *Oh, no you don't.*

"What gives you the right to make any decision for me? Let me make my own choices. You have told me over and over again, what you will and won't do, and I am fine with our arrangement. Now go home before it gets really late."

With Daniel gone, Corinne dropped her bravado. She sat in front of the dwindling fire, glad to be alone. She pulled up the collar of her robe and added a few more pieces of wood. She stayed on the settee until the last log shifted and fell.

The snow fell lightly as Daniel walked the short distance to his new home in town. The accumulating snowflakes outlined the bare tree branches and accentuated the pattern of the wooden fences. As he took in the winter scene, he congratulated himself on his decision to come here, but Suzannah didn't agree. She was miserable, and he hoped their recent move into town would help.

Remorse stabbed at him. At his insistence, they married when Suzannah was too young. In a short time, they were the parents of two boys. Joshua, their youngest, was a difficult and painful birth for Suzannah, and it took her months to recover. Almost as soon as she had, he was offered the job as Chief Mining Engineer and they packed for Crystal Creek.

There had been tearful pleas not to accept the job. She had begged and begged him not to go. But, finally, with great reluctance, she left behind family and friends to accompany him west.

He climbed the porch steps, trying not to make any noise. As he opened the door, he found himself staring at a shotgun pointed at the center of his chest.

"Suzannah, put the rifle down, it's me," he shouted as he ducked to the side.

She lowered the rifle and flung herself into his arms. "Thank goodness, it's you. I was so worried."

She held him tightly and managed to say, ""I'm so glad you're all right."

"Are you mad? What are doing with a loaded rifle?" he asked as he took the gun and hung it back on the wall.

"Daddy told me I needed to have a gun loaded and ready when I was alone. He said it isn't safe out here."

"Daddy has been reading too many magazine stories. We don't live out in the middle of nowhere, we live in a civilized town."

"Where were you?" she asked. "I was worried sick. It's so late."

"I told you I had a meeting, and then we were all going out for some drinks."

He sat down at the table and started to pull off his boots.

"No meeting lasts that long," she said, as she re-belted her bathrobe which had come undone. The tone of her voice warned him this wasn't going to be an easy conversation.

He yanked at his second boot so hard it went flying across the room.

"Suzannah, please," he said, his sense of contentment rapidly dissolving.

"You didn't answer me, Daniel."

She sank into the rocking chair. He listened to the slow

repeated rhythm on the wooden floor. Each thud was an accusation.

"The meeting I went to was at The Laughing Ladies," he said quietly.

She visibly blanched when she heard him. He walked towards her, but stopped when she cowered at his approach.

"Suzannah, I'm a man. Try to understand, I have needs. Sexual needs."

She didn't move. She didn't make a sound. And then a soft, low wail escaped.

"How could you do this to me?" she asked. "Do you want to bring home all kinds of diseases from those dirty, filthy whores?"

"They're neither dirty nor filthy, Suzannah. They have a doctor who checks them regularly. The Laughing Ladies are sophisticated women who happen to make their money in a parlor house."

"Why are you telling me these things?" she asked.

"I'm telling you because it's what I did. We have not slept in the same bed for months. I can't go on like this."

"But, I'm a good wife. I gave you two sons. What more do you want?"

"Sex can be enjoyable," he said. "Haven't you ever liked it?"

Appalled, she jumped up and paced from one end of the room to the other, her arms wrapped around her body as if to ward off his evil words.

"Daniel, how can you talk such nonsense to me? I've done my duty. Maybe, when Joshua is a little older, but now it's too soon to have another child."

"I'm not talking about children, I'm talking about sex. You could learn to enjoy yourself. I can show you, if you let me."

"Don't talk to me like this. I'm a respectable woman, not some indecent slut."

"And I'm a man and your husband. I expect you to act towards me like a wife. Something you have chosen not to do."

"It's too soon. I don't want another child. There's no one to help me with the two I have. You made me leave everyone I love. I'm all alone. I hate it here."

She burst into tears. "What do you want from me?"

Daniel watched her unhappiness spill out. Overwhelmed by guilt, he tried to comfort her. She flinched when his arms encircled her and she pulled away. She walked as far from him as she could and turned.

Her face was scarlet with anger. Daniel thought of the beautiful woman he had barely left. She would never make a scene like this.

"I forbid you to go there anymore," Suzannah said.

She stood there defiantly, with her fists clenched at her side.

"I will forgive you this time, but you may not do this to me again."

He crossed to her and grabbed her by the shoulders. Holding on with one hand, he lifted her chin with the other to make her look directly at him.

"Maybe you don't get to decide what I may or may not do. I am not your four year old son. I'm your husband, and I demand to be treated like one."

She shook herself loose from his hold and walked to the table in the center of the room. She leaned across it using both hands to brace herself and said, "Do you want me to die? I gave you two sons, and I don't ever want to go through that again."

He tried to reason with her. "There are ways not to get pregnant, Suzannah."

She put her hands up to her ears. "Stop it," she pleaded. "Stop it. I refuse to take any chances."

He dropped back down into the chair across from her and took a deep breath before he spoke, "I've given you a choice and you've taken it. I promise not to touch you again."

Relief, then realization, followed by fear, assaulted her.

"What has come over you? Why are you doing this to me? Has one of those tramps bewitched you? How long have you been visiting those filthy prostitutes?"

"That's enough, Suzannah. I won't listen to this name calling anymore. Corinne is a lovely woman, and if you don't want to share a bed with me, she does."

Suzannah leaned against the wall when she heard what he said.

"Corinne? Is that her name? Is she the woman you go see?"

Daniel cursed his foolish mistake. Suzannah now had a name. The whole conversation was a disaster, and he decided to end it. He snatched his boots and started to pull them on again.

"Where are you going?" she cried as he grabbed his hat and coat.

She followed him to the door.

"We're not finished. You can't leave now."

The slamming door was his answer.

As he strode across the yard towards the stable, the beautiful night was now only darkness. The magic of the falling snow was gone. It was cold and wet, and he didn't care. He headed to the stable. He had to ride off his anger at Suzannah and his feeling of being trapped by a woman he no longer wished to be with.

Chapter Twenty-five: Encounter

Encounter - to meet somebody unexpectedly

Corinne stared out the window at the bright, sunny day. Last night's early spring snow had melted, and today it seemed as if winter might finally be over. She grabbed her cloak, hoping a long walk might shake off her lethargy. As she headed towards the mountains, she noticed that Felicia's Snow Angel had recently formed there. Feeling foolish, Corinne spoke aloud to her.

"What am I doing with this man? All I can ever expect from him is the little time we snatch together. Even though he denies it, I'm the outlet that makes his marriage bearable. He can avoid facing Suzannah's refusals. Snow Angel, I think about him constantly. He's become an obsession. What am I going to do?"

She continued down the path, the light demarcation formed by the many riders who previously had gone into the mountain. She crossed to the rubble at the base of the cliff and continued upwards. Around the second turn, she reached a large flat rock, her usual resting place. She tucked her hands inside her woolen cloak and inhaled the crisp mountain air. She loved this time of year, when the air became invigorating rather than chilling.

She looked down at the town and realized how much it had grown in the time she lived here. Main Street had expanded to include many new shops and rooftops extended in three directions now. Not even the ugly tailings of a mine could spoil her appreciation of her surroundings. *I love this place. It's so open and clean, not like the crowded city I left behind.*

Corinne climbed upward, but eventually the trail turned too rocky, and she was forced to go back. As she retraced her way across the open space to the edge of town, a tow-headed boy ran up to her. A woman carrying a small child on her hip tried to catch up with him.

"John," she called out to him. "Come back here right now!"

He hesitated a moment, and then continued on towards Corinne.

"Look at what I found," he said and held up a rock which sparkled with bright metal flecks.

"Oh, I'm so sorry," the woman apologized. She tried to catch her breath and to juggle the child on her hip at the same time.

"I hope he didn't disturb you. You looked lost in thought."

Corinne took the stone he extended towards her. She turned it around and around and admired it as he watched her closely.

"It's lovely. Aren't you a lucky boy to find it," she said as she returned it to him.

"This is my son John and his brother, Joshua," said the woman. "And I'm Suzannah Gibson. We've just moved into town and John doesn't know his boundaries yet. It seems like I've spent the entire morning chasing after him."

Corinne looked down at her chest, sure the hammering of her heart was visible. She forced herself to breathe normally as she considered Daniel's wife.

She's not even that pretty. Her nose is sharp and her lips are too thin. So mousy in a brown woolen dress and heavy overcoat. I bet she didn't spend much time in front of a mirror this morning.

It felt like a hard stone was lodged in her throat. Corinne wondered if she would be able to speak. She wiped her clammy palms on the folds of her skirt and forced herself to say, "I'm Corinne Sullivan."

The reaction was immediate. Suzannah Gibson's friendly demeanor disappeared. She pulled John close to her as if to ward off some contagious disease and quickly hustled him off.

She knows who I am, thought Corinne. She watched Suzannah hurry away, pulling her son who protested their hasty departure. *I wonder if Daniel did tell her about me last night or maybe she only knows I own The Laughing Ladies.*

She shouted silently at Suzannah's back. "What is wrong with you? Don't you see what you have? I would give anything to wrap myself around Daniel at night and have him be the first person I saw in the morning. Why aren't you deliriously happy?"

She was overwhelmed by a powerful longing.

I've got beautiful clothes, lots of money, and a good business. But, I can't have the one thing I want most.

Suzannah Gibson was married to the man Corinne desperately yearned for.

She needed to rid herself of the intense physical pain she felt. She picked up a rock and threw it as hard as she could. She watched as it hit a boulder and flaked off a chip. Then she threw another. And another. And another. And when her arm grew too tired to continue, she sank to the ground and gave in to the frustration which assailed her.

Corinne held herself tightly as sobs racked her body. Overwhelmed by the intensity of her emotions, she rocked back and forth as she tried to stem the tears undoing her tough resolve. Hopelessness engulfed her, and she wept until she was hiccupping and gasping for air. She gradually regained her composure and her tense body relaxed. Then, she sat for a long time, staring at nothing.

When she felt back in control, she wiped her face with her sleeve and made a concerted effort to straighten up. She re-pinned her hair which had come undone and brushed off her skirt. She was irritated with herself for losing control and deliberately filled her head with business details.

She had an appointment with an accountant coming to help Abigail, and she needed to freshen up before he arrived. She walked slowly back to the house and let herself in the rear gate.

A horse's whinny made her look down the side of the house. She saw Cameron tying up his buckboard in front. When he saw her, he waved and headed to the back.

"Corinne, what's wrong? What happened?" he asked when he got closer.

"Why would you think anything happened?"

"Look at you. You're a mess."

"You sure do know how to sweet talk a woman."

"Seriously, Corinne, are you all right?"

"Except for being caught when I don't look my best, I'm fine. I took a walk and I guess I went too far up into the mountain. I fell over a couple of rocks on the way down."

He looked dubious, but the look on her face told him he had heard the only explanation he was going to get.

"Why are you here so bright and early?" she asked in an attempt to steer the conversation away for her appearance.

"I'm on my way to New Mexico to look at a new breed of cattle. Why don't you come with me? You can leave The Laughing Ladies for a couple of days. Abigail can run it for you."

"Oh, Cameron, thank you. It does sound lovely, but the place isn't open long enough for me to leave. I can't go."

"Yes, you can. I have it all planned. We'll take the train to Chalma and stay at a hotel. Maybe go on to Albuquerque. We'll make a fun trip out of it. Say you'll come."

"I'm tempted, but the answer has to be no," she said.

Corinne walked towards the house.

"I'm sorry, but I've got to get ready for the accountant I expect."

He tried to wear his disappointment well. He had hoped once Corinne's business was running, he could convince her to spend more time with him. The possibility of a life with her would not die.

As she watched him leave, Corinne thought how easy it would be to let it happen. She knew how Cameron felt about her, but she also knew how she felt about Daniel. *Oh, why can't it be easy? Why can't Daniel be the one who is free?*

Corinne entered the house and moved silently along the hall. She was thankful Abigail was absorbed in her work and did not look up. She was in no mood for conversation.

A few minutes after Corinne passed by, Abigail threw her pencil down. She had added up the columns three times and three times they hadn't matched. Like a petulant child, she leaned back, crossed her arms and tapped her foot.

"What is wrong with me?" she asked herself, completely frustrated. "Maybe, some fresh air will clear my brain."

When she began keeping the books, Abigail made two neat columns, one for "Income" and one for "Expenditures." With no problem, she added her lists and gave Corinne the numbers. But, as the business grew and money was spent in so many different ways, her "expenditures" entries got confusing.

Certain bills, if paid immediately, would give Corinne a discount. Others needed payment before delivery. Some purveyors bartered and no money was exchanged. Where did those transactions go? When Corinne offered favored clients complimentary drinks, in what column should she record that?

She finally acknowledged she needed help. Abigail hesitated to ask, because for the first time in her life, as she sat behind a desk, dressed in businesslike attire, she felt important. But, she was in over her head and told Corinne she needed a real accountant, not some runaway house servant and ex-prostitute.

Abigail walked to the front door and pulled it open with a yank. She was so busy chastising herself she walked right into Aaron Wakefield.

Embarrassed, she stepped back and asked, "Can I help you?"

"My name is Aaron Wakefield, and I have an appointment to see Miss Abigail Evans."

"I'm Miss Abigail Evans, and you do not have an appointment to see me."

"Oh, yes, he does," said Corinne as she appeared at the door. "Abigail, this is the accountant you asked for."

Abigail, taken aback, apologized and gestured towards her office.

"Then, please come with me."

Corinne indicated that Mr. Wakefield should go ahead of her and followed the pair across the main parlor.

"Thank you so much for coming, Mr. Wakefield."

Abigail entered the room first, but was confused as to where she should sit. *Mr. Wakefield is the accountant, should he sit behind the desk? Or should I sit there to appear more professional?* He solved her problem when he pulled out the desk chair for her.

True to her word, Corinne gave Abigail the room at the back of the house and paid her an excellent salary. Together, they picked out the large, oak desk which, at Corinne's insistence, they positioned to face the window. When Abigail's head was not in her books, she could look at the Sawatch Range of 14,000 foot high peaks.

A tallboy cabinet with doors which opened to reveal hidden drawers stood against the rear wall. Two comfortable brown leather chairs were placed in front of the desk. Mr. Wakefield settled into one of them.

"Miss Sullivan explained the business has grown more rapidly than your bookkeeping skills, and you need a bit of help to keep a set of books which accurately reflect her costs," the accountant began.

Corinne interrupted him. "All I really want you to tell me is how much money am I making?"

Imagine, a woman who runs her own business, he thought. *I wonder if she knows what she is doing.*

"In order to know that, you must know what your costs are. It's called cost accounting," he responded.

"You can call it whatever you want, but the bottom line is I want you to tell me my profits."

"That's what I'm here for," he said pleasantly as if he had not heard those exact words many times before.

While Corinne and Mr. Wakefield spoke, Abigail studied her potential rescuer. He was definitely tall, she only came up to his shoulders. His dark blonde hair was cut short and he was clean shaven. She couldn't decide if his eyes were blue or green. She guessed he was older than her, but not by much. As she inspected his clothes, she thought only a custom tailored suit could fit so perfectly. He looked rich. She wondered if he lived in Crystal Creek.

"I'm sorry, what did you say?" Abigail apologized as she realized she had been spoken to.

"Mr. Wakefield will stay for lunch, Abigail. You should have sufficient time to show him whatever he needs to get started."

Corinne closed the door and left the two of them alone.

Abigail didn't mind one bit and neither did Mr. Wakefield.

Chapter Twenty-six: Infatuation

*Infatuation - the early stirring of
feelings of love and fascination*

It soon became apparent that Aaron Wakefield was interested in more than The Laughing Ladies' books. Corinne noted he always appeared well dressed, newly shaven and smelling from liberally applied soap and water. She also noticed that as time went by, Abigail arrived earlier and stayed later than usual. Corinne and Felicia passed many an afternoon discussing the romantic possibilities and tried to come up with a plan to move it along more rapidly.

"At the rate those two of them are going," complained Corinne, "we won't live long enough to see a wedding."

"Do you really think that's where it's headed?" asked Felicia imagining Abigail as a bride. "I would love to see her married to him."

"He's perfect for her. Sweet, caring, considerate and rich," Corinne agreed.

She sprang up and headed towards the hall. She grabbed her heavy woolen cape from the hook near the back door and slipped it around her shoulders. She pulled on her fur lined hat and reached for her leather gloves.

"This waiting for Mr. Shyness to do something is ridiculous. I'm going to throw them together for an evening out. Two box seats for tonight's performance at the Opera House should do the trick."

Corinne decided 5:00 was the right time to make her appearance in Abigail's office. With the opera tickets hidden in her pocket, she knocked and entered the room. Abigail and Aaron were seated across from one another. Two heavy ledgers lay open and sheets of paper were scattered across the desk. It looked like chaos to Corinne.

"Abigail, Aaron. I hope neither one of you has plans for tonight. I have two box seats to the opera and just found out I can't use them."

She paused to gauge their expressions. Abigail tried to suppress a smile. She knew exactly what Corinne was up to, but Aaron didn't have a clue.

"I would feel terrible if I had to return them after all the trouble I had getting them. Please tell me you can both make it."

Abigail answered first. "I can take one of the tickets, Corinne. I would love to go."

Aaron's affirmative quickly followed. "Thank you, Corinne. It would be a nice break from all these numbers."

He looked at the desk strewn with papers and then at Abigail.

"Why don't you put the ledgers away? I'll get the rest of this mess picked up, and we can head out right away."

Corinne stood in the doorway and watched them tidy the office. She casually mentioned she had a dinner reservation at the Wildflower Inn and thought perhaps they would like to use it before the opera. They both readily agreed and Corinne said good night, trying not to look as smug as she felt.

When Felicia arrived soon after, Corinne told her what she had done.

"And they took the bait," she said. "Let's hope our Abigail can reel him in."

"Oh, Corinne, they don't stand a chance with you on the case," Felicia laughed.

Both women smiled with satisfaction and proceeded to the parlor, each hoping Abigail would at last get the rich husband she longed for.

They headed towards the main part of town. Aaron took her elbow and Abigail carefully raised her skirts. After a winter of contending with icy walkways, it was a relief not to worry about falling. They were both bundled up warmly, prepared for the unpredictable Colorado weather. An unseasonable cold snap enveloped the town. It was chilly as they walked through the long, darkening shadows and the tip of her nose grow numb. She rubbed it with her fur muff.

When he saw her gesture, Aaron slipped his arm around her shoulders. Abigail looked up, but did not protest. Aaron had not enjoyed female companionship for a long time, and it felt good to hold a woman, even if just to keep her warm.

They walked silently for a while and then Aaron said, "You know, Abigail, you've never talked much about yourself. Our conversations have always been about me. What I've done, where I've traveled, what schools I went to. Why don't you tell me something about yourself?"

Abigail shivered when she heard the question. Aaron mistook her tremor as reaction to the cold and said, "We should be there soon, let's walk a little faster."

She was reluctant to talk about her past. He didn't know she worked at Mrs. Woodley's and she would certainly never reveal how she ran away from the Hales. She had yet to figure out a way to sound revealing about herself without actually being so.

"Where back East are you from?" he asked, a common enough question in the West.

"New York State," she said, making her answer general.

"And what did you do in New York State?" he persisted, oblivious to the discomfort he was causing her.

"Don't you think a little mystery makes a person more interesting? I prefer to think my life began when I stepped off the train in Crystal Creek. I left my old self behind when I climbed aboard."

Much to her relief, Aaron chuckled at her evasiveness.

They arrived at the inn and were greeted with much enthusiasm. Abigail untied her hat and handed over her jacket and muff to the eager hands of their host. He returned a moment later to take Aaron's long overcoat and fur hat.

The numbness of her toes soon disappeared in the warmth of the room. Their host lit two long tapered candles and handed each of them menus before he backed away. Abigail was pleased with the attention, unaware fawning was necessary to establish a new place's reputation.

Unlike Abigail, Aaron was used to good service, and his thoughts were different than hers. *I hope the town can finally support a fine restaurant.* He looked around. *Not the same quality of places I ate in back home, but it's a start.*

The rawness of Crystal Creek had always grated on him, but he would not admit, even to himself, how much he missed the accoutrements of his wealthy upbringing. Pride would never allow him to do that. It would mean he made a mistake to come west.

Aaron was born into a legacy of lawyers. Three generations of Wakefield men had entered the legal profession, and it was assumed each succeeding generation would follow. His older brother worked in their father's law office, and it was expected that Aaron would do the same. But Aaron decided to strike out on his own. Competitive by nature, he did not wish to spend his life being compared to his older brother. His quick temper exacerbated many discussions about his future and finally, against his father's strenuous objections, Aaron relocated to the West.

"Would you like to order something to drink?" the waiter asked. He was dressed all in black, his clothes covered by a long white apron. He offered the wine selection card to Aaron.

"Shall we have a bottle of wine?" Aaron asked. "They seem to have a good selection. Do you like California wines?"

"You choose, Aaron. I'm sure you know more about wines than I do," Abigail said. "Although I do know Corinne always orders wine from the Clovis vineyards in California."

"Then Clovis zinfandel it is," said Aaron, handing the wine list back to the waiter.

"Why did you pick zinfandel?" she asked. "I know that name because Corinne mentioned it to me when she ordered it. It sounded odd to her, but Mr. Clovis promised it was the newest wine."

"Zinfandel is a uniquely American wine," Aaron said, welcoming the opportunity to show off his knowledge. "A number of years ago, the California Legislature commissioned a representative to go to Europe and collect vines to be brought back. Although California vineyards produced mission wines, they wanted a more sophisticated grape. Well, he was there for four years and when he returned, the legislature didn't want to pay him. Instead of turning over the vines to the government, he stood on the dock and gave them away to whoever wanted them. One of those vines became the stock for zinfandel and some claim the original vine may have been a cutting from the Austrian imperial collection."

Abigail listened with rapt attention. "Fascinating. How do you know all that?"

"Wine is a hobby of mine. It got started when I was doing work for Andrew Clovis. He always talked about his vineyards in California and how he looked forward to moving there as soon as he had enough money."

"How much more does he need?" she laughed. "He owns half of Crystal Creek already."

The waiter returned with the bottle of wine and placed the glasses on the table.

Abigail took a slow survey of the room. An uneven stone wall surrounded a large fireplace to her left. The rest of the walls were roughly plastered and whitewashed above dark stained wainscoting. A number of Colorado landscape paintings were strategically placed around the room.

Well-dressed men and women occupied several tables. Abigail was relieved she had selected her dark violet dress to wear this morning. The starched white trim on the collar and cuffs was still crisp even though she had worked in it for hours. She looked well-turned out and ladylike. Under Corinne's tutelage, she became selective in her wardrobe. Her clothing was fine and expensive, but demure. Seeing the other women's attire assured her she was dressed appropriately for this unexpected night out.

Aaron's raised voice broke into her reverie.

"Look at this glass. It's filthy."

Abigail, dismayed at his tone, said, "It's just a little smudge, why are you so angry?"

"At the prices they charge, there's no excuse for dirty glasses."

The waiter cautiously approached the table with a clean goblet in his hand.

"Sorry, sir. Here's a clean one for you."

When Aaron saw the glass, he slammed his hand down with such force the dishes rattled. The hum of conversation abruptly stopped and the room grew silent. All heads turned towards their table as the host hurried over.

"Is there a problem, sir?"

"I should think so. First I am served a dirty glass, and now I'm given the wrong glass. I ordered red wine and this one is for white."

"Please allow me to pay for your wine, sir. I apologize for the mistake."

"Thank you, but that's not the point. You should train your waiters properly."

The host hurried off, giving hushed directions to the waiter.

Abigail sat quietly, her head bent, surprised by the display she had just witnessed. She had never seen this side of Aaron before. He was usually mild mannered and his short fuse disturbed her.

She raised her eyes at the touch on her arm. Aaron looked at her, his anger gone.

"I'm sorry I embarrassed you, Abigail. I apologize for that quick temper of mine. But, if they expect to cater to a high class clientele, they've got to get these things correct."

"It's all right, Aaron," she said, but that was not what she thought. *No one should yell at a person who is trying his best to serve.*

Aaron began talking non-stop to alleviate any discomfort he had caused. He ran on about the weather, the new saddler's shop that had opened and the latest arrivals to town. He told her amusing stories about his clients and Abigail listened as he rambled on, making such an effort to please her. Flattered that he was doing so, she shook off her doubts and joined in the conversation. By the time dinner was served, the tension was gone and they were both enjoying themselves again.

"I think we'd better head over to the Opera House soon," Abigail suggested as she finished her coffee.

He called for the check and then added, "I enjoyed dinner so much, I completely forgot we had other plans."

A nervous host brought their coats and Aaron assured him that despite the wine glass incident, everything else had been satisfactory.

They quickly dressed for the short walk to the theater. Since the tickets were unexpected, neither of them knew what they were about to see. And neither of them cared as long as they saw it together.

Abigail braced herself as she entered The Laughing Ladies the following day. Not ready to face Corinne's certain interrogation, she stalled by sharpening pencils, aligning papers on her desk and rearranging the leather chairs at different angles to her desk. Finally, she took a deep breath and pushed open the kitchen door.

"Good morning, everyone."

Corinne and Lili were head to head conferring about the evening's menu. They gave her a perfunctory greeting and went back to their plans.

Feeling a small reprieve, Abigail searched for the "something buttered" as Lili called it. She found freshly baked croissants on a tray near the oven. As she reached for the strawberry preserves, Corinne asked, "What did you think of the restaurant? I've heard a few good comments about the food."

The question caught Abigail off guard. It was not the one she expected.

"We both liked it. But, Lili you are still the number one cook in Crystal Creek," she responded.

"Thank you. That is good to hear," Lili answered and then sat down at the long table in the middle of the kitchen. She began to write a shopping list in her distinctive European hand which made common words look like calligraphy. Abigail thought of her own poor handwriting, self-taught because she had no formal schooling.

"And the opera? Did you like that as well?" Corinne continued.

"Oh, yes."

Corinne congratulated herself. She didn't need to ask anything else. The expression on Abigail's face showed the evening had gone well.

Abigail looked over the rim of her mug as she blew on the hot coffee. *I wonder how many questions Corinne plans to ask before she asks the one she's really interested in. Might as well get it over with.*

"I like Aaron very much and hope he feels the same way about me. I think he probably does because he asked permission to kiss me good-night."

And then, she put her coffee mug down and started to cry.

"What am I going to do?" she sobbed. "He doesn't know I worked at Mrs. Woodley's. If I tell him, I'll never see him again. But, if I don't tell him, and he does find out, it would be worse. Oh, Corinne. What should I do?"

Without a moment's hesitation, Corinne said, "You tell him the truth. If you really care about him, you can't lie to him."

"Is it a lie if you just don't tell? He's never going to ask me if I worked at Mrs. Woodley's."

Lili looked up from her list making. "*Mon chérie*, you must listen to Corinne. You cannot build a house with a shaky bottom."

Corinne and Abigail looked at each other. Corinne was first to realize what Lili meant. "You can't build a house without a strong foundation. Oh, I just love your English, Lili."

But, humor did not relieve Abigail's anxiety.

"Corinne, do I really have to tell him everything?"

"You asked me and I'm telling you. The next time you see him, you must let him know what you did and especially, why you did it. Tell it like a woman who made a deliberate choice. It may be a choice some people wouldn't approve of, but you were on your own and trying to piece together a good life for yourself. It was a fast way to make money. You didn't enjoy it. As a matter of fact, you didn't like it at all and you only did it for a short time to buy yourself a new life. Now, you have a respectable job and you only want to put the past behind you. Above all, you are a good woman and don't let him make you feel otherwise."

"You make it sound so easy, Corinne. Will you help me learn what you just said? I want to sound as confident as you do."

"Abigail, you are a great mimic, it shouldn't be any trouble for you."

"It's just that I want to sound proud, like you sounded. You are so good, Corinne. I wish I could imitate you exactly."

"But you can and you will," Corinne insisted as she turned to face Abigail. "Now, listen again and watch my attitude. Attitude is as important as words. That's what men admire, even if they don't want to admit it."

"C'est la vérité," said Lili.

Chapter Twenty-seven: Surprises

Surprise - to come upon or catch somebody unexpectedly

Felicia loved this time of night when the house belonged to her, quiet returned after the dining, drinking and dancing. She was alone until Philip arrived to walk her home and free to play whatever she pleased. After an evening of popular ditties and sentimental songs, she relaxed to the sounds of her classical favorites.

As she played a Mozart piano sonata, she smiled thinking about Philip. He had asked her to move in with him, but she turned down his request. She treasured her newfound independence. It was heady to wield the power and to answer to no one. She couldn't bear the thought of losing that if they lived together.

She recalled how fine her life was when she initially lived with Stewart. Then, her grandmother unexpectedly died. When he saw how little Felicia inherited, he completely changed. Stewart had married her for her money and now all he had was the ability to punish her for his mistake.

Heavy knocking surprised Felicia. She rose to answer it, assuming Philip had forgotten his key. The smile on her face disintegrated when she pulled the door open. She grabbed the edge of the table behind her to make sure she didn't topple over. Felicia could only stare, shocked into silence by the presence of the man in front of her.

The man was equally surprised to see Felicia, but he had no difficulty speaking.

"Felicia Welles," he said in the same unctuous voice she remembered so well. "Aren't you going to invite me in?"

Felicia moved aside, afraid he would create a commotion and disturb the household.

"This is The Laughing Ladies Parlor House, isn't it?" he asked, not even trying to hide his disdain. "I was told this was the place to come when I was in Crystal Creek."

"You're too late. Come back tomorrow," she managed to whisper.

"Well, you're still here sweetheart," he said as he gripped her arm. "You, Miss High and Mighty. Must have been a long road you traveled and looks like it went straight downhill. Let's see what you've learned."

He pulled her roughly to him. Waves of nausea hit her as she breathed in his whiskey soaked breath. She managed to wriggle free and shove him aside.

"Don't play hard to get with me," he sneered. "This is a parlor house and you're here to service the customers."

He reached out and grabbed her, roughly groping her breasts. Then he forced her to him and she was horrified to feel his erection. She pushed against his chest as hard as she could and extracted herself from his grasp. She tried to back away from him, but he was too fast.

"My money's good," he said and threw a wad of bills on the floor. He caught hold of her again, this time ramming his hand up her skirts.

As he did, he felt a strong grip on his shoulders and was thrown against the wall, held there by Philip's hand on his throat. Although he struggled to free himself, he could not. Fury was on Philip's side.

"Thank goodness you're here," Felicia said and began to sway. Philip let go of his victim to catch her. He helped her over to the couch and ordered her to stay there.

He returned to the entryway, surprised to see the stranger still there, waiting.

"What do you think you were doing?" Philip yelled at the man who was rubbing his bruised neck, glaring at the two of them.

"Wonder what her husband will think when he finds out where I found her?" the man asked, his menacing tone causing Felicia to moan.

"Philip, this is my brother-in-law, Hoyt Welles."

Hoyt moved uninvited into the parlor and sat down on the couch directly across from Felicia. He leaned back, knowing he held the advantage. Both Felicia and Philip remained silent, waiting to hear what he had to say.

"I think we've got a little talking to do, *Mrs.* Welles. Stewart has been searching for you since you left. He even had some Pinkerton detectives asking around, but you did a damn good job of disappearing. He may not be too happy to hear where you are, it's a long trip out here to get you. I'll be over to the telegraph office first thing tomorrow morning."

"Please don't, Hoyt," Felicia pleaded. "I'm not going back."

"Stewart's my family, Felicia," Hoyt insisted. He was deriving great pleasure from their conversation. He had always felt inferior to his sister-in-law, like he was a bug she was unable to squash because he was her husband's brother. Now, he had the upper hand. He decided to leave and let her wonder what he was going to do next.

"I guess if no *lady* is available tonight, I'll go find myself a poker game. Good night, Felicia."

He tipped his hat with mock sincerity and strode to the door.

"Please wait, Hoyt," she begged. "Don't do anything until we talk."

Desperate, Felicia made the only offer she knew would interest him. "I have money. Just tell me what you want."

He stopped and made a great show of considering her offer. Then he smirked and answered, "Money talks. See you tomorrow."

"Philip, what am I going to do? I can't let Stewart find me. What will happen to me if he comes here? Can he make me go back? Don't I still have some rights even if I'm married to him?"

Philip recognized she was on the verge of hysteria. He poured her a glass of sherry and watched as she drank it down.

"Another?" he asked.

She nodded and fell back against the couch pillows, repeating the same question, "What am I going to do?" over and over.

"First thing you are going to do is pack up some things and come to my house. You can't talk to Hoyt again until you've thought this through. He doesn't know who I am or where I live, and you want to make sure he can't find you until you're ready to see him."

"But I've got to talk to him before he does anything. I bet Stewart has a reward out for finding me. I need to offer him more money than Stewart does. Hoyt always disliked me because my family was rich. He thought I put on airs. He would send that telegram just to spite me if I can't buy him off. I've got to get to him before he sends a telegram."

"Felicia, you've got to trust me. If you give him money, there's no guarantee he won't send the telegram anyway. And even if he doesn't, he'll be back for more money. Blackmail never works. You just wind up paying and paying and paying. You'll never be free of him."

"But, what am I going to do?"

"First, you are coming to my house tonight," Philip insisted. "We can't have him come looking for you again. I didn't like what I saw when I got here."

At her house, she woke Abigail and explained what had happened. She tossed nightclothes into a satchel and asked Abigail to bring more of her things in the morning.

She had barely settled in when there was a pounding on Philip's front door. Convinced Hoyt had found her again, Felicia panicked and looked for a place to hide.

"Felicia, calm down. I'm here. I'll take care of you. Just stay upstairs and don't make a sound," Philip said as he left the room.

He hurried down the stairs, anticipating the usual emergency at the saloon. It was not uncommon for him to be awoken in the middle of the night to patch up some drunken poker player who thought draw poker, meant using your gun.

And sure enough, when he opened the door, there was Spike panting unevenly. A sallow youth in his late teens, Spike worked for Sven doing odd jobs, delivering whiskey and fetching the doctor when needed. Sven had hired him because, although he was a little slow, he was dependable. Spike's mother had been so grateful she insisted on doing Sven's laundry as her way of saying thank you.

"Doc, Sven needs you over at the saloon. Some new guy in town, drunk as a skunk, didn't know who he was sitting at the table with when he drew his gun. The new guy missed, but Old McGraw didn't. Guy's shot in the shoulder and hollering up a storm.

Philip grabbed his bag and yelled up to Felicia that he would be back as soon as he could. The only newcomer he knew was Hoyt Welles. Thoughts raced through his mind, not one of them compatible with his Hippocratic Oath.

The two men hurried through the deserted streets. Worry about Felicia quickened Philip's steps. He wanted to do what he had to and get back to her as quickly as possible.

When he entered Big Swede's Saloon, he saw Hoyt Welles laid out on one of the gaming tables. Sven had put a thick blanket under him, and Philip wondered whether it was to make him more comfortable or to protect the green felt table top. Hoyt was holding a large wadded handkerchief to his shoulder and cursing up a storm. Except for the watchful eye of Sven, the men had resumed their drinking and gambling.

"Mr. Welles," said Philip when the swearing momentarily stopped. "Looks like we meet again. I don't think we were properly introduced earlier. I'm Dr. Meyers and I'm here to see to your wound."

Philip was having difficulty maintaining a professional manner. His hands were eager to hit, not heal. If he could have figured out a way to avoid treating Hoyt, he would have taken it, but doing so would have raised questions he didn't want to answer

"I don't want this doctor. Is there any other doctor in this two bit town?" Hoyt yelled to the crowd.

Sven sputtered with laughter. "Sure do have another doc. He's a vet and even if you look strong as a horse, it's not the same thing."

He grinned at the image crossing his mind.

"This here's our doc. What've you got against him?"

Lying in pain and knowing he needed attention, Hoyt gave in.

"Okay, Doc. But you've got to take good care of me, right?"

Philip leaned over to look at the wound and saw immediately it was nothing that merited all the carrying on Hoyt was doing. But, he had to get out the bullet which was still in his shoulder.

Hoyt had certainly had enough alcohol to dull the pain, but Philip called for a bottle and a stick for Hoyt to bite down on. Spike was already on his way over with a bucket of boiling water to sterilize the instruments. All the regulars at Big Swede's knew the routine for gunshot wounds. More than half of the poker games ended with Spike making the run to Philip's house to get him.

When he saw the preparations being made, Hoyt yelled, "Changed my mind. I'll take my chances with the vet. Someone get the vet."

He rose and made an attempt to leave.

Hoyt's actions attracted the attention of the men in the saloon. There was something going on between him and the Doc and no one was leaving until they saw the outcome of the exchange.

"Looks like it might be lead poisoning," said Philip. "Your arm is starting to swell already. We'll have to get the bullet out immediately if you don't want it to spread."

Hoyt had a fit of anger when he heard those words.

"Are you hoping I'll die? Would sure solve the problem, wouldn't it?"

Philip, just barely holding his rage in check, picked up his bag and started to pile his medicines back into it. This unexpected turn caused a murmur to go up from those watching. The Doc couldn't be leaving. He wouldn't abandon a wounded man. And what problem was the stranger talking about?

When he saw what Philip was doing, Hoyt called, "No, wait, Doc. You're can't let me die. You're a doctor. You have to take care of me."

Philip put his bag down and leaned over to speak into Hoyt's ear, making sure no one else could hear what he was saying.

"Then I'm warning you. Shut up and let me do what I need to do. Not another word out of you or I'll leave. I swear I will."

With no other choice available, Hoyt gave in.

"Okay, Doc. Just get the bullet out."

At a nod from Philip, Spike handed Hoyt the liquor bottle and then the stick.

"Take a big swig and bite down on this," he told him.

Spike had done this so many times he had his part down perfectly. And like a well oiled machine, Sven motioned to one of the men to help him hold Hoyt, Philip picked up the sterilized scalpel and his expert fingers removed the bullet.

"A souvenir of your visit to Crystal Creek," he said, tossing it to Hoyt.

"Go get a room at the hotel. You need to get into bed right now and rest. I'll come by tomorrow morning to check how you're doing."

Philip wound the gauze around Hoyt's shoulder and taped it in place. He nodded his thanks to Spike and Sven and headed for the exit.

"This doesn't change anything," Hoyt called out to the doctor's back.

The following morning, Philip walked into the Crystal Creek Hotel and asked if a Mr. Welles had checked in. Vivian, always eager to share the latest gossip answered, "Mr. Welles? Poor man. He was just about passed out when they brought him in last night and haven't heard a sound from his room since. They said he was shot in the shoulder."

"What room is he in?" asked Philip, not interested in providing her with further details.

"Room 17, top of the stairs and to the left."

Philip knocked gently on the door, and when no one answered, he assumed Hoyt was still asleep. He decided to check back later and not disturb his rest.

"Let me know when Mr. Welles wakes up," he instructed Vivian as he left the hotel.

He headed over to Big Swede's Saloon. Although it was early, Sven was ready to open for the day's business. The previous night's debris had disappeared. Washed glasses were lined up neatly on the shelves behind the bar. A new layer of sawdust had been applied to the swept floor and the brass spittoons were polished. Chairs were neatly positioned under the tables. Philip looked around, always surprised at how clean Sven was able to keep the premises.

"Looks good," Philip said and took his usual seat.

"Coffee?" asked Sven, as he placed a mug in front of Philip.

"What's the story with the guy who got shot last night? How come he didn't want you taking care of him? What was that all about?"

"Any particular order you want those answers?" asked Philip.

Sven chuckled as he held out a tray to Philip.

"Here's an easy one. Want a croissant? Spike delivered some whiskey to Corinne, and Lili sent him back with six of these."

As Philip helped himself to a still steaming roll, he sorted out how much he could tell Sven and not compromise Felicia.

"I caught Welles with his hands all over Felicia last night. He wasn't taking no for an answer. He gave her a good scare. When I saw him here, shot, I thought he got what he deserved."

"How's he doing this morning?"

"I tried to check on him, but he didn't answer his door. Figured I would let him sleep it off. I told Vivian to send someone for me when he woke up."

"Looks like he woke up," Sven said, pointing to Vivian who was standing in the doorway.

"Doc," she said in a voice that immediately alerted Philip something was wrong. "I think you better come quickly. Mr. Welles is acting crazy."

Philip jumped up and grabbed his bag. Sven was right behind him.

"What's he doing?" he asked Vivian as the three of them hurried across the street.

"He's shouting weird stuff and throwing things. I went to his door and he threw the water pitcher at me, screaming I was trying to kill him. I came and got you right away."

Philip raced up the steps and burst into the room. Hoyt stood there facing the door. His face was beet red and when Philip took him by the arm, his body was hot to the touch.

Hoyt tried to shrug him off, but was too weak to put up much resistance.

"What can I do?" asked Sven who had rushed in after Philip.

"Let's get him onto the bed."

Hoyt made another feeble attempt to hold them off.

As soon as he was laid out on the bed, all the fight seemed to go out of him. He lay there with his eyes closed and his breathing labored.

"He's burning up with fever," said Philip. "That's not good. There's nothing I can do for that. All I can do is wait and hope the fever breaks."

He looked at Sven. "It was a simple bullet extraction. You know how many I've done. Where did I go wrong?"

"You didn't. He did. You told him to get a room and go

to bed. He didn't listen to you. He sat there drinking until I finally cut him off. He raised such a fuss that Spike and I had to drag him over to the hotel."

"I should have taken him to the hotel myself, but I wanted to get back to Felicia," Philip said, his voice filled with self-reproach.

"Stop it, Doc. You didn't do anything wrong."

Philip walked over to where Hoyt lay spread-eagled. His breathing had become shallow, and he was still burning with fever. He picked up his wrist and checked his pulse.

"Go on back to the saloon, Sven. I'll stay here with him."

He watched his patient's chest moving slowly up and down.

"I'll send word to Felicia and let her know what's going on," Sven said as he left the room.

As soon as Felicia heard, she rushed over to the hotel and found Philip slumped in a chair next to the bed.

"Felicia, I swear. I didn't mean this to happen. I did all the right things for him," he said with a look of anguish that made Felicia hasten to his side.

"I know you did, Philip," she comforted. "But, what is it? What's wrong with him now?"

"It's got to be an infection caused by the bullet. It looked like just a flesh wound. But you can never tell what the bullet took in with it. There's nothing I can do now, but wait."

"I'll wait with you," she said and pulled a chair next to his.

They kept a somber vigil in the small hotel room. Morning turned to afternoon and the light morphed from bright sunshine to deep shade. As evening fell, shadows lengthened on the spare furnishings. Side by side they sat and watched helplessly as the life eventually ebbed out of Hoyt's body.

Philip buried his head in his hands. When he finally looked up, she saw a look of despair she had seen once before. She remembered the young man who lost his wife and stayed at Mrs. Woodley's only long enough to tell her his story. Now, Philip's face bore that same expression of unmitigated sorrow.

Before she could react, she heard Philip say, "There's something I want to tell you. I've wanted to tell you for a while and you might as well hear it now."

He gripped her hands hard and then dropped them. He got up and walked to the window. He stood there, staring down at the street. Felicia sat silently, waiting. A few minutes passed and then he began.

"A few years ago, when I was living in Philadelphia, one of my patients came to me begging me to do something about her pregnancy. She had three young children and didn't want a fourth. I said no, but she wept and begged and threatened to go to someone else if I wouldn't help her. I still refused. It was too dangerous. But, she was determined not to have the baby and she did find someone else. It was a disaster and I was called to her house when she started bleeding profusely. I did my best, but it was too late and she died."

"Now I understand why you reacted the way you did when I asked you why Livvy didn't come to you instead of going to the Ute medicine woman."

She wanted to go to him, to comfort him, but something in his manner, kept her seated.

"But, Philip that woman's death wasn't your fault."

"Her husband didn't believe me when I swore I hadn't given her the medicine. He was positive I was lying to him, and he made sure everyone knew what he thought I had done. Philadelphia is a small world, and little by little my patients found other doctors. I finally realized I had to leave if I wanted to continue practicing medicine. I came out here because I wanted to be somewhere without women. Ironic isn't it? I've caused the death of a man."

"You did no such thing," Felicia said indignantly. "He caused his own death, and it was really just a matter of time before he did. Hoyt's always been reckless and Stewart was constantly getting him out of trouble."

Her hand flew to her mouth as the realization hit her.

"Stewart! Oh, no. I forgot about him. What are we going to do now? We have to tell Stewart his brother died, don't we?"

"I'll notify him and tell him we've made the arrangements to bury Hoyt out here."

"What happens if Stewart wants to come out here?"

"Felicia, don't get ahead of yourself. Let me first send a telegram to him."

"But, how could you possibly know where to send a telegraph?"

"I'll write to the postmaster and say Hoyt mentioned he had a brother back east in Saratoga Springs. He'll be able to forward the message to him. By then, we'll have him buried and I'm sure Stewart won't want him dug up and sent home."

He closed Hoyt's eyes and pulled the sheet over his head. Then, he put his arm around her shoulders and said, "Go home. I'll take care of everything."

Too upset to return to Philip's house, Felicia went to The Laughing Ladies instead. When she found Corinne, Felicia related all that had happened since Hoyt's arrival.

"This is dreadful. But we've got to make sure Stewart doesn't come out here."

"Philip is taking care of that. He's hoping if he telegraphs that Hoyt has already been buried, that will end it."

Abigail came rushing out of her office when she heard Felicia's voice.

"What happened?"

Felicia repeated what she had told Corinne.

"What are you going to do?" Abigail asked.

Felicia shrugged. "What can I do? Luckily, nothing connects Philip to me. Besides, I'm sure Stewart didn't even know where Hoyt was and if he did, he doesn't have a clue where Crystal Creek is."

"Do you have any idea why Hoyt was here in Crystal Creek?" asked Corinne.

"Probably trying to get rich quick. He likes money, but he doesn't like to work for it."

Guilt stricken, Felicia's said, "That was mean of me, to talk ill of the dead."

"Dying doesn't automatically make him nicer," said Corinne.

The sound of footsteps on the porch interrupted their conversation. Corinne opened the door to Philip who looked relieved when he saw Felicia.

"I figured you were here when I didn't find you at home."

"Any news yet?" Felicia asked.

"Telegraph was sent. We have to wait for an answer," he said. "Are you all right?"

She nodded, but he could see the tears in her eyes.

"I'll get Lili to fix us something to eat," Corinne said as she walked to the door, signaling Abigail to follow her.

They looked back to see Felicia walk into Philip's waiting arms.

Chapter Twenty-eight: Dilemma

*Dilemma - a state of uncertainty about
what to do in a difficult situation*

The next time Abigail saw Aaron, she told him about Hoyt Wells. Omitting he was Felicia's brother-in-law, she related Philip's rescue of Felicia at The Laughing Ladies and the subsequent poker game which led to Hoyt's death. Aaron was intrigued by the story, but more intrigued by Abigail's recital of the events. He found whatever she did, or said, to his liking. And by now, Aaron had figured out things moved quickly in the West.

People dismissed conventional customs and chose expediency. Women were scarce, and if a man wanted a woman as his wife, he announced himself as soon as possible. Aaron decided he wanted Abigail as his wife.

He enjoyed thinking about himself as a husband, and then a father. He hoped Abigail wanted a large family. He had only one brother and the competition between them was intense. He felt compelled to move across the country to escape the pressure that was always present. And, now, he would prove to his skeptical family he had been right to make the move. He would return as a successful businessman with a beautiful wife at his side.

Well-established and making more money than he anticipated, he was ready for marriage. He had guessed right about the wealth in this town and his services were valued. But, he was a loner and had made no friends. The bit of socializing he did was with business acquaintances. Abigail was his first friend and now he wanted more.

Since there were no jewelers in Crystal Creek, he would have to order her ring from a catalog. He had seen a shelf full of them in Corinne's bookcase and headed there to borrow one.

He locked up his office, and as he strolled to The Laughing Ladies he wondered what made Abigail decide to work there. She always avoided giving him a direct answer when he asked her, brushing off his question, airily saying, "When you have to take care of yourself, you take a job when it's offered to you."

Well, I'm going to take care of you now, Abigail, he thought. *And I'm going to take you home with me and show you off to my mother and father. You're my proof I can manage my life without their advice.*

When he arrived at The Laughing Ladies, he knocked lightly at the back door and let himself in. Abigail came out of her office when she heard the door open.

It had been three months since their first night out together, and they had continued to see each other as much as possible. With his arm around her waist, they walked into her office.

"I didn't know you were coming this morning," Abigail said, surprised to see him.

"I'm here to borrow one or two of Corinne's mail order catalogs. I need some things for my office and think that's probably the easiest way to get them."

"Good morning, good morning," Corinne greeted them as she entered the room.

"I didn't know you were coming today." she said to Aaron.

"I was just asking Abigail if I could borrow one or two of your catalogs."

"Come with me," Corinne said. "I'll get them for you, and we'll make a stop in the kitchen and tell Lili you are here. I'm sure she'll be delighted to feed you."

Aaron had to admit, once he got to know them, he liked Abigail's friends. Corinne was an astute businesswoman who ran her operation well and was open to new ideas and innovations. He had a great deal of respect for her even if she was a parlor house madam. He knew Felicia's only involvement was as the "professor" who played the piano. She was so elegant and sophisticated, he couldn't imagine why she worked there. But, he reminded himself yet again, this was the West, people were freer and less critical than back home. He wasn't sure if this was good or bad, just different.

Abigail sat at her desk, daydreaming about a life with Aaron. When he returned with the catalogs, she looked up guiltily, afraid he could read her thoughts.

He gave her a small wave and said, "I've got an appointment at 11:00 with a possible new client, so I can't stay. See you later tonight."

Abigail walked to the window and looked at the Snow Angel holding sway on the mountainside. At first, she and Corinne scoffed at Felicia's sending up prayers to her, but gradually the Snow Angel became a talisman to all three of them. She returned each spring to hear their hopes and dreams.

A rustle of skirts made Abigail look up from her silent

prayer. Corinne stood in the doorway. She carried a tray filled with breakfast offerings.

"What are you wishing for?" she asked setting the tray on the desk. "As if I didn't know."

Abigail left her position at the window. She beamed at Corinne and said, "Yes, you do know. I'm pretty obvious, aren't I?"

"Abigail, tell me you are going to tell Aaron about your past. I'm so worried he's going to hear it from someone who knew you at Mrs. Woodley's. If he does find out that way, it will make it harder for him to accept anything he hears from you."

Corinne sat down in the chair across from Abigail and waited for her to reply. She busied herself arranging dishes and napkins on the desk. She watched Abigail blow on her hot coffee and could actually feel her discomfort.

"Corinne, I just can't make myself tell him. I just can't do it."

Abigail had tortured herself with indecision.

"I'd rather take a chance. Why would anyone be so mean as to tell him about me? They all know I work here now."

She glanced towards the window and said, "I'm going to just pray he never finds out."

"Forget the Snow Angel. You simply cannot continue to take a chance. You never know what is going to happen. Look at Felicia's brother-in-law showing up. What are the odds he would find himself on The Laughing Ladies' doorstep? What if Felicia hadn't already told Philip all about herself? Thank goodness, it all ended well for her."

Corinne's heart went out to Abigail who sat across from her exuding misery.

"Okay, I'm done. I won't say another word."

Madeline found them sitting in silence when she came into the room. She acted hesitant, unusual for her.

"Do you have a minute, Corinne? There's something I'd like to discuss with you."

"You're not leaving are you?"

"Oh, no. Not even thinking about it," answered Madeline.

Corinne rose to follow Madeline into the front room, but paused to say, "Abigail, please think about what I said."

Even though summer was approaching, the day was chilly. Corinne had lit a fire and it was now blazing. They seated themselves close to its warmth.

"What do you need?" she asked Madeline who was staring into the flames.

Men thought Madeline's reserve mysterious and always asked her questions about herself. Most of the time, she deflected them, but occasionally she amused herself by fabricating answers. Once Madeline told a gullible client she worked her way across the country as a magician's assistant. As he stared wide eyed, she dropped the shoulder of her dress to reveal a scar she said was caused by a thrown knife accidently nicking her. Later, when Corinne asked her why she made up such a ludicrous story, Madeline responded most men were disappointed when she appeared too normal, so she told her wild tales to please them.

Now, Madeline braced herself and began to speak in a reticent voice.

"It's Betsy. I think she's using way too much laudanum. She sleeps all day and seems so lethargic. I asked her about it, and she said it was only to make her eyes look bigger. That her pupils get enlarged and she looks more provocative. But, I don't believe her."

"I noticed how tired she is, too," Corinne agreed. "But,

she told me she was taking laudanum for a terrible toothache, and as soon as she could, she would stop."

"I didn't want to say anything, but I like Betsy, and she hasn't seemed herself for the last few days. Will you talk to her?" asked Madeline.

Corinne was troubled by what Madeline told her and promised to speak to Betsy. It particularly upset her that Betsy lied to her. She felt like a fool making an exception for what she thought was simply alleviation from pain.

Never one to postpone an unpleasant task, Corinne went upstairs. *Might as well get it over with*, she thought as she walked to Betsy's room.

Repeated knocking brought no response. She turned the knob, but the door would not yield. She pushed against it as hard as she could, but it still didn't budge. A few of the women heard the noise and now stood in the hallway watching.

"I can't get Betsy's door open," Corinne said. "Someone help me."

With added effort from Annie and Dusty Rose, they managed to move the door far enough to edge inside. Betsy was sprawled across her bed, eyes wide open and staring into space. She had moved her dresser to block entrance to the room. On the table next to the bed, was an array of blue glass bottles.

Madeline walked over to the table and picked up one of the empty bottles. "These are from the Chinese laundryman. I've seen them on his shelf. They had opium in them."

"Poor Betsy," murmured Corinne and then, turning to the women, told someone to run and get Dr. Meyers.

"All right, ladies." she said to the little group gathered in the room. "Who knows about this? I want to know and I want to know now!"

They looked at each other and lowered their eyes. No one spoke.

Corinne angrily pointed to the motionless body on the bed. She couldn't bear to see Betsy in such a listless, drugged state.

"One of you must have known what Betsy was doing. I noticed her behavior and asked about the laudanum, but I had no idea she was using opium as well. Who knows something? Tell me now!"

Her demand was met with silence. Corinne could barely keep herself in check.

"After all my instructions and all my warnings about how drugs wouldn't be tolerated, Betsy, of all people, is the one who ignores me. What a great little actress she is. She had me completely fooled."

"Where is she?" Philip demanded as he bounded up the steps. "I heard what she did."

He walked over to the bed and looked into her eyes and checked her pulse. He put his stethoscope to her chest and listened to her breathing.

"All we can do is let her sleep it off. Her breathing seems steady, and her pulse is all right. Let's get her under the covers. Nothing much else to do except wait until she wakes up."

"And as soon as she does, she's going to pack up and leave," fumed Corinne. "How could she do this to me?"

"Corinne, calm down," said Philip. "She didn't do this to you. Stop and think a minute."

Corinne could hardly contain herself.

"Go, go," she shooed the girls. "There's nothing for you to do. I'll take care of her."

She handed Philip the blue bottle.

"Is it true? Could she have gotten opium from the Chinese laundryman?" she asked.

She yanked back the covers and rolled Betsy under them.

"If she paid him enough. I think it's pretty common knowledge around here."

"But, why would Betsy need to use opium? And laudanum? It's so dangerous. I don't understand."

She continued to settle Betsy in the bed as she spoke, adjusting the pillow under her head and tucking in the quilt around her. Betsy's slight form felt heavy and lifeless, and Corinne's mood was now darkening.

Philip shook his head and snapped his bag shut.

"Not everyone is like you Corinne. You're able to push unpleasant things aside, and dismiss them from your mind if they are disagreeable."

"Of course, I do. Why think about them?"

He put the blue bottle Corinne had given him back on the dresser. Together they pushed it away from the door. Corinne took a final check on Betsy and drew the curtains closed. Philip followed her out of the room.

"You are the only one who could do what you did and not have it leave a mark on you."

"What's the sense of dwelling on the past?" she asked.

"Felicia won't talk about being a prostitute and Abigail has said many times she hated it. But, you...you totally block that time out and think of it only as a means to an end."

Corinne turned to him as they reached the landing and said, "Because that's exactly what it was, Philip, a means to an end. How do you think I got all this? I earned it on my back just like they did. Do you think I never feel anything about it?"

"If you do, you do a pretty good job of hiding it."

She left him standing there, medicine bag in his hand,

and stormed into the parlor. He trailed right behind her, not wanting to leave on such a disagreeable note.

"I'm the boss now which means I can't be soft. I have the responsibility of managing my business, making nice to the powers that be in this town so I can keep operating, taking care of my girls and training them to do their jobs, being responsible for the food and the liquor and God knows what else. When do I have time for emotions?"

She started to pour herself a brandy, but realized the irony of her action. All this talk about how bad it was to use drugs to escape your troubles, and she was ready to do just that. She walked as far away from the bar as she could.

Philip tried again. "I'm not saying your way of handling things is wrong. I'm just pointing out you don't need laudanum or opium to get you through the night."

"And why should she? I provide well for my girls."

"It has nothing to do with you. I've seen this over and over again. Not all women work in a place as plush as this. You know it's not an easy life. A woman starts out using alcohol and drugs to help her socialize and appear lively, and then continues to use them to escape from the reality of her life. Finally, she can't stop herself. I would guess Betsy has done this before. The more you drink and use opium, the more you need to get the escape you're looking for."

"How do you help someone break her habit then?" she asked, concerned this particular scenario would be repeated.

"I don't have answers for you, Corinne. I'm sorry."

She managed a weary smile as Philip said, "I'm going now. Send someone if you need me when Betsy wakes up."

Corinne sat alone in the parlor. Before today, she never knew what Philip thought about her. *I wonder if Felicia and Abigail see me the same way as he does. Do they think I'm uncaring? That I have no emotions? None of them know how I torment myself over my feelings for Daniel.*

She heard someone come into the room and was relieved to see it was Cameron. He never brought bad news.

"Lili told me you were in here," he said.

"Come sit with me," She moved over to make room for him. "What brings you here today?"

"I stopped by because I want to talk to you," Cameron answered. "I was hoping I'd catch you alone."

"Your timing is perfect. I'm having one of those awful days when nothing goes right."

"What's wrong?" he asked and laid his hat on the chair before joining her on the sofa.

"First of all, someone needs to talk some sense into Abigail. I see her headed for disaster."

"But I thought you liked Aaron."

"I do. But, she's got to tell him about Mrs. Woodley's. He's bound to find out and then what will she do?"

"Do you want me to talk to her?"

"Would you? Maybe, if she hears it from you, she'll listen. She's very fond of you."

"And how about you, are you very fond of me?" he asked.

"Cameron, you're a wonderful friend."

"Not the answer I wanted to hear," he said.

"Cameron…." she started, but he knew what was coming next, so he cut her off.

"And what's the second? You said the first was Abigail."

"Oh, the hell with it," she said and jumped up. She went to the bar and poured herself a big shot of bourbon. She drank it down and held out the bottle, asking if he wanted a drink. She poured herself another and brought the two glasses back with her. She handed him his drink and said,

"I really shouldn't be doing this after what happened a while ago."

She took a big swig and said, "Betsy's upstairs sleeping off a combination of laudanum and opium."

"Did you get Philip here? What did he say?"

Reminded of Philip, Corinne asked, "Do you think I'm unfeeling?"

"What do you mean?" he asked, confused by her change of direction.

"Philip implied I was uncaring. Do you think I'm uncaring about people?"

"I don't know about anyone else, but I sure wish you cared more for me."

She wished she could say what he wanted to hear. Her life would be so uncomplicated. He had all the qualities a woman could wish for. He was smart, kind, interesting, well-read, not to mention, very good looking. She always enjoyed his company. Why couldn't she love him? What was wrong with her?

He picked up her hand and said, "I have just the right cure for what ails you. Come out to the ranch this afternoon. I'll have Maria fix lunch and we'll go riding. I promise to have you back in time for dinner."

"It sounds wonderful, but I better stay here and wait for Betsy to wake up. We've got some serious talking to do," Corinne replied. "How could she put on such a convincing act when inside she was suffering so much?"

"She'll probably be asleep for hours. Come with me," he urged.

"No, I better not," she said. "I like her and don't want to fire her, but I can't afford to have someone so unreliable working for me. I really don't want to ask her to leave. When she's not using the drugs, she's such a delight and one of my most popular girls."

Cameron reached for his hat. Not even noticing, Corinne went on about Betsy.

"I don't look forward to confronting her. But either she stops taking laudanum and opium or she will have to leave."

"You'll sort it out. You always do," Cameron said and quietly let himself out.

Chapter Twenty-nine: Hindrance

*Hindrance – something or somebody that
makes it difficult to get what you want*

Corinne sat in front of the mirror trying on earrings. She tilted her head and leaned forward to see the effect of the simple gold pair she chose. Unnerved by the day's difficult conversations, she forced herself to focus on the frivolous chore of selecting earrings. She held a silver filigreed pair to her ears and decided they were a better choice.

Only an hour left to prepare. There would be one less woman tonight as Betsy was in no condition to come downstairs. Thoroughly frightened by her near fatal overdose, she swore to Corinne she would stop using drugs. Corinne hoped Betsy would keep her promise, and made it clear this was her only chance. The conversation upset her because she liked Betsy and found it difficult to be dictatorial.

Unsettling exchanges had taken up her day. The talk with Abigail hadn't gone well, and she'd disappointed Cameron with her refusal to go back to the ranch. She wondered how long it would take until he gave up on her.

He's such a good man, and I love his friendship, but I can't help myself. He's not Daniel.

Thoughts of Cameron faded when she came downstairs and saw Daniel placing a small pile of maps and charts on the hall table. Even though he had come from the mining office, he was immaculately dressed in a starched white shirt under his dark brown suit. His pants were tucked into heavy boots and a wide brimmed leather hat was pushed back on his head. He was removing his gloves when she reached him.

"What a surprise to find you here so early."

"I stopped by because I've got great news."

Unable to contain his excitement a moment longer, he lifted her off the floor and swung her around in a wide arc. Then, he set her down to explain why he was in such high spirits.

"Suzannah and the boys are going to St. Louis to meet up with her parents. Her father finally retired, and her folks decided to make the trip west, but didn't want to come all the way out to Colorado. They sent her train tickets to St. Louis and she'll be gone for two weeks. Do you know what this means?"

"You'll be cooking your own meals?" she teased.

He pressed her close and whispered, "I've got it all planned. I've booked a suite at Hermosa Springs. Say you'll come with me. Abigail or Felicia can run The Laughing Ladies for two or three days."

Without a moment's hesitation, she said, "Of course, I'll go. When do we leave?"

"Suzannah leaves Wednesday on the 10:00am train, and as soon as I see her off, I'll buy us tickets for this weekend. It's not a problem for me to get away on a Saturday and Sunday."

The minute he was gone, Corinne rushed through the

house to gather up Abigail, Felicia and Lili. She asked them to come to the parlor, she needed to speak to them. They wondered what could possibly make Corinne interrupt her last minute routines. She was adamant about keeping to a schedule.

Corinne found Felicia selecting music for the evening and sat on the piano bench to wait for the others to join them. Abigail, hearing the urgency in Corinne's voice, raced in without even putting her boots back on. As usual, she had pulled them off to enjoy the freedom of only stocking feet.

Corinne looked around.

"Where's Lili?" she asked.

The kitchen door swung open and Lili bustled through, wiping her hands on her apron.

"I've decided to take a little break," Corinne began. "I plan to go away next week for two days, and I'm hoping the three of you will take care of business at The Laughing Ladies while I'm gone."

Felicia studied her intently. "You're going with Daniel, aren't you?

It was more of an accusation than a question.

"What does it matter? I want to get away for a few days."

"*C'est l'homme qui vous aimez, n'est-ce pas?*"

Felicia started to translate, "She said…"

"I know what she said," answered Corinne. "All I want to do is leave for two days. Don't ask me a million questions."

It was not going as she intended. *What was wrong with Felicia? What did she have against Daniel?*

"Don't worry, *ma chérie*. I will take care of the dinner. Have a time that's a wonder."

"And I'll stay and greet the guests," promised Abigail.

"I won't leave until I make sure the evening is running smoothly."

"Me, too," said Felicia, willing to help, but still wary.

She felt compelled to add, "You're getting in too deep, Corinne. I'm afraid you're going to get hurt."

"I walked into this with my eyes wide open. If I'm going to get hurt, I want to make some memories before I am. Discussion ended."

She started across the room, but turned to say, "Thank you all for pitching in."

The three women remained where they were, digesting Corinne's news.

"I hate to say this, but Daniel will never leave his family. How long can this go on?" asked Felicia.

"Why do you make this a problem?" asked Lili. "In France, the wives expect the husband to have a mistress."

"Maybe some wives do. But, not Daniel's. She thinks he ended it. I wonder how she would react if she found out he didn't," said Felicia.

Abigail stood up to leave. "Corinne can take care of herself. Let her be happy for now."

Corinne awoke early on Saturday, too excited to sleep. It was the first time she would leave Crystal Creek in almost two years. She walked to the railroad station and saw Daniel at the end of the platform, but did not acknowledge him. They were to board the train separately, and if he didn't see anyone he knew, he would join her. She found his plan degrading, but did what he asked.

She settled into her seat with the assistance of the conductor who placed her bag in the overhead rack. She adjusted the skirts of her traveling suit selected after much agonizing in front of her armoire. The wine color vermicular fabric was perfect for travel. She wore a matching hat, covered with amber bugle beads and embellished with a velvet flower of the same wine color. She waited for Daniel, trying not to appear like a woman on her way to a furtive tryst.

The long low whistle of the departing train echoed through the air, and Daniel, after checking the car, came to join her. She reached for his hand, but he gently returned it to her lap. She understood his caution, but found it humiliating. She made the two hour trip to the Colinas station, trying to convince herself otherwise.

The hotel's four-wheeled brougham met them at the station. It was a beautiful rig pulled by two sleek black horses. The driver tossed their bags onto the seat in front of the coach and climbed back up to his perch. Daniel helped Corinne into the two-passenger coach. A small mirror was mounted on its side and she checked to see how her hair had fared the trip.

The driver flicked the reins and the brougham edged away from the station. As soon as the carriage started to move, Daniel said, "I'm sorry, Corinne."

"Look at these," she said, ignoring his apology. "Dark blue lap robes and the same color as the linings of the carriage."

"Corinne, I'm really sorry."

She pointed to the lap robes.

"They're monogrammed with the hotel's initials."

"I know how you must feel, but I've got to be careful," Daniel said, trying to catch her eye.

She nodded to acknowledge she heard him, but could not bring herself to say any words of assurance.

The carriage pulled up to the Colinas Springs Hotel and Spa, a substantial two story building with a red tile roof and heavy wooden doors. Flowers bloomed profusely in the courtyard defined by low stone walls. The driver told them the owners modeled their hotel after the famous German spas.

As they walked through the massive front doors into the reception area, Corinne looked at the ceiling which towered above them. Broad wood beams crisscrossed the room and the walls were hung with decorative Indian blankets. A massive stone fireplace dominated one end of the huge room. Simple furniture, with well worn cushions, was arranged into small groupings. She heard Daniel ask the age of the hotel and was surprised to hear it was built fifteen years ago.

Their suite was in one of the two long wings which flanked the main building. As they were escorted through the property, they passed a large pool with steam rising from the surface. Corinne dipped her hand into the water and must have looked shocked when she felt how hot it was.

"Don't worry, once you are in the pool, you get used to the heat," said their hostess. "You can also look for the natural pools scattered up in the hills if you want privacy. Folks have marked their location for others to find. They're called hot pots, and you'll recognize them when you see them."

She unlocked the door and handed Daniel the key. "If you need anything, just come find me in the reception area."

As soon as the door closed, Daniel reached for her. "We have two whole days together."

Corinne forced a smile, determined to shake off her sense of degradation, and walked into his waiting arms.

Later in the day, they decided to search for one of the secluded pools. The sun still shone brightly and the air retained its warmth. Hand in hand, they wandered through fields of daisies and other brightly colored wildflowers until Daniel spotted a handmade flag marker. Someone had tied a piece of cloth onto a stick and stuck it in the ground next to a large hollowed out spot. A closer look revealed a rock lined pool large enough for two.

Daniel quickly removed his clothing and slid into the muddy water. Corinne, hesitated, and then took off her light cotton dress. She wore neither stockings nor petticoats and her corset was stashed in her suitcase for the weekend.

Daniel stood up so she could gauge the depth of the pool. She took his hand and gingerly dropped into the water until her feet hit the silky mud bottom. A previous bather had arranged rocks to make a shallow seat and the two of them sat on it, submerged to their necks in the warm mineral spring.

Their eyes level with the ground, they looked through a field of wildflowers, a riot of reds, oranges and yellows amidst the green. In the distance, snow capped mountains extended across the horizon.

Corinne allowed her body to relax in the warm water.

"The brochure said these hot springs are known for their medicinal value. For centuries, the Ute Indians used them for their curative powers."

He picked up a big blob of soft mud and smeared it up and down her arm. "Feeling cured yet?"

"I can't believe how silky that feels. Who would think mud could be so sensual," she said.

"Did you ever make love in a hot pot?" he asked.

"No, but I think I'm about to."

Later, after dinner, they walked the short distance back to their room. Corinne was dazzled by the spectacular display of stars.

"Did you ever see so many stars? Do you think it's been arranged especially for us?"

Daniel pointed at a shooting star. "Quick, make a wish," he said.

Corinne knew how futile her wish would be, but didn't want to spoil the mood. She dutifully closed her eyes and pretended for Daniel's sake.

Late Sunday night, she returned to a quiet house. Corinne wandered from room to room, her hand trailing across the furniture as she walked. She looked with satisfaction at the rooms she had created and then, her thoughts wandered to the life she had created.

What am I going to do about Daniel? This weekend was wonderful, and I feel relaxed for the first time in months. But that doesn't make the problem go away.

Lili, who was a light sleeper, heard Corinne and got up to join her in the front room. She placed a welcome back kiss on each of her cheeks.

Corinne poured two glasses of zinfandel and handed one to Lili.

"Do you have something to tell me? You look like someone bursting with news."

"Abigail is wearing a ring."

"When did this happen?' asked Corinne.

"Saturday night. He took her to the Wildflower Inn and on the table he put a box. When she opened it, he, how do you say it, bounced the question."

"Popped the question. He asked her to marry him?"

"*Oui.*"

"She must be deliriously happy," Corinne said and raised her glass.

"A toast to Abigail and Aaron. Let's plan a celebration for them."

"We have to wait until she returns."

"Returns? Is she going somewhere?"

"Aaron's papa died, and he must go home to help his

mama. He is taking Abigail with him. He will introduce his fiancée to the family."

"I'll get the details from Abigail in the morning. But, right now, I'm exhausted. I need to go to bed. Good night Lili, and thank you for your help."

"*Bon soir*, Corinne."

A radiant Abigail floated in the next morning. Corinne congratulated her and admired the ring Abigail proudly exhibited. A round garnet stone was surrounded by tiny seed pearls in a simple setting.

"Isn't it beautiful?"

"Of course, it is," said Corinne. "See? I knew if you told Aaron about your past, it wouldn't matter to him. I'm delighted for you. You've got yourself a good man."

Abigail stiffened, and Corinne realized at once what that meant.

"Oh, no, Abigail. You didn't tell him, did you?"

"I couldn't, Corinne," Abigail whimpered. "I wanted to tell him over dinner, but before I could, he asked me to marry him. He was so happy when he put the ring on my finger, I couldn't spoil the moment by telling him. Then, he got the telegram from his mother asking him to come back East to help with all the estate arrangements. He asked me to go with him, so he could introduce me to his family. We got all involved making travel plans, so I never found a time."

Corinne tried to think of something, anything, she could say to convince Abigail she had to tell Aaron about her past.

"I think you can get away with not mentioning the Hales, but he lives in Crystal Creek. All the men who walk around here are potential informants about Mrs. Woodley's. Listen to me, please!"

"Corinne, I can't do it. I just can't. I'm too afraid I'll lose him."

"Abigail, if you don't tell him now, you'll always live with this over your head. He's a good man. Try him. If he leaves, it's better to have him leave now than after you're married and have children. Wouldn't that be worse?"

"You can't understand because you don't want to get married. You don't want a family." Abigail lashed out at her, frustrated at Corinne's persistence.

"How do you know what I want now?" Corinne said, more to herself than to Abigail.

Before Abigail could appreciate the significance of her words, Corinne slipped her arm through her friend's and walked her into the kitchen for their morning coffee.

Chapter Thirty: Disillusionment

Disillusionment – disappointment caused by a false belief

Ten days later, Abigail walked through the hotel lobby to join Aaron who was waiting at the front desk. She looked quite proper and felt confident she could impress Aaron's family and friends. As he offered his arm, confirmation was written on his face.

She was dressed from head to toe in an ensemble selected by Corinne. She wanted her help to be certain of perfection. First impressions were lasting ones, and she wanted no mistakes. She made this extra effort for Aaron's sake. She was being shown off as proof he had done well for himself out west.

The brown taffeta gown with the small train drew attention to her hazel eyes. She spent a great deal of time curling her long chestnut hair and artfully arranging it into an upswept hairstyle. The ladies' magazines declared it the latest fashion, and it would show women in the West were as up-to-date as those in the East. Soft brown leather shoes with tiny pearl buttons complemented her outfit. She carried a dark brown velvet cutaway jacket and supple cream colored gloves to wear on the way to the Wakefield townhouse.

She held her satin drawstring purse in one hand and extended the other to Aaron. He helped her into the carriage, and congratulated himself yet again and looked forward to presenting her to his family. To him, Abigail was conclusive evidence he made the right decision when he struck out on his own. His mother had been extremely critical of his desire to migrate west, but now he was returning a successful businessman accompanied by his beautiful bride-to-be. She was validation of his choices and showed how wrong they were to doubt him.

Aaron uneasily played with her hand. "Abigail, don't be too nervous. Mother can be intimidating. She's probably got a million questions and, believe me, she won't hesitate to ask them. Just be yourself."

"Aaron, don't worry. I think you're more anxious than I am."

But she checked once again to make sure her hat sat at just the right angle not to disturb her carefully arranged hairdo.

"I can hardly wait to meet your family."

"And, I know you'll love my father's partner and his wife. I've told you they were like second parents to me. I specifically requested Mother to invite them."

She patted his hand and again assured him, "Aaron, please don't worry so. It will be fine."

The carriage covered the short distance from the hotel to the townhouse in only a few minutes. Abigail was ready. She envisioned herself Aaron's wife, a sophisticated married woman. Her dream, the dream she prayed so hard for, was about to come true. She was going to marry a wealthy man.

The family butler greeted Aaron warmly and bowed to

Abigail. They proceeded to the drawing room and Abigail suppressed a gasp when she entered the elaborately decorated space. She tried to memorize every detail.

She looked up at the ceiling, which was at least nine feet high, and noted the crown molding wrapped around the edge. The floor was highly polished dark wood, and mahogany paneling went halfway up the wall. Above the wainscoting, was a light tan and green wallpaper with an acanthus leaf motif. The pale green drapes were drawn back from the bay window to allow a view of the street. Through the sheer white curtains, shadows on the branches reflected the evenly spaced gaslights.

Aaron took her arm and headed towards the fireplace topped by an intricately carved wood mantle. Above it, hung a portrait of a woman, obviously a younger version of Mrs. Wakefield.

Aaron's mother was seated on a couch in front of the fire. She looked exactly like Abigail imagined she would. Her white hair was stylishly arranged in a chignon, and she was dressed conservatively in a dark gray taffeta dress. Her ankles were neatly crossed exactly as Felicia had shown Abigail many times. Her patrician features well suited the matriarch of the family.

She rose to greet Aaron and then turned cold blue eyes on Abigail. Ever the social doyenne, she carefully scrutinized her and, satisfied she looked suitable, welcomed her into her home.

The couple sat across from Mrs. Wakefield, who resettled herself in preparation to learn as much as she could about this young woman whom her son intended to marry. She had to admit she was pretty, just as Aaron claimed, and well turned out in fashionable attire. Her hair even done in that new style all the young women seem to prefer.

"How did you find the ride across the country?"

"Actually, it was quite pleasant," Abigail replied. "We were well taken care of in the Pullman car and had plenty of opportunity to relax."

"Whatever made a young woman like you decide to live in the West?" Mrs. Wakefield asked.

Abigail had anticipated this question and was ready with a well-practiced answer. She began her fictitious tale in a sincere tone.

"It really wasn't me who decided. My parents moved to Crystal Creek when my father accepted a job as the manager of the Beulah Mines. Unfortunately, the vein ran out and he lost his position, but they dearly loved Colorado and decided to stay."

Aaron listened attentively while his mother unearthed information. Tonight Abigail was not being her usual evasive self.

"And where are your parents now?"

Abigail lowered her eyes and said they had both passed on. After the appropriate condolences, Mrs. Wakefield continued her probing.

"If I'm not mistaken, Aaron told me you work as a bookkeeper for a business in the town. Propriety appears to be different out west. Women don't do that sort of thing here."

It sounded more like an accusation than a question, but Abigail managed to keep her expression neutral. She was relieved when the hubbub of new arrivals distracted Mrs. Wakefield's attention. Her elder son and his wife came into the room followed by their daughters.

Although his hair was grayer at the temples and his middle was considerably thicker, Aaron's brother could have been his twin. The family resemblance was remarkable. His wife was tiny, coming barely up to his chest. Their two daughters were miniatures of their mother.

Aaron, full of pride, introduced Abigail to his brother Alfred, his wife Edith, and their two young daughters.

Abigail complimented the girls on their outfits and smiled at the younger Mrs. Wakefield. *I'm going to be a Mrs. Wakefield, too,* she happily thought.

She was engaged in conversation with Edith Wakefield when she heard the elder Mrs. Wakefield ask, "I wonder what's keeping the Hales. They're usually so prompt."

"The Hales?"

She was so startled to hear their names, the words escaped Abigail's lips before she had a chance to censor herself.

"My father's law partner. I've told you about him."

"I don't think you ever mentioned his name," Abigail said, trying to keep her composure.

She put her hand out to brace herself when she heard the butler announce, "Mr. and Mrs. Hale."

The late Mr. Wakefield's law partner and his wife entered the room.

She stood, clutching the top of a chair, and battled a desire to flee.

It can't be. It just can't be happening, she thought, riveted in place as Mr. Hale spotted her from across the room.

Ignoring the greetings from the others who were gathered, Isaiah Hale made his way to where Abigail was standing and peered closely at her.

"It is you, Abigail. For a moment I thought not, you're dressed like a lady."

He motioned to his wife who was talking to Mrs. Wakefield.

"Helen, come here. I want you to see who Aaron is planning to marry."

Abigail was trapped. It was over.

In an instant, all her plans and hopes and dreams were

gone, as if a magician waved a wand and made them all disappear. Only there would be no sleight of hand to bring them back. She stood there, mute, and completely still, waiting for the worst.

Mr. Hale's loud voice silenced the group, and they all turned to look at him. Helen Hale stood there stunned when she recognized Abigail.

She turned to Aaron. "Don't tell me this is your fiancée. Do you know who she is?"

Aaron walked over to Abigail and put a protective arm around her shoulder.

"Who do you think she is?" he asked.

Mr. Hale said, "Aaron, surely you remember the trouble when one of our servants ran away, and we had a devil of a time finding her?"

Aaron nodded his head, still unsure how this related to Abigail. But her face, completely drained of color, made him realize the veracity of what Mr. Hale was saying.

He tried to bluff his way through. "If Abigail is who you think she is, I have nothing but admiration for her. She's made herself into an elegant young woman. Where I live, we care about who a person is now, not who they once were."

"Then you won't mind that the detectives we hired found her working in a bordello as a prostitute," Mr. Hale continued.

"We didn't pursue her after we heard what she was doing," added Mrs. Hale. "We decided it was punishment enough."

Aaron laughed with relief at the misunderstanding.

"Those detectives gave you incorrect information. Abigail isn't a prostitute. She's the bookkeeper at The Laughing Ladies."

Mr. and Mrs. Hale looked at each other.

"The Laughing Ladies? The name the detectives gave us was Mrs. Woodley's Parlor House."

Aaron processed what he just heard. *Abigail, a runaway, indentured servant. Abigail, a prostitute. How could she not have told me? How could she mortify me like this in front of everyone?*

Trying to maintain a scrap of dignity, he said, "I think you will have to excuse us. Abigail and I have some talking to do in private."

He took her up by the arm and escorted her from the room.

"Please call a carriage for us. We won't be staying," he said as the butler handed them their coats.

Abigail cowered in the corner of the coach, wishing she could make herself invisible. Aaron stared coldly ahead. He hadn't said a single word since they left his mother's house.

"Aaron, I'm so sorry you found out this way," Abigail said to his stony countenance. He did not respond.

"Aaron," she tried again. "I wanted to tell you. I really did, but I was afraid I would lose you." Still no response.

"Corinne begged me to tell you, but I was so ashamed, I just couldn't do it." Complete silence.

She realized how useless her pleas were and sat quietly for the rest of the ride. What was she going to do? What could she say?

When they reached the hotel, he took her elbow as she descended the carriage. His grip was unnecessarily strong and Abigail knew he wasn't holding her arm to be polite. He continued his firm grasp and walked her through the lobby to the elevator. The elevator operator pulled the iron cage door shut and looked at Aaron for instructions.

"Three please," he said.

"Yes sir." He remembered the couple from earlier in the

evening, dressed so fine and obviously excited. But, they didn't look like a happy pair right now.

When the elevator doors opened, Aaron dragged her down the corridor to her room.

She reached into her purse for the key and when she unlocked the room, he shoved her forward. The rage she saw in his face frightened her.

"Take off your clothes," he ordered, slamming the door behind him.

"What? What did you say?" She couldn't possible have heard correctly.

"Which part didn't you understand?" He stood there and glared angrily at her.

"No, Aaron," she begged. "Please don't do this. You don't want to do this."

"Oh, yes, I do," he sneered. "I want to see my sweet, innocent, naïve sweetheart without her clothes on. I want you to parade yourself in front of me, just like you did for all those men who paid you."

"Here," he said and threw a handful of money at her. "If it's not enough, let me know. What did you charge anyway?"

She started to cry softly. "Aaron, please don't do this."

"Take off your clothes," he demanded again. He was like a predatory animal circling his prey. He smelled fear and was closing in for the kill.

"Take off your goddamn clothes or I'll rip them off myself."

Abigail backed away from him, putting her arms up. He reached for her, and in a fury, pulled her jacket so viciously, the sleeve came off in his hand. Abigail stood there, looking at him in shock.

"Take off your clothes….now!" he bellowed, and this time she started to hesitantly unbutton her blouse.

"Faster," he said. "You couldn't have been this slow. You never would have made any money. Didn't you have to hurry to make sure a lot of men got their turn?"

She stopped what she was doing and pleaded, "Aaron, I wanted to tell you. But, I just couldn't. Please don't make me do this."

"Keep going," he said. "I want to see what all those other men saw."

Reluctantly, she started to unlace her corset and unhook her petticoats. Her fingers shook so badly she could barely do what he demanded. She couldn't bear to look at him. The face that looked at her with such love was now filled with only contempt.

Aaron sat down on the bed and watched her. Incensed though he was, he was also aroused by her nakedness. She stood in front of him, her body as voluptuous as he imagined it. She was mortified, more ashamed than her first night at Mrs. Woodley's. And, she was scared. His unexpected cruelty terrified her. His eyes were slits in his face and his hands on his knees were rigid. Her fiancé was about to rape her, and there was nothing she could do about it.

He grabbed her and pulled her close to him. His belt buckle dug into her bare skin. He clamped his hands on her behind and ground himself up against her.

"Aaron, please," she begged, but he covered her mouth with his, not caring how he was bruising her.

He wanted to hurt her, the way she had hurt him. He released her, but held on to her wrist as he unbuttoned his pants.

"Aaron, don't do this, please."

Without acknowledging her pleas, and not even bothering to pull off his trousers, he fell on her. She was unable to move with his full weight on top of her. She rolled her head from side to side, but there was no possibility of escaping his brutal attack. He thrust himself inside her and callously moved up and down, trying to cause her pain.

He taunted her. "Is this good? Is this what you like?"

She was helpless beneath him.

As soon as he reached a climax, he pushed her aside and stood up.

She wrapped herself in the bedcovers and stared at him, unable to believe what he just did. *Is this the man I was going to marry? Is this the same man I knew in Crystal Creek?*

She was shaken and dazed, but still found the courage to say, "How could you do this? Whatever you think I did to you is nothing compared to what you just did to me."

"I didn't shame you in front of your family and your friends," he shouted. "How can I ever face them again? You made me look like a complete fool who was stupid enough to be taken in by a scheming, money hungry little tramp."

"That's not what I am. How could you think that?"

"Shut up! I don't want to hear anything you have to say. You've made me the laughing stock of my family. I'll never forgive you for that."

He let himself out without a backward glance.

Abigail sat on the bed in shock. In a few short hours, her life had turned upside down. She was no longer the respected fiancée of a wealthy man. She was once again painted a servant and a prostitute. She let out an enormous sob and began to weep. All her hopes and dreams shattered to pieces, tiny pieces she would never be able to pick up. She would return to Crystal Creek disgraced and abandoned.

When she was too exhausted to cry anymore, she stumbled to the commode to wash her face.

What am I going to do? How can I face Corinne and Felicia? What am I going to do?

She heard a muffled knock on the door. Abigail ran to

the bed and pulled the covers around her as if the person on the other side of the door could see right through it.

"Who is it?" she called out.

"I have a message from Mr. Wakefield," the clerk answered.

"Please slip it under the door."

She watched a long thin envelope appear. She stared at it for a long time before she gathered the courage to pick it up.

Inside, she found her return ticket.

Chapter Thirty-one: Motivation

*Motivation - the act of giving somebody a
reason or incentive to do something*

Abigail rode across the country in a Pullman car, barely
registering her luxurious surroundings. She made the lonely
trip west, thinking how different it was from her original
journey. She was no longer a runaway headed towards the
unknown, instead she was returning to her own home and
to her good friends. But, how was she going to face them?
Oh, Corinne, why didn't I listen to you?

While Abigail's despair followed her across the plains,
Felicia was in a far different mood. She stood at the window,
gazing at the empty street. Since it was two blocks from
the main thoroughfare, only an occasional rider broke the
monotony. Earlier in the day, Janie Vergoeten had come to
fetch Philip. Her little sister, Laura, was running a high fever
and coughing. He had been gone for almost two hours now.
Felicia brimming with news, watched for his familiar figure
to return home.

For the last few months, this had been Felicia's home
as well. She never left after she came to stay with him that

awful night when Hoyt showed up. After he died, Philip took charge. Telegrams went back and forth across the country and Philip convinced Stewart it was unnecessary for him to make the long trip to Crystal Creek.

Relief had turned to gratitude, and gratitude to a desire to always be with him. She felt safe and taken care of. Unlike Stewart, Philip did not want to usurp her life. She trusted her instincts that he was an honorable man.

Acceptance by the townswomen was difficult at first. Eventually, because Philip was so well-liked and the women depended on his medical skills, there had been a bending of the unwritten rule and Felicia was reluctantly allowed into their circle. Although she continued to work at The Laughing Ladies, it was only playing the piano, and they could "overlook" it. A few of the women were curious about what went on in a bordello, but Felicia discouraged their inquiries.

She stood impatiently waiting. She'd kept her suspicions to herself. The tightness when she tried to fasten her skirt, the desire to take a nap in the afternoon, the nausea brought on by certain smells, all confirmed she was right. Now that she had skipped her second month, she was ready to tell Philip.

She saw his long, lanky figure approach the gate. His shoulders were stooped and his dark eyes were weary. His visit to the Vergoetens must not have gone well. She knew Philip, he would worry all night. Laura was a chubby, curly-haired nine-year-old, and Philip took it particularly hard when he could not spare a child any suffering. But Felicia was sure her news would cheer him up.

She let the lace curtain fall and skirted around the settee to wait in the hallway. She stopped at the mirror to give her hair a token pat, then turned towards the door.

The gate latch opened and she smiled at the squeak it

made. *Guess I'm going to have to fix that myself,* she thought. It had squeaked since she moved in. She followed the sound of Philip's footsteps up the path, across the porch and, at last, he opened the door.

When Philip saw her standing in the hallway, he thought once again how lucky he was to get welcomed home by this lovely woman. He still couldn't believe she agreed to share her life with him.

Philip smiled and bent to kiss her. "This is a surprise, finding you at the door."

"I have something to tell you, Philip," Felicia said, "and it can't wait."

"Let me put my bag down and wash up. I'll be right with you."

"No, I want to tell you right now," she insisted, holding on to his jacket so he couldn't move away.

"This must be some important piece of information."

He leaned against the wall dramatically.

"Okay, I'm ready. Tell me."

"You are going to be a father," she beamed at him.

Philip stared at her. Then he pulled her close.

"Not so tight. We don't want to hurt the baby," she said, struggling to get free.

He laughed and set her loose, then hugged her again and shook his head saying, "I can't believe it. I'm going to be a father."

The dining room table was set as if for company. Dinner plates, hand painted with tiny blue flowers, sat on a starched white tablecloth. Silverware gleamed and wine glasses shone. She had saved the beautiful set of imported china that Corinne gave them for a special occasion.

She ladled out chicken stew as Philip poured wine to toast the new addition to their family.

"How would you like a little girl who adores her daddy? Or, are you thinking about a little boy to follow in his father's footsteps?"

"A healthy baby and a healthy mother, that's all I want," Philip said, thinking of the dangers for a woman when she gave birth. He had seen what happened when a delivery didn't go normally. But, he reminded himself, he had also seen many, many healthy births. He swore he would get Felicia safely through the birth of their child.

"Oh, Philip," Felicia said, walking around the table to kiss the top of his head. "I'm so happy about this baby and you're going to be a wonderful father."

She sat down, but did not begin eating. Something was on her mind and she wanted to say it as soon as possible.

"I wish we could get married. When it was just the two of us, I didn't care. But, now I don't want our child to be illegitimate."

"I absolutely agree. I actually came up with a plan I figured we could use someday. Now that we're having a baby, maybe we should do it right away."

Felicia twirled her wineglass around, thinking out loud.

"If I try to get a divorce, then Stewart will find out where I am, and I guarantee he will make trouble for us."

"I know, but I think my plan is a way around that."

"Tell me about it."

He pushed his plate away and leaned across the table to take hold of her hands.

"Suppose we go to Denver for a vacation. We can take the train and stay away for a week. Check into a nice hotel. Maybe do some hiking and sightseeing."

"A vacation sounds lovely, but, what's your plan?" Felicia asked, impatient to hear his idea.

"That is the plan," he said, confused that she looked like she could strangle him.

"Go to Denver? That's the plan?" she asked, still not understanding.

"It's very simple. We go to Denver and when we come back, we announce that the vacation seemed like a honeymoon, and we decided to make it one."

"But, Philip, we can't get married. What are you talking about?"

"We know, but no one else does. Okay, maybe Abigail and Corinne, but they would never say a word. We just tell people we got married. Who will know the difference?"

"We'll know. Do we want to start off our child's life lying to it?"

"Just think about it for a while, Felicia. We don't have to decide this minute."

She carried the dishes back to the kitchen and played with his idea, trying to find a flaw in it. She put the plates into the wide, cast iron enameled sink and turned on the faucets. The running water momentarily sidetracked her.

When Philip installed plumbing in his clinic, he brought the pipes into the kitchen. Then he had a flush toilet and a bathtub put into a small room at the end of the upstairs hall. Felicia, who loved a hot bath, was delighted to find all the indoor plumbing when she moved in.

Denver is far enough away so we don't know anyone there. We come back "married." And, then, If someone comes to Crystal Creek, I'll be introduced as Mrs. Philip Meyers, not Felicia Welles. How could word possibly get back to Stewart?

She wiped the dishes and returned them to the cupboard. Corinne's taste was excellent. She still admired the pattern each time she used them.

Mrs. Philip Meyers. I like that.

She went into the front room and found Philip catching

up on the town news. Pipe smoke drifted above the pages and she could see only the top of his head. When he heard her footsteps, he lowered the newspaper.

"T.J. does a good job with this paper. I remember when he first started it, and now it's four pages long with lots of advertisements."

"When do you want to leave for Denver?" she asked and sat down in the wingchair across from his.

Felicia remembered how they had sat in this same room the day of Livvy's funeral. They barely knew each other then, and now their child was on the way.

"I'll make the reservations tomorrow. You just relax and take care of our baby."

He went back to his paper and Felicia thought about her plans for the next day. She pulled off her shoes and wiggled her toes. Then she stretched out her legs in front of her and noticed that there was a tiny hole in her stocking that needed mending.

"*Well, I can fix that,*" she thought, *but thank goodness Corinne is coming to my rescue tomorrow.* Felicia was baffled by the instructions that came with the new Singer sewing machine she bought. She, who was able to play the most complicated sonatas, found she had two left hands when she tried to thread the machine.

She assumed Corinne would ask her why she suddenly had an urge to sew and that was how she was going to tell her the news. She could hardly wait for Abigail to get home to share it with her.

I wonder how Abigail's trip is going. I bet she's met the whole family by now. The big get-together was almost a week ago. I'll have to ask Corinne exactly when she's getting back."

With a contented sigh, she snuggled into the chair. *I'm going to be a mother,* she thought happily. She wondered how long it would take her to believe it. *How I wish Gran was alive to see my baby. It would have been her great-grandchild.*

Her grandmother had meant the world to her. After her parents died, she felt completely lost and abandoned. It took a long time until she felt safe again, and it was her grandmother who made it happen. She gave Felicia a warm, loving home and when she died, Felicia was bereft. She had no idea her grandmother had gone into debt to provide the best of everything for her. The house turned out to be heavily mortgaged and little money was realized from its sale. Worst of all, she had no one to turn to when she realized that Stewart only married her for her inheritance.

She looked at Philip to reassure herself. *Lucky baby and lucky me.*

She gently patted her stomach and although she couldn't feel anything but her petticoats, she wanted her baby to know she was there.

Chapter Thirty-two: Aftermath

*Aftermath – the consequences of an
event, especially a disastrous one*

Corinne walked around the room opening windows to let in
the fresh air. *That should do it,* she thought as she lifted the
last one. No matter the weather, raising windows was always
the first thing she did when she came downstairs. She found
the lingering scent of cigar smoke disagreeable and wanted
it gone as quickly as possible.

She leaned out the window to inhale the sweet scent of
the honeysuckle vine. Startled by her movements, a white-
tailed Jackrabbit hopped away. She surveyed the landscape
and thought, *I must get those cottonwood branches trimmed.
They're starting to obstruct my view of the mountains.*

She checked that no filled ashtrays or stray glasses
remained from the previous evening. A tasseled pillow had
fallen to the floor, and she tossed it onto the damask settee
where it belonged. Then, she straightened a few bottles
behind the bar.

The sunshine and crisp morning air tempted her

into taking a walk before breakfast. She put on boots in anticipation of the short hike up the trail.

When she approached the outcropping that was her turning point, she found Daniel standing there with his hands jammed into his pockets. She watched him for a moment before she called out his name.

He turned and put a welcoming smile on his face. But she knew him too well.

"What's wrong, Daniel?" she asked, concerned to see him looking so unhappy.

"Come, sit with me," he said and brushed off the ledge with his handkerchief. "It's Suzannah. I don't know how much longer I can go on like this."

"Like what?"

"She wants to go back home. Seeing her parents in St. Louis made her even angrier with me for accepting the job out here. She's threatening to leave."

"What are you going to do?"

"I could never leave you," he said. "Never."

He pulled her to him, needing to reassure himself that she was there. He was torn between obligation and desire, a choice he did not want to face.

The smell of his leather coat mingled with the lingering scent of his shaving cream. She buried her head in his shoulder, trying to slow down the moment.

They sat together, in silence, until Daniel reluctantly moved away.

"It's getting late, I've got to go. I'm due at the mine office for a meeting."

Corinne hung on to Daniel's arm. "Try not to anguish too much. Things have a way of working out for the best."

If only I really thought so, she thought, as she watched him walk down the hill until the path turned away from her.

When he disappeared from sight, she sat motionless for a few minutes. Then, slowly rose and walked home.

She headed to the kitchen anticipating her morning coffee. There, she would perch on a stool, mug in hand, ready to hear the gossip. She relied on Lili to get the latest news from the purveyors who visited her daily. And, after her stop at the newspaper office, Abigail would add anything Lili missed. Their morning ritual was a relaxing start to an otherwise hectic day.

Corinne looked around for the muffins or croissants Lili usually set out on the cooling rack. This morning the rack was empty.

That's odd, she thought, but then heard the door swing open to admit an agitated Lili.

"Abigail is here, and she's in her office working."

"What's she doing here? She's not due home for a few more days."

"*Oui.* I know that."

"Did she say anything?"

"She was crying. I could not understand one word she said."

Corinne hurried to Abigail's office, trying to stifle the unpleasant possibilities crowding into her head. One look told her the worst. Abigail was seated behind her desk, twisting a handkerchief into knots.

"Oh, Corinne," she wailed. "You were right. I should have told him."

"What happened?"

She sat down on the chair facing the desk and leaned forward.

Lili followed right behind her, and stood in the doorway waiting to hear Abigail's answer.

"Come and sit down, Lili. You might as well join us,"

Corinne said. "It'll be a lot easier than putting a glass against the wall."

"Well, at first, everything went well. Aaron's eyes almost popped out of his head when he saw me wearing the outfit you picked out for me. We took a carriage to his mother's townhouse, and, oh, it was the most gorgeous place I've ever seen."

"Abigail!" interrupted Corinne. "Skip the details. What happened with Aaron?"

Abigail couldn't bring herself to tell that part yet. She continued to stall.

"When we first arrived at the house, Mrs. Wakefield was very friendly, and we were having a lovely conversation."

"Abigail!"

"Aaron was so proud of me, and then his father's business partner walked in."

She paused, and tears spilled down her face. "Guess who he was?"

"Just tell us."

"Mr. Isaiah Hale! He was Mr. Hale."

Corinne leaned back, stunned. "Oh, no, Abigail. What did you do?"

Seeing Corinne's reaction, Lili looked from one to the other wondering who this Mr. Hale was and why he was so important. She didn't ask, she just handed Abigail a fresh handkerchief.

"At first, I hoped he wouldn't recognize me. But, as soon as he saw me, he called Mrs. Hale over. They told Aaron I was their runaway maid and that the Pinkerton detective traced me to a parlor house."

Corinne stood up and walked to the window. She knew what was coming. She looked out and saw an eagle soaring high above the town. *How easy your life is*, she thought. *No one to hurt you or disappoint you.*

She leaned against the sill. "What did Aaron do?"

"He put his arm around me and stuck up for me, saying he was proud I had become a lady. And then he laughed, calling it all a big misunderstanding. He told them I was your bookkeeper, and we met when you hired him to help me. But then Mr. Hale said Mrs. Woodley's name and it was over."

"How dreadful for you."

More than dreadful, devastating. Corinne didn't know what to say and just watched helplessly as Abigail dissolved into tears again.

Finally, she asked, "Then what happened?"

"We left and Aaron didn't say one word the whole time we were riding back to the hotel. He was furious at me for embarrassing him in front of his family and friends."

"Well, I can understand that. He always struck me as a proud man and you were his greatest pride. What did he finally say to you?"

Abigail hesitated and glanced towards Lili. Corinne recognized the look.

"Lili, would you bring us some coffee, please? And then you need to get your lists ready. The vendors will be arriving soon."

Reluctantly, Lili got up.

"And bring Abigail a shot of whiskey."

"No, no, Corinne. It's way too early to have a drink."

"Trust me. It will do you good."

As soon as Lili was out of earshot, Corinne asked, "What could Aaron possibly say that Lili can't hear?"

"He said, 'Take off your clothes.'"

"Take off your clothes? What did he mean?"

"He meant 'take off your clothes.' It's hard to screw someone through all their petticoats and underwear. And he wasn't nice about it either. He tried to hurt me."

Corinne shook her head, trying to understand. Aaron always seemed the soul of propriety. He courted Abigail in a gentlemanly, almost old-fashioned way. At times, Corinne even thought him dull. She remembered how surprised she was when Abigail mentioned his quick temper, and how shocked she was at Aaron's loss of control over the wine glass incident. But rape? She couldn't believe him capable of it. And to the woman he supposedly loved?

"Wait a minute. You're telling me Aaron raped you? How could he do that to you?"

"He didn't seem to have much trouble," Abigail answered. "He was so excited by the time he finished mortifying me, he almost didn't have time to get his pants down. And when he was done, he just buttoned them up and left."

Corinne was shocked into silence.

"You were right," Abigail gulped. "I should have told him. But, I didn't deserve what he did to me. It was so awful, the way he turned against me."

Angry and upset, Abigail stood up looking around the small office for somewhere to go. Corinne opened her arms and Abigail collapsed into them, asking with a sad little voice, "How could he treat me the way he did? How could he be so cruel?"

She sobbed inconsolably. Corinne pressed Abigail tightly to her and let her cry it out.

Abigail resolutely wiped her eyes. "I've learned my lesson. So much for my silly hopes and dreams. I'm no lady, and I'm never going to be one. I might as well just go back upstairs again and earn lots more money."

Corinne banged her fist on the desk when she heard Abigail's words. Her face turned beet red.

"Don't say that, Abigail. Don't you dare ever say that again. You *are* a lady now. It's Aaron who's no gentleman. You should be proud of yourself and what you've accomplished.

Those damn rich men think they're so much better than us. But, they're not and neither are their wives. I wonder what they'd think if they knew some of the things their depraved husbands like to do."

Her tirade abruptly ended when Lili knocked on the door. She set down a tray filled with coffee and muffins. She handed a tumbler of whiskey to Abigail and started to say something, but Corinne's raised eyebrows changed her mind. She turned and silently left the room.

Corinne gratefully took a few sips of coffee.

"How did you get home? Did you have to buy yourself a ticket?"

The smell of the food made Abigail realize how hungry she was. She buttered a corn muffin and took a few bites before she answered.

"No, he had my return ticket slipped under the door to me."

"How thoughtful of him."

Corinne picked up the glass that Lili had left on the desk. "Here, drink this."

"I'm okay now, really," Abigail said, "I don't need it."

"Well, if you don't, I do," said Corinne and drank it down.

"Abigail you'll get over this. You really will. I know you don't think so now, but I promise you, you will."

"How can you ever get over a man who was so horrid to you?"

"Felicia did."

"I'm not Felicia."

"Which reminds me. I'm supposed to go to her house this morning to show her how to use her new sewing machine. Come on. You're coming with me. Give me ten minutes to get changed."

Chapter Thirty-three: Diversion

*Diversion – something that moves attention
away from something unpleasant*

The town was quiet, the day's activities about to begin. Mr. Wilson was sweeping the steps in front of his general store, and they called out their good mornings to him. One of the original store owners in the town, Mr. Wilson had built a successful business making sure he provided his customers with the goods they wanted. He was Lili's favorite shopkeeper.

A few doors down, T.J. was at his desk in the newspaper office. He was using a newly purchased typewriting machine.

"Let's make a quick stop," said Corinne when she glanced in the window. "I really want to see his typewriting machine."

They walked into the office and T.J., surprised to see Abigail, said, "I thought you were away with Aaron."

Faced for the first time with the need for explanation, Abigail answered, "I came back early. Aaron and I are no longer engaged."

Out of the corner of his eye, T.J. saw Corinne bring her finger to her lips, signaling him to not ask any more questions. Stifling his newspaperman's curiosity, he said, "I'm sorry, Abigail."

Corinne wanted to see the new machine, and he proudly showed it off.

"Look how clever this is. You press a key with the letter on it and a little bar comes up and strikes the paper and prints the letter. The salesman told me this was the latest model, with the keys all re-arranged. The most commonly used letters are not close together anymore, so the type bars don't hit each other and jam the machine."

"Can I try it?" asked Corinne.

"Just let me put in a fresh piece of paper," T.J. said, and he deftly rolled a new sheet into the typewriting machine.

Corinne slowly typed her name onto the blank paper, hunting for each letter on the keyboard.

As Abigail watched, she asked T.J., "Do you still use all your little wooden letters?"

"Yes, I still do the typesetting by hand. But, not for much longer. I have my eye on another machine. It's called a linotype machine because it produces one entire line of type at once. That's going to allow me to do faster typesetting and…"

"This is getting far too complicated for me," said Corinne, interrupting him. Once T.J. got started talking about newspaper production, they could be there for hours.

"Come on Abigail, we better go."

With many thanks to T.J., they left to continue their walk. Corinne looked over at Abigail, and decided her little diversion helped improve her mood.

"Looks like Clovis snagged another building," she said,

pointing to what had been Mrs. Woodley's Parlor House. "He's going to own this entire town soon."

Abigail nodded distractedly, not wanting to be reminded of anything to do with Mrs. Woodley. She took a deep breath as they passed the next building where Aaron had his office. The shades were down and the sign on the door was turned to "Closed."

"Do you think Aaron will come back?" she asked Corinne as they walked past.

"I would bet he doesn't," Corinne said.

"I hope you're right."

They reached the end of Main Street and turned the corner to Felicia and Philip's house.

When Felicia opened the door and saw Abigail, she exclaimed, "Abigail! I didn't think you were coming back so soon. What happened?"

Corinne walked into the house still holding on to Abigail's arm. She steered her into the parlor and Felicia followed.

"Did something happen with Aaron?"

Corinne squeezed Abigail's hand and said, "If you want to just give Felicia the bare details, I'll fill her in later."

"No, I want her to hear it all from me," Abigail said, and she related the events of the trip and her return trip home.

Felicia was outraged by Abigail's account.

"He's a cad. That's the most polite word I can find for him."

She sat down beside Abigail who started to cry.

"You may not believe me, but you're better off knowing beforehand who you are marrying. Once you get in front of the minister and take those vows, it's hard to make any changes. You're lucky you found out now when you can get him out of your life."

"I know you mean well, but I don't feel very lucky."

"Anyway, we're glad you're back safe and sound," Felicia said and started walking towards the door.

"Come on. We can have lunch right after Corinne shows me how to work this darn machine I've been struggling with."

The three women headed to the kitchen. Felicia removed the lid from the treadle cabinet. Then she pulled up the sewing machine and set it into the oak table top. A base of heavy cast iron scrollwork held the weight of the machine.

"Oh, this is beautiful," said Corinne as she ran her hand over the black metal machine, lavishly decorated with gold leaf flowers.

Two wooden drawers, with ornate pulls, were located on each side of the treadle cabinet. Felicia rummaged in one of them for some thread and a small piece of cloth which she handed to Corinne.

"Here, Corinne. Please do your magic."

Corinne seated herself in front of the machine. She lightly tested the treadle with her foot, raised and lowered a few levers and then threaded it quickly. Manipulating the cloth under the presser foot, she touched the flywheel and a neat, straight line of stitches formed.

"How did you do that?" asked Felicia. "I read the instructions a few times and still couldn't figure out how to get it threaded."

"It's easy when you know what you're doing."

She got up and shook the lint off her skirt, then handed Felicia the stitched piece of material.

"But why did you buy this any way? Since when are you interested in sewing?"

"Since I have someone to sew for," said Felicia, barely able to restrain herself from blurting out her news.

"You're sewing for Philip?" asked Abigail. "Why do you want to do that?"

"Someone much, much smaller," Felicia answered and watched as recognition dawned on her friends.

"Yes, I'm having a baby," she announced, unable to wait another minute. "I still can't believe it."

"This is so exciting," said Corinne. "When is it due?"

"Sometime in February."

"Turn sideways. Let us look at you," said Abigail twirling Felicia around.

"You can't see anything yet," Felicia laughed. "But you will soon."

"I'm going to make a party for you and Philip," Abigail announced. "I need something to celebrate. Say you'll let me do it."

"We'd be honored," said Felicia. "Let's make plans over lunch."

The table was set for two and Felicia reached into the brightly painted blue cupboard for another plate. Then she ladled hot potato soup into the three bowls.

Corinne struggled to find the right words to bring up her unexpected predicament.

"Felicia," she started, "I'll need to find another piano player soon. You're not going to be able to continue once your condition becomes obvious."

"Oh my goodness, I didn't think about that," gasped Felicia.

"Whatever happened to Grady, who played at Mrs. Woodley's?" Corinne asked. "Is he still in town?"

The mention of Mrs. Woodley's name set Abigail off on another crying jag, and she ran out of the room.

When she returned a few minutes letter, blowing her nose, she toyed with her food, hardly making an effort to eat. After pushing the soup around the bowl one more time, she looked up at her two friends.

"Remember when we were on the train coming here

and we shared our hopes? Well, Corinne, you got what you wanted. You're making more money than you could have imagined. And, Felicia, you got something you didn't even know you wanted. Do you think it will ever be my turn?"

Felicia answered immediately, "Abigail, this town is crawling with men and when you are ready, you will have your pick."

Corinne remained silent, debating whether she should say what she was thinking. But, Abigail knew exactly what Corinne was thinking.

"And I promise you Corinne, I will never keep who I am or what I was a secret again."

Chapter Thirty-four: Camaraderie

*Camaraderie - a feeling of close friendship
among a group of people*

Lili's day began early in the morning. Today was Sunday, her day off, but her routine didn't vary. First came the coffee. She spooned beans into the grinder and cranked the handle. Then she emptied the contents into a pot of water and lit the stove beneath it. Soon, the rich aroma of the fresh brew filled the kitchen.

Next, she gathered the ingredients for her "something buttered." Yesterday, when she was in his store, Mr. Wilson gave her a few cinnamon sticks and she wanted to use them while they were fresh. She decided to make Claude's favorite, *raisin au pan.*

They'll be ready by the time he arrives, she thought, counting down the hours until he got there.

Corinne groggily pushed open the kitchen door. With her hair in a plait down her back, and still in her nightclothes, she hardly looked the sophisticated proprietor of an expensive establishment.

Lili looked up from her mixing.

"You're early," she said when she saw Corinne.

"I couldn't sleep, and I smelled the coffee."

She sat down on a stool next to the huge wooden block Lili used for her work space, and watched Lili slowly twist the dough and roll it around into small rings. When she was satisfied with the shape, Lili carefully shook the now pulverized cinnamon onto it and added raisins.

"What are you making?" Corinne asked.

"*Pains au raisin*. Claude loves them."

"That's right, today's Sunday. When does he arrive?"

"He comes on the 10:00am train."

"How long will he be staying?"

"Staying? Claude does not stay, he blows in and out like the wind," laughed Lili and carried the tray of neatly arranged buns to the oven.

Corinne poured herself a mug of coffee and took it with her when she left the kitchen.

"I'll go put something on and be back in time to sample a *pain au raisin*."

Lili sat down to finish her coffee, her thoughts focused on her baby brother. *Not a baby any longer*, she reminded herself. *A handsome man.*

Claude was six feet tall, unusual for a Frenchman. His coloring was also unusual, a striking combination of jet black hair and piercing blue eyes. Perfect English, spoken with a slight French accent, added to his attraction.

He is such a restless spirit. I wonder how many places he's been since he left Crystal Creek. I must have six months of adventures to hear about. I don't know why he can't just settle down here instead of wasting time searching for gold.

Corinne re-appeared just when Lili was shaking the rolls onto the cooling rack. She reached for one before she realized how hot they were.

"Ouch, ouch," she cried, sucking on her finger.

It was not the first time Corinne burned herself. Sweets were her weakness, and Lili's baking her downfall.

"Where is Claude going to stay? Does he have a room somewhere?" asked Corinne, shaking the affected finger.

Lili handed her a small piece of ice and said, "I do not know. Why?"

"Because there's an extra bedroom in Abigail's house, Felicia's old room," said Corinne. "Do you want me to walk over and find out if he can stay there?"

"*Oui*, please do. Perhaps Claude can charm her out of her bad mood," said Lili. "She has a lengthy face since she came back."

Corinne giggled. "Long face, Lili. It's called a long face."

At precisely 10:00am, she heard the shrill whistle broadcast the train's approach. She arrived as the locomotive noisily steamed into the station, billowing large clouds of white smoke. She anxiously scanned the alighting passengers for Claude and spotted him amongst the well-dressed people streaming down the platform.

"Claude, Claude," Lili called and ran towards him. With his free arm, he effortlessly lifted her off the ground and soundly kissed her on both cheeks.

Lili pulled away, fanning her nose. "*Mon dieu*, you smell terrible," she said.

Claude sniffed his sleeve and smiled, "Haven't washed for over a week."

She examined him closely. A dark beard covered his face and dirty hair fell well below his collar. His clothes were filthy, and he carried a satchel badly in need of repair. But he was here, next to her, and she didn't care about anything else.

"In here," Lili said and pushed him through the back door. "I don't want anyone to see you in such a state."

She led him right to the bathing room. He watched her turn the handles atop a spigot and hot water flowed into the tub.

"What a contraception," he marveled and started to remove his jacket.

"They're called faucets and you turn them to let in hot or cold water," she said. "I'll be right back with some towels."

"*C'est magnifique*," he called out, luxuriating in the steamy water. Lili could hear Claude splashing, and it brought back memories of him as a little boy when he would sink ships made of soap chips.

She returned to the kitchen to fix him a sandwich. She was slicing the bread when she heard a knock on the back door. It was Sven. His bulky shearling jacket made him look even larger than usual.

"Come in," she invited, and he followed her into the kitchen. He found the warm room, filled with the smell of freshly baked cinnamon buns, especially inviting after the chilly morning air.

"Would you like something?" Lili asked as he made himself comfortable.

He shook his head and said, "I just stopped by because I was hoping you'd like to take a ride over to Langley Falls. We can stop at the Wildflower Inn on the way back."

Before she could answer, Claude walked into the room.

"Oh, I am sorry. I cannot go today, and here you see the reason," she said, indicating her brother. Lili noticed Claude had shaved off the beard and trimmed his hair.

"Where did you put my clothes?"

Sven looked at the handsome man who had entered, wrapped only in a large towel, and dripping water all over the floor. He jumped up so quickly he knocked over his stool.

"I didn't realize you had company."

Lili, amused at his misinterpretation, said, "Sven Thorson, meet my little brother, Claude Marchand."

A red faced Sven put out his hand as Claude struggled to hold up his towel and shake hands at the same time.

"Claude, I will not give you back those smelly clothes until I wash them."

"But, Lili they're all I have."

Sven broke into their dialog. "I can loan you a pair of pants and a shirt until your sister gives you back your clothes. We look about the same size. It'll only take me a minute to get them."

"I think I embarrassed him," said Claude after Sven rushed off. "Is he your beau?"

"No, no. He is only a friend," Lili protested and busied herself at the counter.

"But, I heard him asking you to go for a ride with him," teased Claude, enjoying his sister's discomfort.

"Sometimes we spend Sundays together," Lili admitted, blushing.

Claude rolled his eyes. "I think you are keeping something from me, big sister."

"Claude, I am not," she insisted and began to assemble the slices of ham and the cheese into a thick sandwich.

A few minutes later, the rattling of a wagon told them Sven had returned.

"Keep them as long as you need them," he said and handed over the clothes. "I brought some extras just in case."

Claude disappeared into Lili's bedroom carrying the shirts and pants.

Lili placed another sandwich on a plate and got down some mugs.

It's different feeding men than women she thought, pushing the food towards Sven. *They'll eat anything as long as they don't have to make it.*

The back door opened to admit Corinne and Abigail. It didn't surprise either of them to see Sven sitting at the counter. He frequently visited on Sundays.

"We stopped in to check on Felicia," said Abigail removing her gloves and stuffing them into her coat pocket.

"Any news?" Sven asked. He knew how nervous Philip was.

"You'll be first to know," answered Corinne stomping her feet to warm them up. "Brrr, it's cold out there today."

A horse's whinny was followed by the clattering of boots on the front porch. Corinne shrugged her shoulders and left to see who it could be. She returned with Cameron in tow. Lili automatically began to slice more ham.

"I thought I'd stop by and see if there's any news about Felicia," he said.

"You'll be the first to know," Abigail said in a perfect imitation of Corinne, causing them all to laugh.

"Come sit with us," Corinne invited, and he joined Abigail and Sven who were helping themselves to the ham as fast as Lili sliced it.

A warm camaraderie filled the kitchen. They sat on an odd assortment of chairs and stools pulled over to the large counter in the middle of the room. As they shared food and drink, the women talked excitedly about the imminent birth.

Cameron said, "Let me know if there's anything I can do for Felicia. You can always count on me."

"I usually do," said Corinne, looking up at him and smiling.

"And I'll always be here," he said, knowing full well the futility of his feelings.

Corinne looked around at the people sitting in her kitchen. *All the people I care about are here,* she thought. *Except the one person I care about the most.*

"I'm sorry, Lili. What did you say?"

She realized Lili was looking at her expectantly.

"How much longer do you think it will be?" Lili repeated.

"Philip says it's any day now," said Corinne.

"What's any day now?" asked Claude as he entered the room.

Cameron looked up at the tall, handsome man who was obviously at home in Corinne's kitchen.

"Meet my baby brother," said Lili proudly. "Claude, this is Judd Cameron."

Claude looked around, surprised to see the small crowd gathered at the counter. He counted three additional people who had arrived in the short time he was gone.

"Looks like a busy place you have here," he said to Corinne who greeted him with a big embrace.

And, then, he saw Abigail.

He lifted her hand to his mouth and said, "We have not been introduced yet. Lili, why are you hiding this charming young lady?"

Abigail was thinking how right Lili was when she said he was handsome.

"Welcome Claude. Lili has told us all about you."

"Certainly not all. I hope she left me something to tell you," he answered with a wink.

"Claude will be in town for a little while," Lili said gazing at him happily. "You will, won't you?"

"At least until I can raise some money," he answered as he got himself a chair. He chose to put it next to Abigail's, and she moved over to make room for him.

"Do you have a place to stay? I can always use another hand at my ranch," offered Cameron, wanting to get Lili's handsome brother as far away from Corinne as possible.

"Or if you'd rather stay in town, I've got a spare room over the saloon," Sven added.

Lili broke in saying, "Thank you gentlemen, but I've already made arrangements for Claude's lodging."

Abigail looked at Corinne, who shrugged.

Cameron finished his coffee and said, "I've got to be getting back to the ranch. Nice to meet you, Claude."

He swung his leg over the stool and reached for his jacket.

When Cameron stood, Sven decided to leave as well.

"Don't forget. I've got that extra room, Claude."

He raised his hat and said, "Morning, ladies."

After the two men left, Abigail turned to Lili, "I'm confused. Corinne asked me if I could put Claude up at my house, but if you've made other plans…."

"No, no. Your house is the plan. He will stay with you. *N'est ce pas?*"

"Sounds good to me," Claude said, silently blessing his sister. "When should I come by?"

"Would 6:00 be all right?"

He looked at Lili. "Do you want me here for dinner?"

"I don't cook on Sundays," she said. "Dinner tomorrow will be fine."

Chapter Thirty-five: Compatibility

Compatible: comfortable, well-matched, like-minded

Claude arrived as the grandfather clock in the hall chimed the hour. He carried his borrowed belongings over one arm and balanced a large casserole with the other.

"Lili insisted I bring food. She didn't want you fussing over me," Claude said, and then he laughed. "Actually, she was making the casserole while she told me how she doesn't cook on Sundays."

He looked around for a place to set it down.

"Just give it to me," she said, reaching for the pan. "Your room is the first door on the right at the top of the stairs. Go on up and get settled while I put this in the oven to heat."

When she heard Claude come down, she called out from the kitchen, "I've got the table set in the front room by the fireplace. It's the warmest spot in the house. I'll be right in. Make yourself comfortable."

Instead, he followed her voice into the kitchen. She was about to reach into the ice box for the butter. The ice box was a first in Crystal Creek, and when it arrived from St. Louis, the large oak cabinet created a sensation. Mr. Wilson debated whether or not to order one for his general store. He was one of the first to stop by for a closer inspection.

"What is that?" asked Claude, surprised to see such an elegant piece of furniture in the kitchen.

"It's my ice box," said Abigail. She opened the door, so he could look inside.

"I've never seen one. What do you use it for?"

"It keeps what you put in it cold."

Abigail was delighted with her modern appliance and eager to show it off.

"It's insulated with sawdust," she explained and pointed to the tin walls which lined the inside. Then, she demonstrated how the drip pan caught the water beneath the ice box.

"I empty it every day so it doesn't overflow," she explained. "But it's worth it. As soon as we had it for only a week, we considered it a necessity. I can't tell you how many trips we saved going to the cold storage in the cellar. Philip had to buy one for Felicia when she left here to move in with him."

"Can I help you with something?" he asked.

"No, I can manage. Go get warm, I'll be with you in a minute."

The living room was simply furnished with a couch and two chairs. The wide pine floorboards were newly waxed and partially covered with a colorful braided rug. A red ceramic vase filled with dried flowers stood on the mantel, and ladies' magazines were stacked next to the couch. He noticed a *McCall's Magazine* tucked into the crevasse of a chair.

An oil painting of a Colorado sunset, all reds and golds, hung over a bookcase on the long wall. He was crouched down beside it, trying to read the titles, when Abigail came in.

He stood to take the bottle she held out to him. She

watched as he unfurled to his full six feet and thought again how good looking he was.

"Dinner will be ready in a few minutes."

She handed him a corkscrew. "If you will do the honors."

He put the bottle on the table and moved closer to the fireplace. He added a fresh log and watched the flames lick around it until it caught with a crackle and a spray of sparks. He sat down and stretched his legs out in front of him. It felt good to be in front of a fire again, and an upholstered chair was preferable to a sleeping bag on the hard ground.

When she returned with the food, he rose to join her at the table.

"It's been a while since I felt so comfortable," he said.

"Where have you been prospecting?" she asked.

She filled their plates with the delicious smelling food. Anything Lili made was a guaranteed treat. He poured two glasses of wine and passed one to her.

"Up at Butte, doing some placer mining, but not much there to bother about."

"Placer mining? I've heard the term, but I'm not sure what it means."

"Panning the sand or gravel looking for gold. There was some rich, rocky soil up there, but no gold."

"Then where did you go?"

"To a place I think is loaded with gold. If I could stake a claim, I know it would make me a rich man. But, I ran out of food and supplies, so I'm back in town trying to find someone to grubstake me."

"And what does grubstake mean?' she asked.

"It means I agree to give a portion of my findings to someone in exchange for them providing me with tools and supplies. I'm forced to do it because I have no money to buy what I need."

At Mrs. Woodley's, prospectors had occasionally shown up to celebrate their finds, but she had never spoken with any of them about what they actually did.

"And you really think you know where to find gold?"

"Yes, I do, Abigail. I'm sure there's a rich vein right near where I was panning. I want to go back to make sure, and then I'll stake my claim."

He studied her as he spoke. Her face, reflected in the light from the fire, showed an intensity of concentration which surprised him. Prospecting was a topic women usually found of no interest.

I like this woman. No pretenses about her. If she doesn't know what I'm talking about, she asks. And very pretty. Wonder why she's not married.

"But, enough about me. Tell me about you."

"What do you want to know?"

"Where do you come from? What made you choose Crystal Creek? When did you get here? How did you meet Corinne and Lili? Do you like men? Do you like one special man?

"Which question would you like me to answer first?"

"You don't have to answer any if you don't want to."

"But, I do."

She proceeded to tell Claude the story of her life starting with the Hales and ending with her broken engagement. As she spoke, she remembered Corinne's advice to sound proud. It was the first time she had told a man about her background and was curious to see his reaction. When it came, it was completely unexpected.

Claude stood up and bowed to her. He lifted his glass and said, "Abigail, I salute you. You have told me a most marvelous tale. I congratulate you."

Bewildered, she stared at him.

"You are an adventurer. You do not let others stop you. Look what you have done."

"Done? What have I done?"

"If you hadn't told me, I would never have guessed you were not what you look like to me."

"And what do I look like to you?"

"A smart, proper, well-dressed young woman. Definitely, not someone who came from a poor background."

She was embarrassed, but pleased, and eager to hear his story.

"When you were in France, what made you want to come to America? How did you even know about this part of the country?"

"Like you, I am a poor boy with rich dreams. I'm not like Lili, who is content to forever serve others. I don't want a life of getting nowhere. I want to be rich, and I read about the fortunes being made out here. I came to find gold and I will, I promise you I will."

Abigail started to gather up the dinner dishes, but Claude told her to sit, he would clean up.

"I insist. Lili trained me well. She cooked and I cleaned. It was only fair. When we ran our mother's restaurant, she couldn't do it all by herself."

Abigail moved to the couch and made herself comfortable. She propped a cushion behind her head and closed her eyes.

How easy he is to talk to. And he thinks I'm to be congratulated. Aaron felt so dirtied by me when he heard my story. But, I don't think I'm so bad, and Claude doesn't seem to think so either.

She began to let go of the despair and anger she had lived with since her return.

For the first time in months, she felt hopeful about life again.

Chapter Thirty-six: Repercussions

*Repercussions – the unforeseen aftermath
that results from an action.*

The day started off well. Corinne hummed while she folded her first gift to baby Emily. She wrapped the tiny dress in a large square of pink cotton. As she tied it all up with a white satin ribbon, she recalled how Philip arrived, exactly ten days ago, to tell her the exciting news.

"It's a girl!" he proclaimed proudly.

"How is Felicia? When can I see her and the baby?"

"Later. She's sleeping now and Emily is too."

The excited voices brought Abigail and Lili charging into the parlor.

"Have a cigar," offered Philip, passing them around. "If it was good enough for President Cleveland, it's good enough for me."

"What does President Cleveland have to do with Felicia having a baby?" asked Abigail, staring at the cigar in her hand.

"After the birth of his daughter, he gave out the cigars

he kept locked in a case on his desk. That's how the custom got started," Philip answered.

"*Mon dieu.* You Americans!" Lili muttered.

"Good-bye, ladies. I'm on my way to tell the immediate universe about my daughter," and he practically danced down the lane.

"What in the world do I do with this?" wondered Corinne, dangling the cigar from her fingertips.

"Give it to me," said Lili. "Claude enjoys smoking them."

At the stroke of noon, Corinne set out with the pink and white package tucked under her arm. She walked quickly, eager to see Felicia and to hold the baby. Emily now waved her tiny hands in the air, accidentally grasping an extended finger. It surprised Corinne how much she enjoyed playing mother.

She returned at 2:15 in the afternoon. Corinne remembered the exact time because the grandfather clock chimed the quarter hour as she walked up the porch steps. She had just placed her gloves on the hall table, when she heard the screen door open. Philip walked into the room. The grim set of the doctor's face alarmed her.

"Is Felicia all right?"

"Felicia's fine," he answered. "Why don't you sit down Corinne?"

He crossed the room and poured two large brandies.

Her heart started to pound. "What is it Philip? You are worrying me."

"Here, take this,' he said handing her the snifter.

Instead of sitting, she stood behind the settee as if to protect herself from what he was about to say. Philip definitely had his bad news face on, his eyes signaling his great distress.

"I'm afraid it's Daniel. There's no easy way to tell you

303

this. He had a fatal accident this morning. I thought it best if you heard it from me."

"Oh, no, no. How? What happened to him?"

Corinne looked down at the amber liquid in her glass. Time became suspended. Everything happened in slow motion. It seemed like an eternity before Philip continued.

"From what I could get from Suzannah, they had a terrible quarrel and Daniel stormed out of the house. He must have tripped on the steps and landed in a way that broke his neck. It's just a tragic, freak accident."

"Did he say anything to you or was he gone when you got there?"

Corinne felt like she was watching from outside her body. She heard sounds overhead as the women walked around. The clock finished chiming another quarter hour. Tree branches scratched at the window. Cooking smells emanated from the kitchen.

How can the world keep going? she wondered while she waited for Philip's answer.

"He wanted to die. He couldn't feel or move anything from his neck down. When I got there, he said, 'Give me something to kill me. I don't want to live like this.'"

She gasped.

"What a hideous way to die. How long were you with him?"

"It was a matter of minutes. He closed his eyes and simply slipped away."

Philip wanted to give Corinne details, but struggled not to upset her more than necessary. He did not intend to mention Suzannah's state. She had starting screaming and cursing Corinne, saying it was all her fault. Daniel wanted the town whore. Corinne had bewitched him. Corinne had stolen her husband. And if it was the last thing she ever did, she wasn't going to let Corinne get away with it.

He watched the color drain from Corinne's face and her eyes glaze over. She held the couch so tightly that her knuckles turned white.

He asked, "Do you want something to calm you down?"

Corinne shook her head, her throat so constricted she could barely speak.

"If you need anything, have someone come get me."

"Thanks, but I think I'd rather be alone."

After Philip left, Corinne paced through the house moving aimlessly from room to room. It wouldn't sink in.

Dead. He's dead. I'm never going to see him again. She tried to conjure up every moment they spent together, but could only repeat, *Dead. He's dead.*

She looked down. Daniel had died without knowing a little piece of him was growing inside her. And now, she could never share her news with him. Now, there would be no next time together. *Dead. He's dead.*

She couldn't stop moving, the house wasn't big enough to contain her grief. She would go outside, up along the mountain path and scream her sorrow to the hills. She grabbed her woolen jacket and left using the front door so she wouldn't be seen. The back way went past the kitchen and Abigail's office. She wasn't ready to tell either of them yet. She needed time alone to try to absorb what she had just heard.

She walked to the edge of town and then across the flat, rocky stretch of land at the base of the mountain. She followed the path she had walked on many times before. When it narrowed, she climbed over rocks until, exhausted, she stopped to rest on an outcropping overlooking the town. She hugged herself tightly and bent over until her head touched her knees. *Dead. He's dead. Gone forever. I don't know how I can bear it.*

As she sat there, trying to force herself to accept the unacceptable, a sharp whistling sound whizzed over her head, and something hit the rock above her.

Those are bullets, she realized when another one passed by. She jumped up and waved her arms.

"Stop, stop," she yelled, trying to see the direction of the shots.

Then, she saw.

She saw Suzannah Gibson aiming a rifle directly at her.

"I see where you are," Suzannah called.

She looked like a mad woman. Her hair, completely unloosed, streamed down her back. Her dress, with all its tucks and pleats, was now torn and streaked with dust. Anger contorted her face into a mask of hatred. Her hands shook as she reloaded and aimed at Corinne, who ducked down behind the ledge.

She crouched down as far as she could. *Maybe someone will hear the shots. But, even if they do, it won't help me. The boys come up here all the time for target practice.*

For the moment, Corinne chose to stay put. *At least I have some cover here,* she thought, looking around for a safer place. *But, if Suzannah climbs higher, she can shoot down at me. I wonder how much ammunition she has with her.*

She studied the barren landscape and realized she had nowhere to go.

Suzannah began shouting at her.

"My husband is dead. My children have no father. And it's all because of you."

Should I answer or stay right here? Corinne wondered. *Can you talk sense to a crazy person?*

Before she had a chance to decide, Suzannah yelled, "You tramp. You home wrecker. I'm going to kill you."

She fired another shot.

Corinne didn't know what to do.

How long can I stay here before she comes up to get me? I'm trapped.

Trying to time it so Suzannah would be reloading, Corinne stood up with her hands in the air.

"Don't shoot," she called to Suzannah. "Killing me won't bring Daniel back."

A shot rang out and Corinne felt a sharp stab in her shoulder. Blood oozed through her jacket, turning it crimson. She grabbed for her shoulder to try to stop the bleeding.

When Suzannah saw the blood rapidly spreading, wild, piercing cries of anguish erupted from her. Clutching the rifle to her chest, she turned and dashed down the rocky surface, putting distance between herself and Corinne.

Corinne, left alone and bleeding, could only think of lying down. But, she knew if she closed her eyes now, she might never open them again. Instead, she deliberately concentrated on feeling the pain to keep her conscious.

She had to get to help, but found it difficult to navigate the rocks without the use of her hands. Her left hand held on to her right shoulder to stem the bleeding. If she tried to put weight on her right hand, an excruciating pain ran up her right arm to the wounded shoulder.

She staggered across and around the boulders as she tried to move downward. She lost her footing on the loose rocks and caught herself before she fell too far forward. Her long skirt ripped when she hit against the rocks' jagged edges. The rims of her leather shoes bit into her ankles. She didn't care. She didn't care about anything as long as she could keep moving down and down and down.

She slowly dragged herself to less rocky ground, and relieved to have gotten this far, she stopped. By now, blood completely soaked her jacket and the front of her dress.

She needed something more to press into her wound. She had to stop the bleeding. She pulled at her skirt and held it up to her shoulder, unconcerned that her petticoats were showing.

Afraid to delay any further, she made herself move and continued unsteadily along the path. She paused, lurched a short distance more and paused again. She was exhausted. Her body begged to lie down and rest.

I will make it, she told herself. *No, we will make it. Suzannah's not going to kill the last part of Daniel I have left.*

She felt a small surge of hope when she came to the flat part of the trail. *I'll go right to Philip. He's in his clinic today.*

As she moved across the piedmont swaying unsteadily, she kept the roof of his house directly in her line of vision. She managed to stagger down the street to his office. She pulled herself up the porch steps and collapsed before she reached for the door. She fell heavily against it and Felicia, hearing the sound, went to investigate.

"Philip, Philip," she called frantically when she saw Corinne. "Hurry! It's Corinne, and she's covered with blood."

Philip rushed to the door. Corinne lay unconscious, in a heap on the floor. He lifted her gently and raced down the hall to his examining room.

"Get some hot water," he yelled to Felicia and started to strip off Corinne's bloodied clothing. He exposed the wound and applied pressure until Felicia arrived with the water. He saw with relief that the profuse bleeding had now become a gentle seepage.

After washing the immediate area and probing gently, he told her, "She's been shot, and I've got to get the bullet out. You're going to have to help me."

He opened the glass doors of the cabinet in the corner and removed a metal box. He arranged his operating knives, a pair of tongs and two long, thin needles on a wooden cart. He glanced over at Felicia, knowing how worried she was.

She stood next to the examining table staring down at Corinne's unmoving form. A strand of hair was matted to her face and Felicia lightly pushed it away.

"She'll live, won't she?" begged Felicia. "What happened to Hoyt won't happen to her will it?"

"Felicia, try to calm down. I'm doing everything I can."

He reached behind him to the apothecary jars filled with medicinal powders and herbs. He found the one he wanted and added it to the cart.

Taking Felicia's arm, he pointed to the chloroform inhaler with its absorbent cotton gauze and said, "If she starts to wake up, hand me this."

He continued his instructions in a voice meant to calm her. He could tell her nerves were making it difficult for her to concentrate and he needed her assistance.

"Ready?"

Felicia nodded her head and Philip picked up his scalpel.

Mercifully, Corinne remained unconscious throughout the procedure.

Philip was taping a bandage around Corinne's shoulder, when Emily started to fuss in the other room. Felicia picked her up from her bassinette. She inhaled Emily's sweet baby smell and felt her warmth. *So unlike the still form in the other room,* she thought.

"Abigail!" she suddenly remembered, and still holding Emily, rushed to grab her coat.

"What are you doing?" Philip asked when he saw her frantic activity.

"I'm going to get Abigail," she said and started to bundle Emily up.

"Why take Emily? Leave her here."

"You need to concentrate on Corinne."

"Go, Felicia, go. I'll be all right."

Chapter Thirty-seven: Secret

Secret - intentionally withheld from general knowledge

Felicia lifted her skirts and tore through the darkening streets, ignoring the startled looks which followed her. Her mind was intent on only one thing, she had to find Abigail. Although she lived only two streets away, Felicia felt like she was running forever. As she neared the house, she called out Abigail's name. Hearing the shouts, Abigail ran out and down the steps to meet Felicia. The look of fear and worry on her face made Abigail grab hold of Felicia's shoulders to steady her.

"What's wrong? Is Emily all right?"

"No. I mean, yes, Emily's all right. It's Corinne. She's been shot."

"Shot? Who shot her?"

"I don't know. Hurry get your coat. Let's go."

They almost collided with Cameron's buckboard when they turned the corner.

"What's the matter?" he asked seeing their agitated state.

"Corinne...shot...my house," Felicia blurted out, sounding like a telegram, using only necessary words.

Cameron reached down and pulled them both into the wagon and flipped the reins.

No, no, not Corinne, he prayed. *Please dear God, let her be all right.*

On the mountainside, high above the town, the Snow Angel watched over them as they headed towards Corinne.

For hours, Felicia and Abigail sat together, holding hands and intently watching Corinne, willing her to live. Abigail had long ago removed her shoes, and then her corset, as she kept the long vigil. Except for the times she slipped out to feed Emily, Felicia never moved from the bedside.

Abigail rested her head on Felicia's shoulder. "Do you think she's going to be all right?"

Felicia answered with more confidence than she felt, "The three of us will always be together."

When Corinne finally opened her eyes, she saw Felicia and Abigail sitting side by side next to her bed.

"I must be in heaven," Corinne murmured, "because I'm looking at two angels."

Abigail squeezed Corinne's hand. "Oh, Corinne, you gave us an awful scare. Thank goodness you're awake."

She watched Corinne weakly smile and close her eyes.

Felicia nodded her head unable to say anything. She held back a sob until she ran out of the room to get Philip.

She found him in the kitchen sitting at the round oak table, smoldering pipe ashes dumped into a piece of crockery in front of him. A fresh pipe had been lit and wisps of smoke rose from it.

Across from him, Cameron slumped in his chair, bent forward, his haggard face supported by the palm of his hand. He reached for the half-empty bottle of bourbon and was about to pour himself another drink when Felicia burst in to tell them the good news.

"Corinne's up and she's talking and she even cracked a joke. Does this mean she's going to be all right?"

Philip smiled and nodded, but Cameron looked grim. He would continue to look grim until he heard the words from Corinne herself.

"How's my favorite patient doing?" Philip asked as he crossed to the bed and reached for Corinne's wrist. She had regained consciousness, and he knew the worst danger had passed.

"To tell you the truth, I don't feel so good. I can't move my arm."

"I've bound you up to keep you immobile for a few days. It gives the wound a chance to start healing."

"I'm so tired, Philip. For a while there, I didn't know if I could make it to your door. The last thing I remember is seeing your house."

Felicia laughed and said, "Let's just say you dropped in on us."

Cameron moved to the foot of the bed so Corinne could see him. His clothing was rumpled and the long night of no sleep showed on his face.

He walked over to her and smoothed back the hair from her forehead. She looked up at him and watched the conflicting emotions play across his face.

"What happened? Who would want to shoot you?" asked Felicia.

"I don't know. I didn't see anyone," she said.

She glanced at Philip, and then back at her friends.

Philip looked steadily at her, but didn't say a word. He would keep his suspicions to himself until he could speak to Corinne privately.

"Just tell me who used you for target practice," Cameron demanded. "I want to get my hands on the person who did this to you."

"Not now, Cameron," said Philip sharply. "Leave it to the sheriff."

"I think I want to sleep. Can we talk later?"

And, Corinne closed her eyes.

When they left the room, Abigail said, "Why doesn't she want us to know who shot her? I could tell she was lying. She's a really bad liar."

"What do you mean? Who would want to shoot Corinne?"

Felicia was amazed at Abigail's suggestion.

"I don't know. That's why I'm asking."

"I'm going to find the lowlife who did this to her. And I guarantee you, my aim will be better than his," said Cameron seething with anger.

"Let's wait until the sheriff gets here and talks to Corinne. I'm sure things will get much clearer then," said Philip.

Corinne awoke early the next morning. She lay propped against the pillows watching the sunlight stream in through the curtains. She half expected a swelling of music when the sun rose above the horizon. She was in what Felicia called her "music room".

She rested comfortably, surrounded by colorful Crystal Creek Opera House posters and stacks of sheet music. Across from the bed, a tall bookcase held an inventory of novels, biographies, and the 9th Edition of the Encyclopedia Britannica. The woodstove in the corner gave off plenty of heat, but Felicia had piled extra quilts onto the trunk at the foot of the bed.

Philip allowed Sheriff Tremont in to question her, but cautioned him not to be long.

Felicia and Abigail hovered nearby, anxious to get answers to their questions. Yesterday, Philip had told them about Daniel's death, but neither of them connected it to the shooting. But, Philip did. He remembered Suzannah's threats and wondered if there could be a connection. *If Suzannah shot her, why wouldn't Corinne tell anyone?*

They looked expectantly at Sheriff Tremont when he came out of the room shaking his head. "She didn't see anyone, and she didn't hear anything. All she knows is she was sitting on the outcropping, you know the second one when you come up the mountain path, and all of a sudden, she felt a stabbing pain in her shoulder. She looked down and saw the bleeding. Her only thought was to get here so the doc could take care of her."

"But, it's so wide open there. She must have seen something," Abigail insisted.

"She's got her story and she's sticking to it," the sheriff said. "Nothing I can do if she can't tell me anything. But, I'll check around. Maybe someone heard the shots."

He put on his hat and headed towards the door.

"I'm just glad she got here in time for you to fix her up, Doc."

"Thanks, Sheriff. If she remembers anything at all, we'll get in touch."

Philip looked at the two women and said, "There's nothing to do right now, and the best thing is for her to sleep. I'll just check one more time and be right out."

When Corinne saw Philip firmly close the door behind him, she knew what he planned to ask. She thought about feigning sleep, but decided she might as well get it over with because Philip would insist on an answer.

"Corinne," said Philip. "Did Suzannah shoot you?"

"Why would you pick on Suzannah, of all people?"

"You're not answering me," he said.

"And you're not answering me."

Philip sat down on the edge of the bed. Her evasiveness convinced him he was right about Suzannah. He couldn't imagine why Corinne would want to protect the person who almost killed her.

"Okay. I think Suzannah shot you because she practically told me she planned to."

"When did she tell you that?" asked Corinne.

"I answered your question, now please answer mine."

He was prepared to sit there until he got a response from her. He knew how obstinate she could be, but he planned to outwait her.

"Why does it matter who shot me?"

"Because it is a criminal act, and whoever shot you has to be punished."

She shifted uncomfortably on the bed. He reached behind her and straightened the pillow that had fallen.

"Punished? You mean go to jail, don't you?"

"Yes."

"And if Suzannah did shoot me, she would go to jail and then what would happen to her little boys? They just lost their father, and you want me to take their mother away from them, too?"

Now, he had the reason, but it didn't matter. Suzannah was guilty of attempted murder.

"So, it was Suzannah."

"Philip, I will only answer if you agree never to tell anyone what I tell you. Do you promise?"

He heard the determination in her voice. Weak though she was, she would hold back the truth if she thought Suzannah would be taken from her boys.

"Yes, I promise," he agreed, although it made him angry to do so. "It's called doctor-patient confidentiality, like a priest or a lawyer."

"Then, yes, it was Suzannah. But, she was out of her mind. When she saw the blood, she completely lost control and ran away. I managed to get myself back to town. You fixed me up. I'll recover. End of story."

"Corinne, you've got to tell the sheriff," Philip insisted.

"No, I don't. Suzannah will leave Crystal Creek as soon as she can. She hates it here, and now, there's no reason for her to stay. It will all blow over and no one needs to know. I will not take those boys' mother away from them. A child needs his mother."

She started to cry. Philip was startled to see Corinne with tears streaming down her face. Knowing how proud she was, he started to leave, but she held on to his arm.

"Don't go. I have something else to tell you."

He sat down without saying a word. He handed her his handkerchief and waited.

"I'm expecting a child," she said.

His eyes widened, but he remained silent.

"I don't want to tell anyone yet," she said. "But, I thought you needed to know. I don't want anything to happen to my baby."

"Don't worry," he smiled. "This part is also covered by doctor-patient confidentiality."

She reached out for his hand.

"Thank you, Philip, for being such a good friend."

Chapter Thirty-eight: Proposal

Proposal - a suggestion put forward

Cameron appeared in the doorway, almost hidden behind a huge bouquet of pink coneflowers and baby's breath. Tiny white blossoms cascaded to the floor, creating a floral snowstorm as he walked to the desk where she sat.

Corinne reached for the flowers and felt the pinch in her shoulder. Some pain still persisted, but she refused to take medicine. Since Betsy's near fatal overdose, she was deathly afraid of any kind of drugs.

Two months after the shooting, Corinne found herself relying more and more on Abigail and Lili. She was tired all the time, and didn't know how much longer she could blame her fatigue on recovering from the wound. Very shortly, she would be forced to reveal her pregnancy.

"These are beautiful, Cameron. What's the occasion?"

"I have a proposition for you," he said, "And I want you to hear me out before you answer."

"I'm not going anywhere," she said. "But, would you please ask Lili to bring in a vase? When you get started, you can take a while, so I'd like to get these into some water."

He leaned over, kissed her forehead and carried the flowers to the door.

"Lili," Cameron called. "Would you take these from me please?"

Lili bustled out of the kitchen, wiping her hands on her starched white apron. One day he would ask her how she could do the amount of cooking she did and still never get a spot on herself.

He returned to Corinne's office and closed the door behind him. He wanted this conversation private. He sat down in the chair next to her desk and looked directly at her. She was much too pale and her long hair, usually so carefully done up, was casually tied back with a blue ribbon. She was wearing an unflattering dress which hung loosely on her frame.

This isn't like Corinne. She usually pays more attention to her appearance. But, I guess it's too early in the day for her to worry about how she looks.

He could see much of his mother in her. Another feisty woman, but diametrically opposed to Corinne in physical appearance. His mother was a large blue-eyed blonde, but with that same determined, high spirited, don't mess with me attitude. Julia Cameron had been a mail-order bride and much to their surprise, his parents fell deeply in love. Theirs was a true partnership. They built a small empire together and by the time they were finished they had accumulated 5,000 acres of land and countless herds of cattle.

When his father died, his mother was devastated. She seemed to shrink in size before his eyes. She finally pulled herself together when she realized her seventeen-year-old son was trying to keep the ranch intact. It was then she treated him as her full partner and taught him how to manage the business. He, in turn, became the well respected man he was today.

He took Corinne's hand and cleared his throat. Suddenly he was nervous, but he barreled ahead in his usual direct manner.

"Corinne, honey, I'm not going to get down on my knee, but this is a proposal just the same."

He waved his arm around the room.

"Why don't you give all this up and marry me? I promise I'll take good care of you. You can have whatever you want. I wouldn't expect you to do any of the wife stuff you hate so much. I have people cooking and cleaning for me now, and I don't see any reason for that to change."

He paused and tried to gauge her expression, but he didn't see any reaction. Corinne closed her eyes for what seemed like a long time. He waited patiently.

This is one time I have no intention of letting you off, he thought, looking at the woman he wanted for his wife with all his heart. After the shooting, he discovered a vulnerability he had never seen before. It touched him more than any of her sassy remarks and strong opinions ever did. Today, he planned to stay until she said yes.

Corinne's mind was racing. *Marrying Cameron would make all my problems disappear. It would be so easy. I could stop all this agonizing over what to do when the baby is born.*

Other madams raised their child in a bordello, but she didn't want to do that. Or, they sent their child away to a boarding school because the townspeople would never accept a brothel baby. She didn't like that option either. The only solution she could think of was to move away, go where no one knew her. She could say she was a widow raising her child alone. With her substantial bank account, she could even open a different kind of business. Something respectable this time.

If I marry Cameron I could stay in Crystal Creek. But,

what's he going to think when he hears about the baby? Will he still want me?

Corinne searched for the words to tell him.

She opened her eyes, but did not look at him. She couldn't bear to watch his face when he heard what she was going to say. She stared at the far wall instead and said, "Cameron, I'm going to have a baby."

He sat there numb. Of all the answers she could have given him, he didn't expect this one.

"I know who the father is, but I haven't told him," she continued.

He couldn't stop himself. The words spilled out in an angry rush.

"I know who the father is, too, and that mining engineer would never have left his wife to marry you. You know it, and I know it, and that's the reason you didn't tell him."

She turned to face him.

"You're wrong. I didn't tell him because he died."

The two of them sat in silence. She couldn't bring herself to look at him. Cameron turned his hat around and around in his hands and tried to put his thoughts in order. *I'm too close. I'm not going to lose her now.*

"Well you just told me, and here's what I say. Your son or daughter is a part of you, and I'd be mighty proud to claim him or her as my own."

"Cameron, you realize people know who I am. Do you really want to marry a pregnant ex-prostitute who now runs her own parlor house? Fancy as it is, it's still a bordello."

"I just said it, didn't I? You'd be Mrs. Judd Cameron. Who would dare to say anything about my wife?"

Mrs. Judd Cameron, she repeated to herself. *I'd be Cameron's wife, I would be accepted. People would forgive my "past sins" because they all love Cameron so much. And my child would be accepted as well. No one has to ever know it's not his.*

A faint smile appeared. "You mean you're willing to take a package deal?"

"Willing? Try and stop me."

He leaned over and kissed her, hardly believing she'd finally agreed to marry him.

"We're going to make the biggest shindig wedding this town has ever seen."

"We better hurry," she laughed. "Or your bride will need a very big dress."

She inhaled sharply as an unbidden longing surfaced.

Oh, Daniel, I wish it was you.

Shame overwhelmed her.

What kind of person am I? How could I think that? I just accepted a proposal from this wonderful man. Besides, I could never have married Daniel. Even if he had lived, we never could have been together. I've got to say good-by to him so I can concentrate on being a good wife to Cameron.

Taking his hand in both of hers, she said, "I promise you won't be sorry. I just need some time to get used to the idea."

He jumped up and threw open the door.

"Lili," he shouted. "Bring us a bottle of Corinne's best champagne. And a big bucket of ice to chill it in. Can you do that for me, sweetheart?"

"I am not your sweet tart," she answered as she came into the office. "Corinne, please tell me why I am doing this."

"Do you let me taste the food before it's served?" Corinne answered with a big grin. Revenge was sweet.

"People drink champagne for only two reasons," Lili insisted. "A wedding or a baby. Am I right?"

Corinne and Cameron exchanged glances. "Up to you, darlin'," Cameron said.

"No, Lili. You're wrong. We're celebrating because I am finally feeling better. You know Cameron loves an exaggerated gesture."

He stared at her when Lili left the room, the question hanging in the air.

"I can't tell Lili before I tell Abigail and Felicia," laughed Corinne. "Do you want them to run me out of town?"

Morning brought a beautiful Colorado spring day. New leaves suddenly appeared, brushing the tree branches with a pale chartreuse haze. In the garden, green stalks burst out of the ground, harbingers of the flowers to come. The fresh smell of a new season blew in on the mountain air.

Felicia happily pushed Emily's brand new baby carriage along the street. A large wicker carriage rested on four metal wheels and today the baby was taking her first ride. Felicia had selected the newest model with a reversible hood so she could place Emily facing her.

As she walked, Felicia sang softly to baby Emily who was lying on her back. Her large brown eyes framed by long, thick eyelashes, were focused on her mother. Her wispy strands of light brown hair were covered by a lace cap. Felicia still couldn't believe she was the mother of this perfectly formed miniature human being. She never tired of counting her tiny toes or looking at her plump little fingers. Today, Emily wore another of Corinne's special creations.

"Surely, I'm looking at the best dressed baby in Crystal Creek," Felicia told her daughter, smiling at the number of little dresses Corinne had already sewn.

"I would smile, too, if I was wheeling such a beautiful little girl," said Sven as he stepped aside to avoid bumping into her.

"Say hello to Sven," she instructed Emily, who continued to stare complacently at the two of them.

"Look at those round cheeks."

He peeked into the carriage and offered Emily a large finger to hold.

"Sure she doesn't have two of Lili's biscuits tucked up in them?"

Felicia laughed and squeezed Sven's arm. Although she had no fond memories of the time she worked in his saloon, she liked Sven from the first day she met him. And, when she came to know him better, her initial impression was confirmed.

She remembered the long discussions between the two men when Hoyt died of his bullet wounds. Sven finally convinced Philip he couldn't have done anything differently, especially when an obstinate patient didn't follow his doctor's orders. She would always be grateful to him for that.

"I was hoping the Doc would be in," said Sven. "Saw a story in the latest *National Geographic* and I wanted to talk to him about it."

"I just left him in the clinic. I'm sure he's still there because he has nothing on his schedule today. I'm on my way to The Laughing Ladies."

"How is Corinne doing? She sure scared a whole lot of people when she got shot. Did the sheriff ever find out who did it?"

"Completely recovered and, no, she never could remember anything but what she told him."

"Say hello to Lili for me."

He hesitated, as if he wanted to ask Felicia something else, but then changed his mind and continued on down the street.

Come on Sven. Say something to Lili. I'm going to have to put Corinne on his case. We don't want Lili to wait forever.

Felicia pulled the carriage up the steps and wheeled it to the end of Corinne's porch. She carefully lifted Emily out and carried her into the dining room where Corinne was just putting the finishing touches to the table setting. Felicia, unnoticed, stopped to watch her.

She's putting on weight. Strange she's not complaining to me about the extra pounds. She's so vain about her figure. Maybe coming so close to death changes you.

Corinne fussed much less about everything since the shooting.

Felicia wondered what this lunch was about. She was puzzled by Corinne's evasiveness. She had invited Felicia to join her at noon and refused to say anything further.

Corinne looked up and saw Felicia watching her.

"Let me tell Lili you're here," said Corinne. "And I'll go get Abigail."

As soon as the three of them were seated, Corinne popped open a bottle of champagne and poured each of them a drink.

"What's this for?" asked Felicia.

"I'd like to propose a toast," said Corinne and held her glass aloft. "To Mr. Judd Cameron, whose proposal of marriage I accepted yesterday."

"It's about time!" exclaimed Abigail.

"Now talk," demanded Felicia. "How could you hide this from us? How long have you known?"

"Before I answer, drink up," Corinne prodded as she waited for them to drain their glasses. "I have another toast to make."

"Hurry up and drink, Abigail," said Felicia. I can't wait to hear the other news she's going to spring on us."

"To Emily's new best friend, who should be arriving in about four months," Corinne said, waiting for it to sink in.

"Now I know why you looked like you were gaining weight. I was wondering why it didn't bother you," said Abigail.

"Me too, but I thought it was just from laying around so long," said Felicia, then added, "Corinne, have you told Philip yet? You have to take especially good care of yourself now."

"I made him swear not to tell anyone."

"That rascal! Wait until I get home."

"Felicia, I didn't want anyone to know. Especially Cameron. He would have been out of his mind with worry. It was bad enough when he thought he was just worrying about me."

Corinne thought her remark a rather nice touch. Although she hated to deceive her friends, she wanted this unborn child identified as Cameron's, with no suspicions otherwise.

'It's Cameron's baby?" asked Abigail. "I didn't realize you and he...you know what I mean."

"Well, it wasn't planned," Corinne admitted, deliberately confusing what Abigail was asking. "But now I'm pregnant and we're going to make us a family."

"What good news! We both adore Cameron," said Felicia as Abigail nodded her agreement.

"I'm not done ladies. One more round," Corinne said, and she re-filled the champagne flutes.

Mystified, Abigail and Felicia dutifully brought their glasses into the air and waited.

"Let's drink to the new manager of The Laughing Ladies."

"What are you talking about? Are you going somewhere?" Abigail asked, stricken she might be losing her job.

Corinne didn't allow her to worry long.

"To Abigail, who has proven over and over she knows

how to run my business," toasted Corinne, enjoying Abigail's astonishment.

"First of all, thank you," said Abigail. "I'm honored you trust me. But, where are you going and how long will you be gone?"

"I just told you, silly. I'm going to the ranch. For good."

"You're leaving The Laughing Ladies for good?" asked Felicia. "Are you sure that's what you want to do?"

"More than anything," Corinne answered as she patted her protruding middle.

"I'm so happy for you. Cameron is a wonderful man," Abigail said, and quickly added as she turned to Felicia. "And so is Philip."

"How about Claude Marchand?" Felicia asked, winking at Corinne.

Abigail's blush told them both what she thought of Claude.

But, she did not intend to let either of them know that she gave Claude his grubstake. He'd left Crystal Creek to return to the place he'd described to her. If he found gold, there would be time enough to tell them what she'd done. For her $25, which paid for his new tools and other supplies, she would get part of his claim. If she told them now, Felicia would say she didn't know him well enough, and Corinne would scold her for throwing away her money. It was a discussion she did not wish to have.

"And Lili. Will she be staying here?" Abigail asked.

"Yes, of course. I can't imagine anyone but Lili in the kitchen," Corinne assured her.

Abigail jumped up from the table and pranced to the doorway. She pulled out a bunch of curls from her hairdo, stuffed two napkins into the front of her dress and returned as Mrs. Woodley.

"Welcome to my establishment," she purred. She then lit an imaginary cigar, inhaled deeply and blew smoke directly into Corinne's face.

Felicia burst out laughing and said, "Corinne, remember how she came into the room when we were celebrating your buying this house? Oh, she was in rare form, deliberately lighting a cigar to bother you."

Corinne laughed, too, remembering the night. She turned to Abigail, "Did you ever think when you boarded the train a runaway servant you would end up managing a successful business?"

"I did not," Abigail answered, aware of the responsibility she was taking on.

Then Corinne turned to Felicia. "And could you imagine you were leaving the worst man in the East to wind up with the best man in the West?"

"Not in a million years."

The baby began to stir and Felicia took her into her lap.

Corinne's tender expression as she looked at Emily made Felicia say, "Excuse me, but are you the same person who said she never wanted to get married and certainly never wanted to have children. I seem to recall hearing you say those exact words. What made you change your mind?"

"Mother Nature," Corinne said. "Or maybe I'm ready for a conventional life."

"Well, you certainly took an unconventional way to get there," said Felicia.

And that made the Laughing Ladies laugh.